SILENT NIGHT

By the same author:

Take These Men

CYRIL JOLY

SILENT NIGHT

THE DEFEAT OF NATO

CASSELL
LONDON

CASSELL LTD.
35 Red Lion Square, London WC1R 4SG
and at Sydney, Auckland, Toronto, Johannesburg,
an affiliate of
Macmillan Publishing Co., Inc.,
New York.

First published 1980

ISBN 0 304 30656 8

Printed in Great Britain by
Richard Clay (The Chaucer Press) Ltd.
Bungay, Suffolk.

'The right end can only be achieved
by the right men serving it in the
right way and at the right time'

Laurens van der Post
A Far-off Place (Hogarth Press)

To the hope that it will never happen in any form
and
To my wife who gave me every encouragement
to put my ideas in writing.

ACKNOWLEDGEMENTS

The facts and figures regarding the forces of the North Atlantic Treaty Organization and the Warsaw Pact are based on the information contained in "The Military Balance," published by the International Institute for Strategic Studies, at 23 Tavistock Street, London WC 2E 7NQ.

TUESDAY

Casteau, Belgium

At Supreme Headquarters Allied Powers Europe, a Belgian Army duty officer glanced at the clock on the wall of the Operations Centre, saw that it was almost 1800 hours, and busied himself collecting his belongings and tidying the desk, ready for his relief's arrival. His twenty-four hour watch was at an end. Throughout the Centre, the other officers, NCOs and men who had been on duty with him were also preparing to hand over their sometimes tedious, always taxing tasks, monitoring and collating the regular reports of the subordinate commands from the North Atlantic Treaty Organization, and sending a digest of the information to the Military Committee of NATO and to Defence Staffs of the Alliance nations.

Prompt on the hour, the bell at the locked main door of the Centre rang. It was immediately opened to allow the next duty watch in. As each individual entered, his special identification pass was vetted by the two armed military policemen, posted at each side of the heavy door.

Commanded this time by a colonel of the German Army doing his turn on the roster of duty, the new watch moved in without ceremony, hung their heavy winter coats in the closets adjoining the Centre and then immediately settled down to take over the telephones, teleprinters, viewing-screens, data-banks and the other equipment crammed round the walls and stacked in rows down the centre of the sound-proofed hall.

'Glad to see you,' said the Belgian. 'We can't wait to get home. Nothing unusual to report. All the last situation reports have been received. No unusual movements. The traffic at the crossing points is still heavy, but it seems to be the normal pre-Christmas amount.'

'Still the same friendliness at the frontier?' asked the German, a note of disbelief and some anxiety in his question. He had been suspicious from the start of the change in behaviour of the Russians and East Germans during the last few months.

'Still the same friendliness, perhaps even with a touch of the

1

Christmas spirit, though I know they don't believe in it now. Don't worry. It might be that the recent friendliness is an effort to make up for their other activities round the world. Don't be so suspicious — be thankful for it.'

'I would be if I could believe in it,' muttered the German. But it was hard for him to accept the outward show of less hostility, and that there was no ulterior motive behind what had been to him an inconceivable change. It had happened gradually. The checks of vehicles and documents had become less protracted, the searches of luggage had become more considerate and careful, there had even been occasional smiles of welcome or dismissal when the formalities had been completed. As a small boy in 1945 he had experienced the ferocity and cruelty of the Russian soldiers when they swept across East Prussia, killing and looting.

He reassured himself that he could put his anxieties to rest, at least for the time being, and could feel fairly confident that, in mid-winter, he had less reason to worry about a possible Russian invasion, except that it had been at Christmas that they had invaded Afghanistan.

He and the rest of the NATO staff could reasonably assume that, in the last half of December, the best campaigning periods for a large-scale invasion had passed. Only when the snows melted and the ground afterwards dried, could sizeable mechanized forces move in Europe — until the late autumn and early winter rains again made cross-country movement by either tracked or wheeled vehicles difficult, if not impossible.

The short daylight hours of mid-winter were an additional reason for thinking that the Warsaw Pact Forces, heavily mechanized and motorized, and dependent, in their tactical doctrine, on the close support of their Air Armies, would not attack when there were barely eight hours of daylight in which to operate. 21 December was the shortest day when sunrise occurred only a few minutes before 8 o'clock in the morning and sunset just before 4 o'clock in the afternoon. So, for at least a week before Christmas Day, and for at least a week afterwards, the available hours of daylight were the shortest — and therefore, for a period of two or three weeks, most people's minds turned to other more entertaining and less sombre pursuits than the contemplation of the possibility of war.

2

The German duty officer was no exception to the general rule. He knew that the normal detailed procedures for gathering intelligence about the Warsaw Pact Forces would be undertaken with the same zeal and efficiency as at other times of the year. It was part of a duty officer's responsibility to ensure that the information fed into the Supreme Headquarters was properly and completely monitored and examined. Any signs of apparent build-up of enemy forces or any indications of unusual activity would be reported immediately to his superiors.

But, equally, they would want to be kept informed of the normal indicators showing that nothing unusual was afoot, that no sudden twist or turn or attack or surprise was imminent. The job of the duty officer would be to report the absence of movement among the enemy tank, air or naval forces just as much as the slightest indication of unusual activity.

What no one could know were the intentions of the Warsaw Pact, so that neither activity nor apparent inaction was necessarily a clear indication of what might be being planned, unless other more definite clues emerged.

Meanwhile it was the season of joyful festivities which all looked forward to enjoying.

TUESDAY

2100 Hours Central European Time

Police Headquarters, West Berlin

The Intelligence Co-ordination at SHAPE received a phone call from a British Staff Officer in Berlin reporting that an East German defector with potentially important information had crossed to the West. The British Officer asked for a member of the Intelligence Co-ordination staff to travel to Berlin immediately.

In West Berlin, the British Officer on the staff of the three NATO Commandants put down the phone in the office of the Chief of Police and went back to the small medical aid-room where a doctor, two orderlies and three senior policemen were grouped round a hospital bed on which a man lay and mumbled

3

incoherently, saliva dripping from the corners of his mouth, his eyes shut and his fists clenched. The stench in the room was a clear sign that he was incontinent. But none of the men in the room appeared to notice — intent as they were not to miss the brief moments of sanity and clear speech, becoming less and less frequent.

Dittmar Langman was a small, square man, prematurely ageing. He had lived in an official flat of four rooms on the southern outskirts of East Berlin with his wife and two teenage sons, and had held a high executive post in the secretariat of the Ministry of the Interior of the German Democratic Republic Government. His wife and sons were dedicated members of the Communist Party. Langman's interests had lain elsewhere and he had seen progressively less of his family.

For two years he and his secretary had become more deeply entangled in a clandestine love affair. Langman's wife had suspected nothing and did not care that his interest in her and the boys had become less and less. They had their own interests and enthusiasms and were thankful that he did not interfere.

There came a time when Langman and Gerda realized that they both wanted to make a new life together. But as the difficulties and restrictions in East Germany would be so great, they decided to get away to West Germany and start a new life there. They adopted a simple plan. They would each mark down a visitor from West Berlin who was nearly identical in build and facial looks to themselves. At a suitable moment when all their preparations were ready, they would individually entice their victim to a room in a semi-derelict office, drug him or her, change clothes, take the documents and, using them, pass back through the check-points into West Berlin. They reasoned that, ideally, Gerda should go first, as her absence from the office could more easily be explained.

Their preparations were completed and they were waiting for his secretary's West German near-double to visit East Berlin again, when Langman became involved in the final stages of large-scale plans to disrupt Western European society by terrorist subversion, sabotage and assassination, as a prelude to widespread disorders. Realizing that their long-laid plans for a new life away from the prying eyes of the East German Communist state would be ruined if this occurred, they settled that

4

Langman should go first, leaving as soon as possible to warn the West.

A week later Langman's chosen victim entered East Berlin on a visit to an elderly relative, at the usual time and on his usual day. Langman was waiting for him. He produced his official identity documents and ordered Hassler to accompany him. In the office he drugged the man with a cup of poisoned coffee, changed into his clothing, and hid his own identity documents inside the lining of the man's hat.

At 1600 hours, when it was already nearly dark, he walked through the poorly lit East Berlin streets to the border at the sector crossing-point in Bornholmer Strasse.

Langman's liaison with his secretary had not gone unremarked by his superiors nor unnoticed by the security police, who had put him under surveillance. They were intent on guarding against his being blackmailed to give away secret information. The agent on duty was naturally startled to see Langman's contact with Hassler, reported the fact and was joined by two other security men. When Langman, dressed as Hassler, left the building, one man followed him, while the other two broke into the office, found Hassler, still partially drugged and very distressed, and raced to join the man following Langman.

Sweating profusely, his hands damp with apprehension, his breath almost stifled with anxiety, Langman handed over Hassler's papers for inspection, and tried to control the trembling of his hands and legs. After what seemed an age, the East German sentry handed the papers back with hardly a glance at Langman. Just stifling a gasp of relief, he smiled wanly and, tucking the papers into his coat pocket, walked, trying to control himself from running, towards the West German checkpoint, thirty yards ahead.

As he did so he turned to see who was causing a commotion behind him. Three men, in bulky top-coats, had barged their way to the head of the queue and were in deep argument with the sentry. All four were looking in Langman's direction, who was in no doubt that he was being followed. Knowing that his best chance of salvation was to make an unremarked entry into West Berlin, Langman forced himself to walk naturally, to hand over his documents calmly for the almost perfunctory inspection by the West German police, and then to move rapidly away into

West Berlin, as if he had an urgent task to do.

Just when he thought himself safe, and turned into Sonderberger Strasse, a side street off the brilliantly lit main road, the three men caught up with him. He felt a heavy blow to the back of his head and, simultaneously, a sharp stab of pain to the back of the fleshy top part of his right thigh. He woke to find himself in a small room, lying on a hospital bed, surrounded by half a dozen men in strange uniforms.

Struggling to prop himself on his left elbow, and finding that his head was swimming and his vision blurred, he nevertheless managed to explain that he was not Hassler. He told the surprised West German police that his real identity was shown by the papers which he fumblingly produced from inside his hat, handed to him on his urgent demand. In a voice which was already becoming hoarse, and slurring his words, he said, 'They're going to come — hundreds of them — killing and blowing things up — watch out.'

'Who's going to come?' the senior policeman asked.

'Terrorists — agents — like the ones who followed me — bloody hell, why can't I think and see straight — they must have poisoned me.'

'You mean,' the policeman had said, 'that more of them are coming after you?'

'No, no, no, no,' Langman tried to shout back, 'they are coming after all of you — soon — all over West Europe — you're all going to die — I know — look at my papers — see who I am — alert everyone — don't let them do it — we want a good, safe home here — Gerda and me — look after Gerda when she comes.'

After that Langman's speech started to become virtually incoherent, except for moments of clarity when he insisted that there was to be a large-scale terrorist attack and when he pleaded that Gerda should be cared for when she came.

By 1900 hours the police doctor became very concerned about Langman's condition and had him moved to the intensive care unit of the nearby hospital.

Outside the special ward the two NATO officers discussed the defector: was he a plant? Were they on a wild goose chase? Could they put out a major alert just on the basis of what he said in his deathbed delirium?

6

WEDNESDAY

Brussels, Belgium

When the NATO Staff Officer returned to Brussels from Berlin, he drove first to a dress salon in the city, owned and managed by his girlfriend, for a drink and some food.

When he entered her office, she said, 'You remember I told you that we had had orders for dresses from the wives or mistresses of Russian Embassy staff in a number of capitals in Western Europe? And that I had also had cancellations of two orders from girls whose Russian men-friends had suddenly been ordered back to Russia? I told you then that one of the girls had said that new, younger, tougher, KGB men were taking over and the other men were being replaced. Well I have just had three more cancellations — one here in Brussels, one in Bonn, and one in London. What can it mean?'

Later he drove to the home of a Colonel of the German Army. There he found the two most senior officers of the Co-ordination Section of the Intelligence Division at Supreme Headquarters. It was their task to collate into the military intelligence obtained from all sources the relevant details of political, economic, industrial and police information. From this great variety they tried to build up a picture of the total potential of the Warsaw Pact, from which other experts would try to discern its short and long term intentions.

The first officer told of his hurried visit to Berlin adding, 'I don't know what to make of it. The man's probably dead by now — poisoned by being jabbed in the leg with a sharp needle. But he was on about a large-scale terrorist campaign right across Europe — soon I think, but exactly when we couldn't get clear. What do you think?'

'It's possible,' the German Colonel answered. 'They might well have decided that any military campaign would be too risky — might escalate too easily to thermonukes. They might think it possible to take over the West purely by paramilitary forces — depends on what they reckon their existing total of

7

agents amounts to — maybe Interpol can help. Did you hear of anything else?'

'Yes,' the first officer answered. 'This morning I was taken to meet five West Germans who had recently made visits to the East. Each had been told as usual that something was on the cards. Just exactly what they don't know. They had heard that some Soviet military vehicles with skeleton crews have already been moved on to some of the farms and into some of the towns in a 50-kilometre zone between Berlin and the Iron Curtain. They're probably there for the next lot of manoeuvres starting a couple of weeks from now. There's some talk that in the last ten days or so, the full crews of these vehicles have been moved in at night close to where their vehicles are, or, on the farms, actually with their vehicles. The story is that it's all to do with bigger manoeuvres. What seems surprising is that there has been no movement of any heavy tanks. But of course they don't always use them for their manoeuvres.'

Later that night the radio news reported that there would be demonstrations in West Germany against the Soviet invitation for people in the West to have totally unimpeded entry into East Germany and Czechoslovakia to visit friends and relatives. The Soviet announcement had said that the invitation was being made because of the special time of year in the West. The demonstrations were to be against what was described as 'the Soviet trap of bogus *détente*'.

At SHAPE many officers were being brought face to face with the huge Soviet military build-up, which had provided the Warsaw Pact Forces with a preponderance of weapons and manpower, essential for enabling them to make war with NATO with every prospect of success, whatever the circumstances in which they decided to launch their attacks. The momentum of Soviet political, strategic and tactical activities had been such that the increasing pressure to keep the initiative had generated even more momentum, whatever the obvious disadvantages to Soviet standing in the world. With each repressive act in its own country and each one which it supported in other countries, the political credit of the Soviet Union had become less and less. Also, its economic system was proving to be inefficient and insufficiently adaptable to modern techniques and technology.

Many had concluded that the increasing momentum of

Soviet actions had been dictated by the progressive failure of the Soviet economic and agricultural systems to meet the needs of the Communist countries and to support the vast aspirations of the Soviet leaders. Before this situation became unmanageable, the Soviet Union might conceivably have to take the one remaining drastic step which would solve its problems — the take-over, if possible without destruction or disruption, of the whole of Western Europe, with its successful industry, commerce, agriculture, science and advanced technology. Only by such a comprehensive step could the Soviet Union expect to achieve world domination in the face of the power of the United States and the remaining free countries of the world and against the latent strength of China.

The urgency for such action was also dictated by the fact that by the early 1980s the Soviet Union would no longer be able to maintain both its armed forces and its industrial and agricultural manpower at the levels it considered necessary — there would in fact be a severe shortage of Russian labour. A whole generation of young Russian workers, the children of the millions of potential parents killed in the Second World War, was missing from the labour force. The Soviet population was becoming predominantly of Asian stock: European Russians and the Baltic Republics had for years had a low and diminishing birth-rate. The more educated and technically adaptable and adept Europeans were becoming increasingly outnumbered by Asiatics with no capacity for the skills required, held back by problems of language and training. Unless the Soviet Union were to acquire a vast new source of skilled manpower by taking over Western Europe, the changing character of its own population would create stagnation and anarchy.

But it was the generally held belief that whether the Soviet Union actually invaded or used its massive preponderance of forces to blackmail Western Europe into surrender, there would be due warning of its intentions when it mobilized its manpower and moved its ships, aircraft and tanks into positions ready for battle. And when that happened the NATO powers would initiate the measures necessary to mobilize their European forces and to airlift across the Atlantic the huge reserve forces the United States had made available.

THURSDAY

Brunssum, Holland

Throughout the night reports of large-scale demonstrations throughout the Federal Republic reached the Headquarters of Allied Forces Central Europe. By early morning it was apparent that the disturbances were so serious that there was a danger that the civil authorities might not be able to retain control, and that the NATO armed forces should be ready to come to their help if required.

In the incident centre which had been set up at an early hour all was bustle and hubbub — phones were ringing, wireless links were in use, messengers were scurrying in and out, and the latest reports were being pinpointed on a brightly lit map covering one wall of the room.

There were a lot of separate incidents in each place where there was rioting. The worst incident reported so far was in Hamburg where four coaches were driven into each other and set alight. In Bremen two policemen were knocked to the ground by bricks and then badly kicked until they were rescued. In Bonn there was mainly noise — the crowd chanting 'Russians out — Russians out'. In Bremen the crowds massed at the gates to the port and brought traffic movement to a standstill. The crowds in Frankfurt were breaking the windows of banks and hotels. In Mainz there were three incidents of petrol bombs being thrown at the offices of foreign companies. The demonstrations were serious, large numbers being involved in each place. However the incidents were far too well managed to be spontaneous when an overall view was taken of them all. The media, in the thick of the turmoil, were just reporting what they saw and heard — noise, violence, abuse, damage, injuries, some fires, and some petrol bombing. It was all much like many other demonstrations but, to the trained observers, it appeared to be definitely contrived.

The monitors picking up Moscow and East German radio broadcasts reported that the incidents were being given maximum coverage. It was being alleged that the so-called

Neo-Nazi activities were against the peaceful, conciliatory Soviet proposal to open the frontiers at Christmas. Such violent objection to so friendly an act was being quoted as evidence of the serious underlying enmity against *détente* and peaceful co-existence — itself a dangerous threat to peace. Evidence was however emerging that the instigators behind the worst scenes were known left-wing agitators, backed by groups of agitators whose sudden emergence in such numbers astonished the German police.

There seemed to be no explanation for the sudden upsurge of violence on the scale reported, except that it was deliberately contrived. It seemed all of a piece with the defector's warning of widespread disruption to enable terrorists and agents to assume control. And yet, widespread as the riots apparently were, they were still not serious enough to portend a collapse of the West German authority.

Throughout the afternoon, until darkness fell at 1630 hours, incidents continued to be reported. In the early part of the night a few police stations were attacked and set on fire and shots were aimed at some West German Army barracks. By 2100 hours all was quiet in West Germany.

At the Centre camp beds had been placed in the corridors and the restaurant was kept open to feed those on duty and the press. All were uneasily aware of the importance of the build-up of violence and went to bed early to be prepared for any eventuality.

The mobs gathered slowly on the Friday morning. The initial momentum appeared to have passed — there was an atmosphere of lethargy but also of expectation. By midday the violence was as serious as on the previous day, the mobs as large, the damage just as important.

Soon after 1300 hours, a solemn announcement was made on Moscow radio that, in view of the vigorous hostility shown by the hate inspired Nazi masses of West Germans, the Soviet, East German and Czechoslovak proposals to open the frontiers for Christmas visits had been cancelled and the Warsaw Pact would be meeting the following day, Saturday, to determine what further action it should take to safeguard its position and safety.

The mobs dispersed. By 1600 hours, the streets, where the

11

violence had raged for almost the whole of two days, were suddenly deserted and quiet. Relieved, but with a deep feeling of disquiet at the clear evidence of the sophisticated stage management of events, and more than ever worried about the reason for mounting such riots, the Intelligence Staff were informed about the incident in Berlin. They all felt some considerable unease, but there was as yet not enough concrete evidence to lay out before their chiefs. There had been some sort of a build-up of military equipment in the western areas of East Germany and Czechoslovakia, in preparation for yet more manoeuvres, already announced. In recent months, there had been a noticeable reduction of tension, a deliberate effort by the Communists to be pleasant and accommodating. On the other hand some women who had ordered dresses had suddenly cancelled their orders.

But the Soviet Navy had not moved out in strength from its bases, the Warsaw Pact heavy tanks had not left their peacetime barracks, and the Russian Tactical Air Armies had not stepped westwards at all.

In a discussion of recent events with a NATO intelligence officer a French Interpol official reported that they had noticed that in the last six or so months there had been an increase in the numbers of used cars, vans and trucks being taken into Eastern Europe. Most of them had been properly purchased, some had been stolen and obviously furnished with false documents for the journey, others had been rented. It was not very remarkable as there was a shortage of vehicles in Eastern Europe. What had however attracted the attention of Interpol was that some trade vehicles which made regular journeys to the East seemed to have had their scheduled returns delayed for various reasons.

FRIDAY

1600 Hours Central European Time

Wolterstadt, East Germany

Hans Ulrich Unterleib slammed the front door of his flat, took off his hat, scarf, gloves and overcoat, moved down the short passage to his small kitchen and turned on his electric kettle to make himself a cup of coffee. He then went into his compact, furniture cluttered living-room, drew a sheet of clean, lined paper from a pile at the back of his writing-table and sat down to write his weekly report to be transmitted through various channels to West German Intelligence contacts in West Berlin.

He worked as a freelance journalist, scraping a living by his wordy reports on agricultural matters throughout East Germany. He owned a small two-stroke motorcycle on which he travelled long distances to get his stories, and on which a great deal of his spare time was spent on general maintenance and repairs, when he could get the parts. His other income, from his spying activities, he spent carefully and with extreme caution on his collection of books, which he had found he was able to buy at extremely low prices from the farming families he met regularly, or from their friends and acquaintances, all desperate to supplement their sparse incomes.

He had just returned from one of his regular visits to the area between Berlin and the borders of East and West Germany — a visit he had contrived to make whenever the Warsaw Pact announced its annual winter manoeuvres. All such military exercises were of considerable concern to the farmers because of the inevitable damage to their land and fences, which Unterleib faithfully reported, but in the guarded terms on which the censor insisted.

When he had made himself his cup of coffee, he wrote his detailed Intelligence report in longhand.

'As usual,' he wrote, 'the Warsaw Pact winter manoeuvres will take place close to the Western borders of the German Democratic Republic and the Czechoslovak Socialist State. Again as usual, in accordance with the Helsinki Agreement on exercises and manoeuvres, observers from the NATO countries have been invited to attend but will probably, as usual, be impeded from entering the manoeuvre areas. As usual, also, the manoeuvres will take place in the period which coincides with the time when many of the population, and the soldiers, might have wanted to celebrate the rites of Christmas and to enjoy the celebrations. As it is there will be considerable disruption of traffic, family life and commercial business of all kinds as a number of reservists have been called up and some civilian vehicles have been taken over.

'As usual, again, the manoeuvres are based once more this year on the assumption that there is likely to be an invasion of the Warsaw Pact frontiers by the military forces of the NATO Powers.

'This year it has been assumed that the NATO invasion will be carried out by deep-penetration light forces somewhat similar to the Soviet Assault Regiments.

'All seven regiments have been moved to the Western frontiers where they are to advance east at high speed on about twelve of the routes which the NATO forces might use for an invasion. They are without their heavy T-72 tanks.

'On a line about 100 kilometres east of the frontiers, a number of Soviet and East German motor-rifle divisions have been positioned to meet the first impact of the invasion. These motor-rifle divisions have left all their tanks further east. The Warsaw Pact tank divisions are positioned even further to the east.

'There are reports that the call-up of reservists for some East German divisions is higher than in the past, but there are also reports that the Warsaw Pact Forces are intending to test their logistic units more than in previous years.

'There have been no reports of any moves by the Warsaw Pact airforces.

'The attitude of the general public is one of disinterest and some resentment about the inevitable disruption.'

Unterleib finished his report, carefully encyphered it, copied it on to the special thin paper with which he had been provided and folded it painstakingly into one of the long thin envelopes designed for this particular use. He finished his cold cup of coffee, put the envelope into the pages of one of a pile of weekly magazines which, each week, he delivered on a Friday to Frau Henschel, a widow in her ninetieth year, who lived in a tiny flat on the far side of the town. Where his letter would go from there he had no idea and no wish to know.

FRIDAY

1700 Hours Middle East Time
1600 Hours Central European Time

Tel Aviv, Israel

As the mobs dispersed in West Germany during Friday afternoon, in Tel Aviv in Israel the joint five services of Israeli Intelligence were gathered for a specially summoned, urgent meeting to consider the latest information provided by their agencies. They met on the Friday both to evaluate certain serious items of intelligence and to be able to pass their findings to the capitals of Western Europe, before the long holiday weekend leading up to Christmas. And they wanted to clear all urgent business before the start of their own Sabbath. All present were nervously aware that only a matter of supreme urgency could explain the calling of such a special meeting.

The Chairman of the Joint Intelligence Committee had taken his place at the top of the long table in the cool, white-painted room where all their meetings were held. On the straight-backed chairs round the bare stone walls sat the staff officers, clerks and stenographers. At the table sat the Cabinet Minister selected to attend to represent the Prime Minister; the Chief of the Army Staff; the Director of Military Intelligence, responsible for military information regarding Israel's immediate external enemies; the Head of the Security Services, responsible for information about Israel's internal known or likely enemies; the Director General of the Research Division of the Foreign Ministry, responsible for information regarding the political aims and attitudes of Israel's external friends and enemies; and the Controller of Counter-Terrorist Operations. In attendance as observers at the meeting were the Inspector General of Police and the Commander of the Security Forces, combating terrorism inside the country.

Up to that point the meeting had dealt with certain urgent but more minor matters. There came a pause in the discussions and the Chairman, turning to the Controller of Counter-Terrorist Operations said, 'You have a statement to make.' The Controller nodded and started to speak. He spoke slowly and

15

clearly choosing his words with great care. He had been selected for the cool, considered balance of his judgements, and had acquired the regard of those who knew his work because of past examples of the acuteness of his perception of the methods and intentions of the secret, ruthless enemies of Israel.

'I have described for some months now how we have been getting persistent reports that the terrorist camps of the PFLP in Iraq, Aden and the Island of Socotra have been training assassins and saboteurs in some numbers. I would have expected some of these killers to have acted before now, but, when they leave the training-camps, they disappear. I don't know what to make of it — and I have communicated my worry to the Prime Minister. I also reported yesterday that a defector from East Berlin has warned of large-scale terrorist attacks right across Europe.'

'That is what we are here to discuss — the Prime Minister wants us to give him our joint opinion,' the Chairman said.

'I can only add my worry to that of the Controller,' answered the Foreign Ministry Director. 'We also have reports from our agents of the arrival of men and women to be trained, and then they have gone — disappeared.'

'My main concern,' the Controller of Counter-Terrorist Operations said, 'is the potential scale of the terror that could be launched against us. If all the trained terrorists were to concentrate on any one country they could do irreparable damage to Jewish interests in that country.'

'On the other hand,' the Chairman interrupted, 'if they were to attack our diplomatic, financial — even religious, institutions throughout Europe, it would be a very serious blow to Israel. Have we any idea where the blows may fall?' He turned a questioning look at each member of the Committee and stopped at the Head of the Security Services. 'Is it possible that they are preparing a massive attack against targets in this country?'

'It is one possibility,' said the Head of the Security Services. 'But I would say that I am fairly convinced that the threat is not against us here in Israel. My contacts within the country are good, the Arabs are inveterate talkers, unless they are carefully trained like the PFLP terrorists, and any operation on this scale, I am sure, we would have had a whiff of by now. We also know that a defector has warned of large-scale terrorist action

16

throughout Europe.'

The Director General of the Research Division of the Foreign Ministry leaned forward in his chair and, speaking with deliberation, added, 'The Prime Minister, as you know, has taken a personal interest in this affair and has instructed that our Ambassadors warn the Governments to which they are accredited that the Israeli Government reminds them of their obligations to protect the lives and property of Israeli citizens in their countries. Our Ambassador in Washington is seeing the United States Secretary of State today, in about one hour's time, and will raise this particular issue.'

'I can only hope,' replied the Chairman, gathering his papers and rising to his feet, 'that the impending Christmas holiday is not going to be the hour when the blows are struck, because I fear that vigilance in some countries will be relaxed.'

FRIDAY

1000 Hours Eastern Standard Time
1600 Hours Central European Time

Washington, USA

At 1000 hours Eastern Standard Time the Israeli Ambassador, accompanied by his Military Attaché, was shown into the office of the United States Secretary of State. They were old acquaintances and did without elaborate preliminaries, but moved to three armchairs round a low coffee-table decorated with a bowl of bulbs in bloom. They ranged briefly over a number of routine matters and came, at length, to the main matter on the Ambassador's agenda.

'My Government is very concerned,' started the Ambassador, and paused to pick his words carefully, 'because it believes that the terrorist organizations are preparing a massive attack. You have received the latest report from Berlin?'

'Yes,' replied the Secretary of State, 'I have had that report and others that numbers of terrorists have been trained, and have then gone to ground and trace of them has been lost. Even the known terrorists seem to be leading a quiet life.'

17

'That,' said the Ambassador, 'is what we are not happy about. There has been an unusual calm. There have been attacks, it's true — the usual kidnaps and murders — but not on the scale that we have been expecting, knowing the numbers that have been trained.'

'What is your fear, then?' asked the Secretary of State.

'We fear, Sir,' the Military Attaché replied, 'that there will be concerted attacks, possibly all in one country — even here in the US — possibly in a number of countries. And we think that a likely time is over a holiday period — like Christmas or over any week-end before or after Christmas.' The Secretary of State nodded and answered, 'We have alerted all the agencies here in the States. We have no evidence that the attacks will be here, but we shall be ready with extra protection for likely targets. I can't promise more because we have no firm warnings to go on.'

'That is what my Government wanted to be sure of,' answered the Ambassador. 'It is an uncomfortable feeling.'

The Military Attaché interrupted to add, 'We are certain that something is on hand, but we have been totally unable to find out any concrete facts. There has been no loose talk, no hints. There is even a feeling among some of our experts that there is a bigger hand now having closer control over the terrorist set-up. But we cannot get chapter and verse on what is behind it all. Whatever it is — it will not be pleasant — and we want to be prepared — and we want everyone else to be prepared.'

'That's very understandable,' said the Secretary of State, rising from his chair as the two Israelis stood ready to leave. 'And we trust that all our worries are groundless. Perhaps there are other plans afoot and it is not Israel that is in danger.'

'Thank you,' said the Ambassador. 'I hope you are right — but, if you are, I do not envy whoever the target is, if it is not Israel. Good morning to you, and have a happy holiday.'

The Ambassador and the Military Attaché left and the Secretary of State closed the door behind them, and then remained holding the door handle, deep in thought.

If the targets were not Israeli, what would they be? What was being planned and where? Not in the United States he felt sure. But where else and against what and whom? Could the Russians be behind this new massive terrorist threat? Could it be a new way of throwing NATO off its guard? He had had a

18

nagging worry over many months that the situation in Central Europe was not secure, despite the apparent calm of *détente*, and the recent more friendly attitude of the Russians and East Europeans. The warning of large-scale terrorist attacks reinforced his concern about the long-term Soviet intentions, whatever the improvement in international relations in the short term. The American forces in Europe might be at risk.

There were only about six divisions of American ground troops based in Western Europe, together with twenty-eight squadrons of aircraft, which could be reinforced by one division and forty squadrons in ten days.

Was it all going to be too little and too late? wondered the Secretary of State. And what if an emergency occurred without warning? Or if the emergency was totally different — a terrorist take-over instead of the invasion usually envisaged?

He had found that any assessment of the military balance between NATO and the Warsaw Pact involved making comparisons between so many inter-related aspects. It was not just a comparison of the strengths of both men and equipment. But any comparison started from one unarguable premise, that NATO was a defensive alliance and that the intentions of the Warsaw Pact, and especially those of Russia, were unpredictable. This was the main advantage held by the Warsaw Pact. There was no saying when or how or what they would do. Would they attack with nuclear weapons or conventional weapons or unconventional terrorist forces? There was so little depth in the NATO Central Sector in Europe that it was appallingly vulnerable to any sort of attack. The Warsaw Pact had more armed forces at battle-readiness and more to call on from closer distances, so it could easily reinforce anything it did. And, except for the British, with their experience in Northern Ireland, none of the other NATO forces were trained adequately to combat large-scale terrorist action.

And — in every aspect of warlike equipment — guns, tanks, aircraft, submarines and tactical missiles, the Warsaw Pact had three times as many as NATO.

Another considerable NATO disadvantage was that, built in to all the NATO thinking on their defence plans, was the concept of political warning time — that there would be enough warning of a possible attack for reinforcements to be added to the peacetime strength of their forces. This assumed that there would be a confrontation, and that the Western Governments, possibly at the risk of increasing tension, would allow mobilization and the movement of reserves.

But if there was no build-up of crisis, no increase in tension even, the Warsaw Pact might be able to mount a surprise attack, whether conventional or unconventional, having taken precautions to hide their own preparation and movements. The Germans had achieved complete surprise for their attack on Russia in June 1941. Even when an attack was expected, by careful preparation and considerable deception, the Allies had achieved significant surprise for their invasion of the Normandy beaches in 1944.

Inside the Iron Curtain, within societies under the strict dominance of secret police, with interior lines of communication on road and rail, it might be possible for the Warsaw Pact to assemble in secret so many different kinds of forces that NATO, without additional strength, would be overwhelmed and overrun.

In short, the Secretary of State reluctantly concluded, the overall balance, although deemed to be satisfactory by the NATO experts, could be tipped radically in its favour by the Warsaw Pact if it decided to launch a sudden, surprise attack against selected targets — and particularly at a time when NATO might be off guard or might, by deception, be induced to be complacent. It might also be able to devise methods, totally unexpected, to achieve surprise in new ways.

He moved to the windows and stared gloomily out — a very worried man. He decided that, before the day was out, he would talk with the Defence Secretary to check the latest satellite, sea surveillance and military intelligence reports, just to reassure himself that all was well, before going home for the Christmas holiday. The equation of the risk of war depended fundamentally on the balance of power between the United States and the Soviet Union. He knew it and he knew the Soviet Union knew it. But what worried him deep down was that some of his NATO Allies also knew it, and traded on it, by spending less on defence than was sensible and being less alert than was wise.

FRIDAY

1700 Hours Central European Time

Brussels, Belgium

As night fell on the Friday evening eight men met in a brightly lit, starkly furnished room. There was nothing remarkable about any of them except their common tension and wariness, particularly in the eyes, and the meticulousness with which they listed and noted all that was discussed.

'We have much to do,' the leader said briskly, 'and I do not want to waste time. We have not long in which to be sure that all our arrangements are going according to plan. If anything needs seeing to, I want it done tonight. Don't hide anything if it is not right now, because we still have time to put it right. I do not know exactly when we shall be required to act, until I get the codeword, but I know we have not long to wait.'

Although listed as a Senior Secretary in the Russian Embassy, the man was in fact the head of all KGB affairs in Brussels and answerable to no one except his senior in Moscow. On his shoulders rested the success or failure of the campaign of widespread disruption in an important sector of Western Europe. He turned to the man who was responsible for identifying the key Western personalities to be eliminated and for organizing the actions of the carefully trained Special Groups who were to carry out the task.

'In a sense,' he said, 'the major disruption will be the result of the successful actions of the many agents and groups under you. So we will start with you. Have you established clearly where all your targets will be over the next four days?'

The second man cleared his throat loudly and said, 'Where their plans have been made, we already know them for all but a few of our targets. Where we cannot get the plans, we have made provision for the individuals to be closely followed. We have information from all the agents we have been able to recruit about all the individuals who are of interest.'

'Good,' replied the leader, 'because if we can take out all these key men, the disruption that can be caused will be vital. What about the men who might step in? You remember we discussed them at our meeting last month?'

'I remember, Comrade,' replied the second man, 'but that is more difficult. We have been able to determine in most cases who is the nominal successor. What we cannot be sure of is whether they are likely to be the most resolute and will act decisively or, whether, when the disruption is apparent, a stronger personality will emerge.'

'Are your Special Groups all ready?' the leader asked, turning to the man responsible for the recruitment and training of the Special Groups.

'They are all ready, Comrade' the man answered, 'The Groups with only KGB personnel more ready than the others, but the others are learning discipline. The latest arrivals from the training-camps will be the most difficult to control.'

'That brings us to the Spearhead Groups then,' the leader intervened. 'What about your Spearhead Groups?' he said turning to the man responsible for organizing the actions of the groups which were to carry out the tasks of sabotage, of taking and holding key installations and of eliminating, where necessary, the NATO staff of these installations.

'As you know,' the man replied, 'the last of them do not arrive until tomorrow night — Saturday. There have to be many of them and it would have been too risky to have too many near their targets for too long before they are due to strike. We were in danger of having too few for the tasks to be done, but I have got reinforcements. It was very lucky that the Ukrainian bulb growers should want to visit Holland just now. They arrived two days ago and have all been instructed about their targets. Not the bulbs!'

There was a short, subdued murmur of amusement.

'Good,' said the leader, 'have you solved your problems about where to put the crews and vehicles tonight and tomorrow night?'

'Yes,' said the man, nodding, 'and we have planned to take more vehicles tomorrow night so that we can split into more, smaller, groups. We shall have surprise to help us and we do not need large squads.' ·

'Good again,' the leader said. Then, turning to another man, 'Now, what about the targets the Spearhead Groups are to hit?

Are they all clearly ear-marked and directions to them lucidly written up and mapped for the Groups?'

'Indeed, Comrade,' answered the fifth man. 'All is ready and we have been able to arrange in every case that local collaborators in the Support Groups are on hand to act as guides.'

'Can you give us a brief summary of the Spearhead Groups which are coming ostensibly to do other things?' the leader asked, turning back to the man responsible.

'Some have already arrived, Comrade, and some arrive during tomorrow. As you know we have arranged a variety of groups so that they do not draw attention to themselves. A cruise liner docks at Antwerp tomorrow night. Nineteen hundred of the passengers and crew are already ear-marked and Support Groups have been briefed as a safeguard for these Spearhead Groups. The Ukrainian bulb growers you have already heard of. We have two hundred delegates in Paris attending a Conference at the invitation of the French Communist Party. We have a rugby football team and supporters in Toulouse and close to the factories of Aerospatiale. Three ships of the Soviet fleet are on a goodwill visit to Brest. Two ocean fish factory-ships will enter Cherbourg tomorrow night for urgent repairs. We have a winter sports team training in South France, not far from the French strategic rocket sites. There are others, but I will leave out these details. So far as we know, they will be in position by midnight tomorrow.'

'You next,' the leader said, nodding to a short man, sitting behind the other. 'I imagine that you have had fewer problems recently in recruiting the Support Groups — the collaborators in the local population?'

'That is true. Initially we had many problems in trying to contact the silent hardcore of the likely collaborators in each country. There is no difficulty in finding the openly avowed Communist sympathizers. We have had to look for the doers and not the talkers. They were more difficult to find and much more difficult to convince that we were really serious in what we proposed. Gradually, however, through their own underground networks we have got all the help we want. The few Spearhead Groups which have already arrived have been hidden away without trace, men, women, vehicles — the lot. The Spearhead

Groups which have come as teams, tourists, crews of ships, have and will be equally well guided and helped.'

'Good, good,' the leader said, 'now to the problems of making your contacts with the Armed Faction for Peoples Power and the other organized terror groups?'

The man responsible for these activities replied, 'As you know, Comrade, we have tried to get close contacts with the Armed Faction in France and the Red Help in Holland. There is a new group in Belgium too, linked with Red Help in Holland. These groups are fanatical and unreliable. We have given them encouragement, but we have told them which targets we do not want them to hit and we have also stressed that we can only give them two hours' notice to strike.'

'What do you have to report?' the leader said, turning to the last man, who answered slowly, 'My problem is how to sort the real Communists from the loud-mouth Communists first, and then among the real Communists to pick the ones who will have the stomach to accept all that is involved in bringing Communism to the West. We do not want talkers who are intellectual Communists only. We want the Communists who will send their own mothers and fathers, sisters and brothers, even their own wives and children to the firing-squads or the chemical exterminators if necessary. We have picked some and have made useful contacts. Not ones that you will have heard about — the talkers are not very often the doers we want either.'

'The plans seem to be well under control,' the leader intoned slowly. 'If there are any difficulties, any problems at all, I am to be told immediately. I want no delay in informing Moscow if there is any detail going wrong. Is that understood? Finally I must stress again that the character of the whole of this operation at this end must be ruthless terror, terror without hesitation, terror without mercy. We must ensure that there is total disruption, confusion, despair and a conviction that there is nothing the civil population can do to protect themselves. Their only hope must be seen to be surrender.'

However, he had a note of warning to issue before the meeting broke up. 'Comrades, I must tell you to see very carefully to your plans and tell your groups to be ready to meet more resistance than we might have expected. An East German official, who knew a little of what has been planned, defected to

24

West Berlin last Tuesday. We must therefore assume that he has put NATO on the alert. So tell your Groups to be extra prepared and extra alert.'

FRIDAY

1730 Hours Central European Time

Paris, France

As evening drew on in Paris and the crowds made their ways home or to their evening entertainments, officers of the Scientific Section at the Headquarters of Interpol in Paris were conducting their examination of the evidence which had been first given to the West German Police in Hamburg by Laurenti Blok, a defector from the Soviet Union, who had escaped the previous week-end from the Estonian port of Tallinn, in a carefully constructed semi-submersible midget craft, propelled by compressed air, and had been picked up by a West German freighter. After initial interrogation in Hamburg, he had been flown to Paris.

He had been shown the photographs, taken by American spy satellites and widely reported in the Western press in January 1978, of specially built, heavily guarded biological-warfare weapon factories, near Moscow and elsewhere in the western Soviet Union. Expert analysis at the time had shown the factories to be both research and production centres.

'I can confirm,' Blok said, 'that the Soviet Union is breeding new strains of lethal viruses and microbes in large quantities. I have worked in those centres. The Russians are carrying out work on refining and making more lethal the microbes and viruses which produce plague, anthrax, tuberculosis, smallpox, yellow fever and diphtheria.

'I can no longer be involved in such work. I must tell the world that tactical nerve agents and their derivatives are being made in the germ war factories.'

A great deal of the information that Blok was able to give was already known to Interpol, but the officers were reluctant to interrupt him in case he had new information on the subject.

25

'What you almost certainly do not know,' Blok went on, 'is that to meet the need of a close range, highly lethal, fast acting, silent weapon the Soviet Union had merely to develop the inherent properties of the nerve agents and to reduce, where possible, the effects caused by cumulative poisoning of those individuals handling the agents. By early 1978 they had found a type of neutralizing agent similar to that which had been discovered by the British Chemical Defence Establishment. The Russians, as the British have done, have also developed further antidotes in the form of hypodermic syringes loaded with compounds based on belladonna.'

The interest of the Interpol officers intensified as Blok continued, 'One problem remained: to determine the best means by which the nerve gases could be carried and delivered to their targets. The conventional methods of spraying from canisters or of bursting small gas filled grenades have the double disadvantage of being very difficult to conceal and being very inaccurate. What was needed was a small, simple, easily concealed device which could be produced just before use, when within a very short distance of the intended target.

'After considerable research the Soviet Union developed two small weapons very similar in shape, size and method of use to some which they had obtained from the United States used for delivery of their Chemical Mace non-lethal compounds.'

Blok could see that he had the full attention of his hearers. 'The smaller of two Soviet weapons, specifically constructed for precision attacks, takes the form of a pocket size, fountain pen type cylinder measuring about 12 centimetres in length and 1¼ centimetres in diameter, which can be fitted easily into a jacket or coat pocket. It can be used accurately at any range up to two metres, and each cylinder contains enough gas for twelve one-second bursts.

'The larger of the Soviet gas weapons, designed for less precise attacks, is made in two sizes, depending on the number of shot bursts likely to be required in any action. It is made to look like a thick baton or truncheon, about 2 centimetres in diameter, and either 25 or 30 centimetres in length. Both sizes can be used accurately at ranges up to 4 metres. The shorter weapon contains enough gas for twenty shot bursts, and the larger weapon thirty shot bursts. The trigger and burst nozzle are fitted to one end of the stick.'

Blok paused to allow the Interpol officers to make detailed notes and to answer certain queries. At length he continued, 'For use at longer ranges the weapon has been adapted for ranges up to 50 metres in one form and up to 250 metres in another form. The first adaptation consists of putting a thin plastic head on top of the stick, the plastic being brittle enough to splinter on impact with any surface, so emitting the gas under pressure from the compressed air-actuator. This adaptation is fitted into a hollow metal tube, much as the arrow in the tube of an Australian aborigine's woomera weapon, and fired from the tube by a compressed air-cartridge at the back end.

'The second adaptation is very similar to the first except that the stick is made in a better aerodynamic shape, with small clip-on fins at the back end, and is fired from a very powerful cross-bow. At a range of 250 metres it has the accuracy of a rifle, the cross-bow being fitted with a telescopic sight for day use or tele-scopic infra-red sight for night use.

'To evade discovery while passing through customs inspec-tions or any other close security, the shorter length gas stick is made so that it can be fitted inside an apparently normal vacuum flask, in batches of six sticks, or inside the tubular framework of the large coloured umbrellas which are carried to shield photographers from sun or rain. The parts for the cross-bows have been designed to appear to belong either to the umbrellas, or to different types of camera tripods, walking-sticks or shooting-sticks. The telescopic, day or night, sights have been designed to look like a camera optical lens or flash equipment.'

Blok paused, gathering his thoughts, then said, 'One further weapon has also been developed by the Russians. In order to ensure that certain key personnel in vital positions can be replaced, a method had to be devised to eliminate them. A variety of lethal or highly debilitating poisons have therefore been developed from the research carried out into plague, anth-rax, Lassa fever, Ebola fever and Marburg fever.

'There has also been a development programme of the methods by which the poisons can be delivered to selected

27

individual targets. A variety of methods have been found and have been tested.'

The Interpol officers thanked Blok for his information and took him back to the carefully selected and guarded hiding-place which they had provided.

They arranged for Blok's information to be circulated to other police forces in the Western world through the usual channels, and to the Intelligence Division at SHAPE.

FRIDAY

1800 Hours Central European Time

Brussels, Belgium

A senior female computer executive in a Belgian government department called at the home of a Belgian Army officer, whom she had met through mutual friends. After introducing herself briefly, she said, 'During the last ten days I have become very worried and frightened. You know I am a computer executive. I am also a senior member of the trade union branch in the department. I have attended most of the important union committees, but I have just become aware that I have been excluded from certain small, more secret committees. There are three pieces of information which I have been able to piece together because some people I know have not been as discreet as they should have been.

'First of all I have found out that during the latter part of last week and every day this week, special cadres formed from union members and left-wing activists have been carrying out particular assignments. I don't know exactly what, but I understand that they have had to find special hiding-places for groups of men and women and for the vehicles of these special groups. I think the groups have or will come from Germany, possibly East Germany. I think they are terrorist or sabotage groups. But what has worried me now for some days is that it seems that there are to be quite large numbers of these groups, and that they will be moving into the whole of Western Europe.

'I have come to you now because I think I am under observation. There is no one else I can see to pass on my worries. In a civil department of the Government I can't be sure what attitude my superiors would adopt to the sort of report I am making. I don't know what their political opinions are for instance. In your case I feel I can be sure that you will see that my information will get to the authorities who need to know.'

The woman paused and then continued, 'The next thing is that some time tomorrow there is to be an announcement made throughout Western Europe, that the trade unions representing the public services, the trains, the airport workers, the dock workers and so on will insist that, to show friendly solidarity with all workers everywhere, they are declaring a workers' holiday on Monday. And that all services will be reduced to holiday schedules from midday Sunday. They will make it known that this action is in protest against the demonstrations by the fascists, who objected to the friendly gesture by the Communists to open their frontiers for Christmas visitors to Eastern Europe.' She fell silent for a moment, deep in thought.

'The third item of information,' she said, 'is linked to the second. I am in computers — I told you that. I have discovered that, again over this week-end, certain key sections of vital civil and military computer systems are to be disrupted, at about the same time as the strike in Europe. I don't know exactly which parts of which computers will be put out of action and I don't know how and for how long. But the idea seems to be that, to show that the unions running the computers have got to be listened to and taken account of, they will put vital components of important computers out of action for about twenty-four, maybe forty-eight, hours. It won't be just the hard core of militant computer staff who will be taking action. It will also be the militant hard core of electricians, repair engineers, and programmers who might be called in to rectify faults in the software. It will be a very severe disruption. I am sure of that.'

'What proof have you got?' the officer said. 'Can we get any proof? Is there anyone else we can ask to confirm what you are saying?' He paused and stared hard at the woman. 'Now don't get me wrong,' he added quickly as he saw her face flush, her fists clench and her chest heave as she prepared to answer him. 'I do believe you. But how can I convince anyone else that what you say is true?'

29

She could only emphasize her fear and worry and left soon afterwards.

The frightened woman's information was passed by the Belgian Army officer to the Intelligence Division at SHAPE where it joined a growing number of indications that some widespread disruption was about to affect Western Europe. But there was still no concrete evidence to indicate an impending emergency. The Soviet ship dispositions remained unchanged. There was no information that any heavy tanks had moved out of barracks, nor that any large numbers of reserves had recently been called up. There was no sign that the Pact Tactical Air Armies were being moved to airfields closer to the frontier. And there was no political tension between the Pact nations and NATO except over the recent riots, which were against an apparently friendly Communist offer to open the frontiers.

During the night the duty staff of the Operations Centre at SHAPE received a report from Interpol in Paris that there was further evidence to add to that of the defector about large-scale terrorist attacks. Interpol considered that without a further dimension, it could not see how even widespread attacks could be expected to succeed. However, it now had that extra dimension — a new range of very lethal special weapons, using nerve gas which Laurenti Blok, an escaped Soviet scientist, had reported. SHAPE told Interpol what the computer executive had said, which, they both agreed, added yet another dimension to the same equation.

FRIDAY

1800 Hours Central European Time

Western Europe

Preoccupied with their daily tasks and pleasures, impatient for the approaching holiday, the population of Western Europe was largely unaware that war against them had already been in progress for years. Ever since the United States had humiliated the Soviet Union over Cuba in 1962, the driving ambition for world domination by the Soviet Union had been reinforced by an urge for revenge. War was joined on every front with greater intensity — the political front by expansion in Africa and Asia, the economic front by expansion of the Soviet Merchant Fleet and the blocking of vital raw materials from Africa, the military front by a vast expansion of armed forces, the terrorist front by the support given to the forces of international terrorism, the espionage front by a steady increase of penetration from Communist spies, and the subversion and sabotage front by the assiduous, unrelenting, merciless process of turning the loyalties of individuals and recruiting the unsuspecting and the willing converts. The campaign of subversion and sabotage was nowhere more vigorously pursued than in the trade unions of the West.

Throughout previous years, the countries of Western Europe had been hit by a wide variety of strikes, go-slows, work-to-rules, all of which, in one way or another, had hit at their economies, their defence services, and at the fabric of their societies. In Britain, there had been a succession of incidents which had brought major ports such as London and Southampton to a standstill. Disruption caused by industrial civil servants had crippled the naval ship repair and overhaul programmes and had seriously impeded naval operations and, in particular, the overhaul of the nuclear submarines carrying the Polaris ballistic missiles. The civil servants had hindered government business and had stopped the working of ports and airports.

In France and Belgium, workers at the airports, including the air traffic-controllers, had handicapped the functioning of the civil airlines. In a number of countries power workers in the electricity generating industries had virtually halted industrial and commercial activity for periods long enough to cause serious economic damage.

Throughout Europe telephone operators and engineers had disrupted normal, as well as emergency and vital, communications in furtherance of impossible demands for more pay. The mail had often not been delivered.

In some countries the fire fighting forces and the municipal services, which cleared household rubbish and industrial waste, had been on strike for such long periods that men from the armed forces had been diverted from their normal duties.

Political and trade union leaders in some of the European countries had continued their close links, if not more, with the

31

Soviet Union, and had continued to express their admiration for the Soviet system.

Over many years the ground had been carefully prepared by the Soviet Union, so that, at a given signal, their deep-cover agents, the fifth columnists, could act in unison to cripple Western communications and vital installations, and hinder the NATO armed forces.

The secret departments of the KGB and the GRU (Soviet Military Intelligence) had prepared detailed plans of sabotage of the vitals of Western Europe, using agents in the trade unions, to impair not only the military preparations and precautions of the West, but also its political, economic and social life.

Soviet agents had ensured that, with the help of relatively few Western fifth columnists, they could dislocate important components or programmes of the fairly small but vital key NATO computers. Soviet missiles, aircraft, submarines, ships and land forces would not be properly monitored; NATO reserve forces and the shipping and aircraft to carry reinforcements would not be fully mobilized; transport and communications would be impeded; police forces would be hampered.

It only needed careful and judicious tampering with key installations for the Soviet agents to be able to prevent the comprehensive co-ordination by NATO of the mass of facts, acquired by intelligence and surveillance, which would indicate a build-up of Warsaw Pact activity.

FRIDAY

1900 Hours Middle East Time
1800 Hours Central European Time

Beirut, Lebanon

After a short twilight period, night had fallen suddenly in the Lebanon, where a training-camp of Terror International was situated in the foothills east of Beirut. At about the same time as the KGB plans for France and the Benelux countries were being reviewed in Brussels, Zalah Jafid, the Chief of Staff of

Terror International, was meeting his senior assistants to check his end of the elaborate web of plots.

'There is not much time left to be sure that all the arrangements are properly made,' Jafid stated. 'It is essential that no link in the chain of our organization should fail. We are a vital part of the overall plan and, if we carry out our part without fault, we shall have earned for ourselves great importance in the reshaped world that is to come after a fully successful Marxist-Leninist world revolution. Even I am not so fully informed of the great plan that I wholly understand what the importance is of our part of it. But I have a message that without success in our operations, the whole of the rest of the plan could fail. So — we will go very carefully through our check list — first Germany.'

He turned slightly to his right to look towards the centre of a row of rough tables, which formed one side of a square of them, the centre of which was occupied by three small desks where the secretaries were poised to take notes.

'The Red Army Faction is nearly fully ready and will carry out its orders according to plan. All our trained members are back in Germany and have made contact with the Russian agents or our own watchers who have kept the targets under observation. The less highly trained members will be allotted to the less important targets.' He paused.

'Let us be clear on this matter,' Jafid interrupted. 'I laid down some weeks ago that the operatives to be used against the less important targets must be reliable — I want to be assured that this has been arranged. I will not have the whole operation bungled by some hothead like Akache at Mogadishu. Have you seen to that point of my instructions?' he snapped.

'Yes, I have,' the German answered hurriedly. 'I did not mean that our less highly trained members are not reliable. We have eliminated those not to be trusted to stick to the strict letter of the orders. Our hotheads have mostly got themselves killed or captured. We can do without them. Those who have been trained here or in Aden and Socotra have been given the key targets. I shall be able to check final details with each of them when I reach Cologne tomorrow night.'

'Are the details of your return fully planned?' asked Jafid. 'Carlos has already left to see to other matters, but my instructions to him were that the cover plans and disguises for each of you key leaders should be as good as any he made for the "Jackal" in the past.'

'My cover plan is fixed. I fly to Rome tomorrow afternoon. A German doctor who has an Italian mistress will have been taken from his love-nest. His clothes and papers will have been adjusted for my use, and I shall use his home and car as my own.'

'Excellent,' said Jafid, 'and you understand the vital necessity of taking out all your key targets? You have issued detailed instructions as to which they are? You know where they are to be found at zero hour? You have the vehicles to take you to this point? You know the code-words for making contact with the agents who have been watching them? You know what you are to do when you have dealt with them?'

The German nodded vigorously as each question was asked. Jafid then turned slightly to his left and said, 'Next, Holland.' A dark-haired, slim, nervous young woman spoke.

'We are ready too. We have not the same problems as in Germany and we have fewer targets. Our special targets have been under close watch for many days now. We do not intend to allow them to escape. We have worked closely with the German supporters on the frontier and we may be able to give them useful aid. The Red Help is ready.'

Jafid nodded and turned to the man sitting next to the Dutch woman. He was tall, gaunt-faced, with long, straight, fair hair, somewhat rounded shoulders and long-fingered, large hands.

'Is all ready in Britain?' he asked. The man drew a deep breath and spoke in an unexpectedly deep voice.

'Yes, we are ready. The Red-Black Group have been able to recruit the help we needed to have for the tasks which have been set for us to do.'

Jafid nodded and smiled slightly and then said: 'I know you have had problems in getting enough help as there are extra difficulties in getting our agents into the UK. Also since you are isolated across the sea from the Continent there is not much help the other groups can give you and you have your special problems to carry out the tasks. Are you sure you have a solution to all your problems?'

The British man nodded and spread his hands out before him

on his knees. He seemed to use his fingers to count off the points in his reply as he made them.

'We have recruited the full quota of agents we need — there was a time when we thought we would not have enough. We have sent all the key agents through your courses here and all but the last few are back in Britain. We have kept in close contact with the KGB staff of the Russian and other Eastern Bloc embassies. We have identified our targets and we have learnt their habits and movements. We have followed up the peripheral information on our targets so that we can be as ready as possible for any variations in their usual pattern of behaviour. For the most important key targets we have worked out at least two ways in which we can take them out. We have worked out carefully planned alternative methods of escaping when we have taken them out. We have even made lists of alternative key targets if, for some totally unforeseen reason, we cannot take out the first choices. We have at all times used extreme caution to cover our safe houses and our safe routes.' He paused.

Jafid looked up from the pad on which he was taking brief notes. 'You have learnt well and you have been very thorough. Have you anything to add?'

'Yes. We have taken all your instructions to heart and we have taken some steps which you have not instructed us to do. Don't worry,' he added quickly as he saw Jafid about to speak. 'I think you will approve. We have been able to get a line on some of the Intelligence men and women who have been following and watching some of us. We have followed them and we are now sure that we have identified, not the top agents acting against us, but some of the higher up agents who can be dealt with when the time comes, and so remove a part of the chain of agents.'

'That is a good precaution,' replied Jafid. 'I approve. But the most important thing to remember in the UK, as much as in Belgium and Holland where there are as many key targets, is the vital necessity that you succeed and carry out your instructions to the letter. We do not want any of the key targets to be lost or dealt with in any other way than the one laid down in your orders. And finally remember that timing is vital. You must not act too soon and you must not be more than a few minutes later than instructed. Now to France — what have you to report?'

The Frenchman listed the arrangements made by his agents. An Italian girl followed. The interrogations went on for over two hours. As each country's agent spoke and listed the plans and detailed the proposed acts, the other agents checked their own lists and added items to be further verified. Among the senior agents outlining the details, sitting behind them on stools, benches and chairs set against the walls, or crowding in to the doorways at each end of the long room, were other more junior agents. They had all now completed their training, were all ready for the acts required of them, and would all, within a few hours, have left the training-camp behind them and be on their various ways to the hiding-places already prepared for them.

There were the Germans, successors to the original Baader-Meinhof terrorists, their sympathizers from Holland, Belgium and France, the British group recruited from the militant leftist factions, and others who had offered their services for a number of reasons. There were the believers in a Marxist-Leninist world revolution aimed at the imperialist states of the West which was to be the essential step towards the realization of a new kind of world. There were the envious who wanted power in their own lands, whatever the means and whatever the end might be. There were the ambitious, the idealists, the vengeful, the pathological killers. Whatever their aims and beliefs, they had accepted that they could not alone achieve what they wanted by revolution reinforced by terrorism. They had, therefore, deliberately tied their immediate loyalty, temporarily at least, to a power far greater than any they could even together hope to muster — the might of the Soviet Union and its allies.

Jafid had the last word as they fidgeted and made ready to go. 'The revolutionary change which can transform the imperialist West into the socialist West must succeed. Make sure that it does.'

In public the Soviet Union had condemned indiscriminate, extreme, precipitate action — as in the case of the hijacking of the Air France plane to Uganda in July 1976. The Soviets were anxious not to be seen to be on the side of terrorism until it suited their political and strategic plans. It wanted world public opinion to believe that international terrorism was mindless, motiveless, and lacked clear aims or adequate support.

Behind the apparently individual terrorist acts of small groups, a multi-national group was nurtured, trained, tested and equipped. This wider group was guided by Dr Wadi Haddad, the more extreme ex-collaborator of Dr George Habash. As the student riots of the late 1960s drew to an end, and as Vietnam slipped out of their focus for militant actions a new cause developed — world revolution to the operation of which Dr Wadi Haddad later added his energy and expertise. The old national states of the West were seen as irrevocably imperialist obstacles in the path of world revolution. At about the same time one organization, the Popular Front for the Liberation of Palestine, the PFLP, a Marxist-Leninist Group within the structure of the Palestine Liberation Organization, the PLO, emerged. Led initially by Dr George Habash in collaboration with Dr Wadi Haddad, it believed that a Marxist-Leninist world revolution aimed at the 'imperialist states of the West' was crucial to the success of world revolution in the Middle East and Africa.

In Germany the Baader-Meinhof Group declared war against 'smug and complacent' society and 'world imperialism'. In Italy there were the Red Brigades, dedicated to the spread of communism throughout Europe. In France there was the Armed Faction for People's Power, in Ulster the Irish National Liberation Army, in Holland Red Help, in Britain, the Red-Black Group with which Ulrike Meinhof had connections. They and others admired and emulated not only the PFLP's aims for world revolution but its direct action.

These groups and other individual men and women were forged into the weapon of Terror International. Young Germans, Japanese, Irishmen, Frenchmen, Englishmen, Cubans and a Venezuelan called Ilich Ramirez Sanchez, later known as Carlos Martinez or The Jackal, joined the more extreme militants of the revolutionary groups. Trained and disciplined by Dr Wadi Haddad's wing of the PFLP, paid, fed and armed by the Soviet Union and its supporting East European and Arab states, they started to chalk up their battle honours, such as Lod Airport, Vienna, Rome, Athens, Mogadishu. They deliberately spread terror far and wide by assassination, bank raids, ambushes, torture, the whole gamut of cruelty designed to show that resistance was hopeless. Behind the slogans and the banners, manipulating the ideologies, recruiting the fanatically disaffected, encouraging the ruthlessly ambitious and envious, aiding, abetting, arming, and always building a secret army for the chosen moment of attack, was the power and wealth of the Soviet Union and its allies.

FRIDAY
1900 Hours Central European Time

Kirkenes, Norway

At 1900 hours Central European Time, a Norwegian Army sergeant returned to the local Army Headquarters in Kirkenes, after a late patrol to a point overlooking the small Russian town of Pechenga. He went immediately to report to the Garrison Commander.

'It was not possible to see much, but I had the feeling that there was more light in the sky in the distance than there is usually, perhaps due to more than the usual small number of vehicles moving in the streets.'

'Are you definitely reporting the movement of a larger number of vehicles?' asked the Commander, immediately alert.

'No, I can't report movement of vehicles definitely. All I can say is that I got the sense of more than usual traffic because of the greater amount of light and it was a flickering light, as if a number of lights were moving. And there was the noise.'

'What noise?' asked the Commander. 'Engine noise? Track noise from tanks? What sort of noise?'

'Very difficult to say. Engine noise I would guess, but at that distance and distorted by the shielding buildings, it's impossible to say how much more noise there was. The whole patrol agreed that there was extra noise and extra light.'

'Was there enough extra for me to report and, if so, what do I suggest it is due to?'

'No, I don't think there was so much more that you need report it and cause undue alarm. But it did go on for some time

38

and we also thought that there was increased movement west along the road to Nikel.'

'Well, was there enough noise and movement that I should report it?' asked the Commander, exasperated that the sounds of unusual movement could not be clearly categorized as either serious or merely due to some local event. 'Do I report it or don't I? I need your definite opinion.'

The Sergeant pondered for a full minute and realized that, if he gave his decision that there had been enough light and noise to constitute a danger signal, he would have to back his judgement with more definite information than he was able to give. It was a hunch and no more than a hunch, impossible to justify with facts and figures. He had patrolled the frontier often enough however to have acquired a feeling for anything out of the ordinary, but again he could not back such a feel with logic. In the distant far north of Norway it would need only the addition of a few, very possibly totally innocent vehicles, to constitute a significant increase.

'Just report that there seemed to be more light and noise than usual in Pechenga and on the road to Nikel. I cannot give an informed opinion as to what it was caused by. And I certainly cannot say that the scale of the increase should be regarded as serious.'

'All right, Sergeant, I understand your problem, and you were right to report what amounts to your suspicion. I will report merely that there seemed to be more traffic movement. At Base they can log that report with any others they may have from other sources and decide for themselves what importance to give it. I hope you weren't right. We don't want anything to blow up and spoil our Christmas, do we?'

He rose from his chair and smiled his dismissal. As the door closed behind the Sergeant, he fell deep into thought and walked across to the window to gaze out into the dark sky to the east. That afternoon he had received an unexpected request from the Soviet Border Commissioner for an unscheduled meeting at the border at 1700 hours on the following Sunday. The written note arranging the meeting had given no reason. It had caused him no disquiet, just a flash of annoyance at its peremptory tone and the inconvenience of the hour and the place of the meeting. Now, however, he sensed a doubt that the meeting was to be routine.

But he could hardly put two weak doubts together and report them as matters for concern and action.

FRIDAY

1930 Hours Central European Time

Frantiskovy, Czechoslovakia

In the town of Frantiskovy, in Czechoslovakia, lying about 5 kilometres north of Cheb, which was itself about 5 kilometres east of the border post with West Germany at Schiernding on the main road from Karlovy Vary in the east to Bayreuth and Nürnberg in the west, Franc Dubic stopped on his evening walk with his dog to watch the activity in a large warehouse near his home. It was 1930 hours Central European Time and he had just finished his supper. It was a clear cold night, good for a brisk walk, and he was looking forward to the week-end and a quiet, surreptitious celebration at Christmas. But what he saw made him draw a quick breath and hurry on home to his wife, Irma. They were both in their late sixties, a quiet unassuming pair, whose children had grown up and moved away from their parents' home, which Franc had inherited from his own parents and from which they had never moved.

Irma glanced at Franc as, in silence, he hung his hat, coat and scarf on the hatstand in a corner of their cramped living-room. 'What is it, Franc?' she asked. 'You look troubled.'

'I am troubled, very troubled,' answered Franc. 'I've just been past the big warehouse at the end of our street, where they load and unload all the different trucks. Well, you know how they usually put the trucks in at the week-end, so the large lorry park outside is empty, and turn on the big overhead lights all night so no one can climb the fence and get into the warehouse without being seen?' He was white and shaking as he spoke. 'The big overhead lights were out when I passed going to the gardens for our walk. I didn't think much about it except that it was more difficult to see my way as the street lights are so dim. They were still out when I came back and all the trucks from inside the warehouse had been moved outside — twenty or

40

thirty of them, of all sizes.' He stopped to draw breath and to gather his thoughts.

'There's nothing serious about that, Franc. What are you so worried about? Were there thieves? Are they stealing the trucks or the goods in the warehouse?'

'No,' said Franc. 'It is worse than that. Inside the warehouse, and in the lorry park waiting their turn to go in, there were cars, vans and large and small trucks. Twenty or thirty of them. And men and women were climbing out and going into the office block. And in the offices, I could see more men and women moving from room to room and closing the blinds and the curtains. Maybe a hundred of them in all.'

'It must be something to do with the security police, like last year and the year before. They are always going somewhere or coming from somewhere else badgering and frightening innocent people. Why can't they stay in their police stations and keep to themselves?' She rushed on, vehemently airing one of her favourite complaints, and Franc opened and shut his mouth trying to get a word in.

'But,' he said finally, 'you don't understand. This time it is not security police. These men and women are dressed like civilians but fully armed. And they do not look as if they are just going to round up a few people. They were quiet and serious about their business — and being very careful to pack all their vehicles into the warehouse, and very careful to draw all the blinds and curtains in the offices. They looked as if they were on some important duty — not just getting ready for a round-up in a small place like this.'

His wife's mouth opened and she stared at him. Her hands searched her lap for her handkerchief. She cried out as if in pain.

'Oh, Franc, not again. Not another purge, with arrests and doubts about our friends and people being taken away, and never coming back again. Or coming back years later in such a state that they can't be recognized as the same people who went away. Not again. What have we done to deserve that?'

Franc put his arm round his wife's large shoulders as she sat in the chair, and tried to give her the reassurance that he was far from feeling himself. They sat for some moments in silence, remembering the earlier terrifying days of the Communist takeover and the arrests and witch hunts of those years. They were

41

jerked out of their memories by heavy knocking on the front door. Franc opened it and was pushed back into the room by two heavily built men in black coats.

Franc moved back and stood next to Irma's chair. The two men looked at them and one spoke.

'Who lives here? Just you two?' Franc nodded.

'You walked past the warehouse just now?' Franc nodded again.

'Why were you out at this time of the night? What were you looking for?' the second man snarled.

'I was taking my dog for a walk as I do every night about this time — sometimes I go a little earlier. Sometimes I go a little later, sometimes I just put the dog out and she comes back after about ten minutes,' said Franc firmly but fearfully.

The two men looked at each other.

'You saw what was in the warehouse?' Franc nodded.

'You will both come with us,' the first man barked, as he and his companion grabbed Franc and Irma and pushed them out of the door into the street.

FRIDAY

2000 Hours Central European Time

Tarvisio, Italy

At Tarvisio near the Italian border with Austria, half a dozen members of the Red Brigade met in the darkened attic room of a rented house on the outskirts of town to receive their final orders. It was a cold frosty night, the dim light of the waning moon hardly illuminating the snow covered slopes of the surrounding mountains. The streets of the town were blanketed with fog, and deserted. The room had been warmed by two paraffin stoves, which cast a warm glow from their large reflectors. Their leader spoke first.

'We shall not take long with this meeting. It is simply to check that all is ready and that you are all clear about your orders. I will just summarize. We are to await a signal at any hour after midnight tonight. The signal will come to me and I

42

shall call for each of you by the various methods we have already arranged. From tonight you are not to be away from your alert positions for more than a few minutes at a time. Understood?'

There was a murmur of assent and a middle-aged woman, sitting cross-legged and half hidden in the shadows behind a main rafter, answered, 'After all these years of waiting, we shall be ready, don't you worry.'

The leader of the group frowned and nodded impatiently. 'I know you are awaiting our deliverance. That is not what I meant. I wanted to be sure that you all realize that from tonight we must all be on the alert. We have to be ready at a few minutes notice to overpower the frontier posts at Coccau, on the Italian and the Austrian side. We must be ready to block the side roads and patrol the railway crossings so that the traffic is not delayed at any point. You all have your orders. Are there any questions?'

A man's voice from the back of the gathering asked, 'Do we know yet what is going to happen? Have you been given any idea what is planned?'

'No,' the leader answered, 'I know no more than you do. I can guess, but I am not sure my guess will be any more accurate than yours. All I can tell you is that we are not alone. Other groups, in Rome, in the ports, in the Army and Navy base towns have also been alerted. They have their orders which they cannot divulge any more than we can speak of ours.'

'It is a big operation then?' another voice asked.

'Yes,' was the decisive answer. 'Yes, it is big. How big I do not know. But big enough, I think, to mean that before the end of the week we will be finally in control of Italy.'

A few minor details were dealt with, some timings checked, watches were set and the meeting broke up.

FRIDAY

2100 Hours Central European Time

Cologne, West Germany

Ludwig Braunitz and Hans Collmar had waited for two hours

after the last lights in their school buildings had gone out. They checked their watches and together climbed over the outer fence of the school grounds, at a point which they had marked previously and where a large tree branch made the climb a simple matter.

Once over the fence, they crouched for a moment or two to make sure they had not been seen. Then, bending low, they ran across a football pitch to the side wall of the single-storey building which housed the school kitchens leading into the dining-hall and so into the rest of the school. Before leaving school two days earlier, when the term had ended, Ludwig had gone to the kitchens, after an evening game of netball, had loosened the catch of one of the windows, and had wedged it shut with a piece of wood.

A hard push on the window frame from outside and it swung inwards over the worktop next to the long kitchen sink and draining-boards. Ludwig bent over and the smaller boy, Hans, climbed onto his back and darted in through the window. He turned and pulled Ludwig up behind him and then carefully shut the window. As carefully, they both climbed down onto the kitchen floor, paused to take out their flashlights from their trouser pockets, then, shielding the lights with their hands, moved across the tiled floor to the food preparation room. Here they knew they would find the row of cupboards where the stores were kept. They were after the sweets and chocolates which were kept to be sold to the children. They planned to take tinned fruit, dried fruit and sugar for their families too. They also planned to go into the school offices for pencils, pens, writing-books and paints. Their Christmas presents were going to be provided free of charge by the school.

At fifteen years of age they were familiar with most of the school premises. The buildings were three-storeyed, U-shaped with the open side of the U away from the road, facing a wooded hillside. The school's offices and paper and pencil stores were on the top floor at the front. Ludwig and Hans went there and took their time making a careful selection of the wares, and prying into rooms and cupboards which were normally out of bounds to the students. They were so engrossed in their investigations that the time flew by, and they were unaware of activity in the back courtyard. Only when they had decided to make their way

44

back to the kitchens, and were at the top of the staircase leading down to the front hallway, did they realize they were not alone.

Hans stopped abruptly as he heard the sounds from below and whispered to Ludwig behind him, 'I hear footsteps. There must be someone in the hallway.'

Ludwig moved alongside him and together they edged carefully down the stairs to a point where they could look over the balustrade into the hall below. There they could see the vague outlines of ten or twelve men and women, moving quietly into the building through the door from the back courtyard. Each person was carrying a large bundle of what looked like clothes and bedding, which they were taking down to the cellars. Hardly a word was being said. Only carefully shaded torches were being used, and the figures below were taking care to ensure that no doors banged and no undue noise was made.

As Hans and Ludwig watched, the figures below stopped what they were doing and gathered together in a group. There was a short discussion which neither boy could hear and then the group below dispersed to its tasks.

Ludwig pulled at Hans's sleeve and moved carefully back up the stairs. At the top they went into the nearest room and closed the door quietly behind them.

'What's happening?' asked Hans, a note of panic in his voice. 'I wonder if they are criminals — but what on earth would so many of them be doing here?'

The two boys moved across the room and peered out of the window into the courtyard. Parked close up against the building and largely out of their line of sight they could just make out part of the top of what looked like a Volkswagen minibus.

They moved back to the door, opened it carefully and moved down the stairs again to the point where they could overlook the hallway. There was still movement below. They were cut off from the kitchen and their escape route. They went back to the top floor room. For some time they sat in silence, abject, dispirited and increasingly desperate. At length, Hans jumped up abruptly from his seat, grabbed Ludwig's arm and said, 'The fire escape.'

They tiptoed along the corridor. Hans slid back the catch to the emergency door, which Ludwig closed silently behind him. Moments later they were on the ground and making their way back to the fence where they had climbed into the grounds. Once outside they ran back to the front gate of Ludwig's house. They paused for a moment and gasped at each other. 'We can't say anything about this. Just keep quiet,' Ludwig said and turned to go indoors.

Then Hans ran on to his home.

Both families noticed how unusually quiet the boys were for the rest of the evening.

FRIDAY

1600 Hours Eastern Standard Time
2200 Hours Central European Time

Washington, USA

At about the time the two German boys reached their homes in Cologne, the United States Secretary of State in Washington remembered his earlier worry about Europe, lifted his phone and dialled the Defence Secretary.

'Before I go off for the week-end, I wanted to ask what the latest intelligence reports are. Anything to note?'

'No,' replied the Defence Secretary, 'nothing unusual has been reported to me. I haven't asked specifically, but I am sure I would have been told of anything out of the ordinary. Why do you ask?'

'The Israeli Ambassador called here earlier today and reported that his Government is concerned about a large number of agents who have been to PFLP training-camps in the last few months, and have then disappeared without a trace. His Government has warned all the Western states that it expects an attack on Israeli targets some time.'

'Yes, I see that figures,' said the Defence Secretary, 'but you asked me if we had any unusual reports, or did I get you wrong?'

'No, you got me right,' answered the Secretary of State with a guilty laugh. 'I was just wondering if the targets to be hit aren't the Israelis. But I've been a bit jumpy, lately — I think I need a vacation. Still I think we're all getting a little too complacent. So I thought I'd check with you to see if anything unusual had shown up. Forget it though. Sorry to have bothered you.'

The Defence Secretary mumbled a reply and put down his receiver, deep in thought. A moment later he jabbed at his intercom and, when his secretary answered, said, 'Get me Strategic Air Command, I want to speak to the Commanding General.'

A moment later his phone buzzed. He picked it up and a voice said, 'Omaha, Commanding General SAC, you wanted me Mr Secretary?'

'Just a check up before I leave town for the week-end. Anything unusual been picked up by satellites? Any troop moves, out of the ordinary activity, anything to report?'

'No,' said the General slowly, turning over the papers on his desk, 'no, nothing remarkable. You know the Soviets put up two more Cosmos satellites about a week ago — we spoke about that. During the last week or so there has been an increase in night traffic on a lot of roads in East Germany, Poland and Czechoslovakia. The character of the traffic has been indistinguishable at night and no evidence of a big build-up of vehicles has been seen by day.'

'Which way was the traffic going — east or west?' asked the Defence Secretary.

'All ways,' said the General, 'east and west, and north and south to some extent. Of course some of it could be a cover for westerly movement, we know that, and we've looked by day to see if there has been any build-up.'

'And has there been?' asked the Secretary. 'Have any of their tanks moved?'

'No,' replied the General, 'as you know there are a lot of tanks west of the Soviet Union as they have never moved east the T62s which have been replaced by the T72s. No, there's no sign of them having moved tanks. There has been no increase in wireless traffic either. We have the full monitor on that and on most of the messages which have been passed. Probably the increased night traffic has got something to do with their holidays — they do have some, you know — or maybe it has to do with preparations for their manoeuvres.'

'OK, General,' said the Defence Secretary thoughtfully. 'It all sounds pretty ordinary to me. We have had some reports of some classes of reserve soldiers being called up, but that

47

happens so often we can't tell from that whether it means anything. It may just be to let some of the other poor bastards get home leave for a change. And we know that they have their annual winter manoeuvres about this time, as you say. Keep me informed if anything unexpected turns up. Thank you.'

'Thank you, Mr Secretary,' answered the General.

The Defence Secretary buzzed again and said, 'Get me NORAD Commanding General please.' He picked up the phone and waited for a reply. A moment later a voice said, 'North American Air Defence, Commanding General here, you called?'

'Yes, General, anything to report before I leave for the weekend? I know about the two Cosmos satellites which the Soviets launched a week ago. Any sign of their purpose?'

'No, sir, they have remained in the same orbit as at launch, but of course that doesn't mean anything as we know from experience that they can change orbits very quickly. I imagine you want to know if these are two killer satellites. All I can say to that is that they could be. They may be just surveillance ships but you know as well as I do that they could just as easily be killers.'

'Yes, I know, General, and we won't know what they are until it's too late. Too bad we didn't start our killer satellite building programme sooner. But we didn't and that's that. How many in orbit now do you estimate could be killers?'

'Well,' said the General slowly, 'you know it's only an informed guess but right here we are working on about twelve being potential killers and in orbits which could be easily adjusted to converge on some of our most sensitive satellites, and by that I mean the communications ones.'

'Sure, sure, I know,' the Defence Secretary answered. 'And there's no way we can do anything but hope for the best. But you have no reports as of now which indicate any unusual activity?'

'No, Mr Secretary, we have no indications of anything unusual. I'll sure as hell report them if we get any.'

The Defence Secretary said good-night to the General and put down his phone. He stood for a moment pondering. Then he buzzed his secretary again. 'Get me SACLANT, Commanding Admiral please.'

He picked up the phone when it rang. 'Office of the Supreme

Allied Commander Atlantic — Commanding Admiral just coming, sir.' There was a pause. 'Commanding Admiral here, Mr Secretary. What can I do for you?'

'Admiral, I'm just off for the week-end — I'll be at home if you need me — but I just called for the latest reports.'

'Nothing unusual to report, Mr Secretary. Soviet Navy ship movements are standard, the usual submarines on passage outwards and inwards. No build-up outwards, I mean, Mr Secretary, and that's what we are on the look-out for. Is that the information you wanted?'

'Yes, thank you, Admiral. All seems as normal then?'

'The only changes are that some of their cruise liners have started out on their winter voyages and will be calling in at various ports over the Christmas holiday. Some of their deep sea fishing and whaling factory-ships are also on passage to their usual stations and they will be making standard port calls too. I think we have a pretty good check on all movements. Standard procedures will show up any unusual changes, though surveillance is always more difficult at this time of the year with the long nights and bad weather.'

The Defence Secretary thanked the Admiral and put his phone down.

FRIDAY

2230 Hours Central European Time

Cherbourg, France

A large Soviet ocean fish factory-ship, on passage to the fishing grounds in the South Atlantic, diverged from its normal course and put in to the French port of Cherbourg on the western tip of the Normandy peninsula. As SACLANT was speaking to the Defence Secretary a man darted across the deserted quayside and climbed quickly up the ship's gangway to the dimly lit bridge. A member of the French Communist Party, he was keeping a rendezvous on board with the ship's second officer, a senior member of the KGB.

Below decks in the cold, cavernous factory section of the ship,

49

six hundred picked men and women of the Soviet forces waited for the orders to disembark for the tasks already allotted to them. The Frenchman's duties, and those of his local Communist Party cell, were to arrange the transport for the various groups and to provide the guides to take them to their targets, the military and communications centres west and south of Paris.

FRIDAY

2145 Hours Greenwich Mean Time
2245 Hours Central European Time

Cork, Eire

At twilight a Soviet container ship drew slowly into the quayside in the port of Cork. The Eire authorities had given permission for it so that the steering gear, on which a fault was reported, could be repaired. Below decks, ninety men of the Soviet forces, huddled in cramped damp corners of the hold, waited for their final orders. Four hours after docking had been completed, an agent of the Irish National Liberation Army slipped furtively up the gangway and down to the hold. He conferred with the Soviet Force Commander and confirmed the details of the port take-over operation, the code-words, the vehicles which would be needed, the names of the guides being provided by the INLA, and the meeting points. Only the hour of the attack was left undetermined, and for that both he and the Russian would have to maintain a silent listening watch for the coded time to be transmitted from Moscow.

All round the coasts of Europe, on one pretext or another, large and small ships of the Soviet Merchant Navy were entering port, carrying with them specially selected and trained forces, to take over ports, installations, communications centres and NATO naval ships and shore establishments. In most ports similar visits had happened before. The arrivals of Soviet vessels were no longer unusual. The Soviet crew members were good spenders in the local shops, and seldom caused any trouble in the bars and dance halls they visited. It

50

looked innocent enough and not unexpected at Christmas time, even though the Russians did not take part in the festivities.

So it was that Soviet ships, apart from visiting Cherbourg and Cork, also put into Bodö in North Norway, into Reykjavik in Iceland, Plymouth in southern England, Oporto and Lisbon in Portugal, Bordeaux in France, and Genoa in Italy. And the small armada of fish packing and fish processing ships, usually stationed in the estuary of the Fal at Falmouth in Cornwall, had its crews altered and augmented, without the local population or the port authorities being aware of any changes.

FRIDAY

2201 Hours Greenwich Mean Time
2301 Hours Central European Time

Atlantic and North Sea

In December 1977 the Soviet Union announced that CTC Lines — short for Charter Travel Company Limited — would be operating seven passenger liners of different sizes out of United Kingdom ports, calling usually at London and Southampton. They were to offer cruises and a transatlantic services to New York and Montreal.

Three of the liners were modern ships built in East Germany, the *Shota Rustaveli* of 20,000 tons, the *Alexandr Pushkin* of 19,890 tons, and the *Mikhail Lermontov* of 20,000 tons. A fourth large ship was the *Leonid Sobinov,* 21,400 tons, built in the John Brown Shipyard on the Clyde, and originally the Cunard liner *Carmania.* There were also three smaller ships, the *Baltika* of 8,468 tons, the *Litva* of 5,000 tons and the *Mikhail Kalinin* of 4,722 tons. The *Litva* had been in the news in September 1978 because three passengers had been found to have typhoid, when the ship berthed in England.

At 2201 hours Greenwich Mean Time, the *Leonid Sobinov* and the *Shota Rustaveli,* almost visible to each other, were passing the Rhine Estuary in North Holland, the *Leonid Sobinov* bound for Southampton and the *Shota Rustaveli* for Antwerp. A hundred miles astern of them was the *Alexandr*

51

Pushkin, bound for Tilbury, the port of London. Ahead of them was the *Mikhail Lermontov* bound for Le Havre.

Near the Faeroe Isles north of Scotland were the *Baltika* bound for Belfast, the *Litva* for Dublin, and the *Mikhail Kalinin* for the Clyde.

The blaze of lights of the three Russian ships passing north of Scotland were clearly visible to the captain and his crew of the RAF Nimrod, a long-range maritime reconnaissance aircraft, flying north from the RAF base at Kinloss in Scotland, to take over surveillance on a Soviet C-class nuclear-powered, cruise missile armed submarine, reported earlier by the Norwegian Air Force which had tracked it round the North Cape and into the Atlantic.

The Soviet submarine had first been detected by the Norwegian scanning radar at its isolated site at Vardö in North Norway, having sailed from the main Soviet Navy base at Murmansk. From there by visual contact and by the use of sonar buoys dropped from aircraft, the submarine had been tracked to a point in the deep ocean trench of the Norwegian Sea, about 300 miles south-east of Jan Mayen Land. It was essential to maintain contact at this stage of its journey, because it was from there that it would either go due west to the Denmark Strait between Iceland and Greenland, or turn south to pass between the Faeroe Isles and the Shetlands. In the deep waters of the ocean trench leading south to the Rockall Deep and then into the North Atlantic, that submarine, and others like it, would try to evade surveillance by the NATO maritime reconnaissance aircraft and the surface Allied naval ships which might be in the area. It had been so much of a problem that, to ensure detection of Soviet submarines, on passage outwards and inwards, a string of underwater sonar detecting devices had been laid on the sea bed between Greenland and Iceland, and between Iceland and the United Kingdom. The system known as Submarine Ocean Sonar Underwater Surveillance (SOSUS) was a vital link in the detection barrier. But it was only a link, and the men aboard the Nimrod knew that their essential task was not to lose track of the submarine, whose course would eventually be confirmed by SOSUS.

FRIDAY

1715 Hours Eastern Standard Time
2315 Hours Central European Time

Norfolk, Virginia, USA

The NATO Supreme Allied Commander Atlantic (SACLANT) at his headquarters in Norfolk, Virginia on the East Coast of America, and the Commander-in-Chief Channel (CINCCHAN) at his headquarters at Northwood, near London, received all reports of the movement of Warsaw Pact Naval ships, both surface and submarine. All information was fed into computers so that at any time, on video display units in these headquarters and in the major ships at sea, there was an instant display of the position of all known Pact ships at sea and in port.

When the Defence Secretary put down his phone, the Supreme Allied Commander Atlantic checked again for himself that nowhere in his area of command was there apparent cause for concern. The Commander-in-Chief Channel confirmed the situation, having first checked the latest reconnaissance reports from the Norwegian Air Force Headquarters at Bodö, from the RAF base at Kinloss, from the United States Air Force base in Iceland and from the collated intelligence summaries of NATO Naval and merchant surface ships.

FRIDAY

2330 Hours Central European Time

Casteau, Belgium

The ripple of last minute contacts continued round the remaining NATO commanders, each checking with one another and with their lower commands. The Supreme Allied Commander Europe (SACEUR) at his headquarters at Casteau had already completed his survey of the up-to-date situation. He had seen his immediate staff and issued his orders. His Chief of Staff had earlier delivered to him a first draft of a situation review which

53

SACEUR himself had initiated to summarize some of the more glaring inconsistencies of the strategic and tactical concepts in the NATO theatre.

He had watched with ever increasing concern the massive building up of the Soviet Army — an increase since 1965 of 800,000 men, almost as large as the entire United States Army. At the same time he had had to draw attention to the dangers inherent in the failure of many of the Allied Governments not only to match the Soviet increase, but even to continue to spend the same amount on defence as in previous years. Some, preoccupied with domestic economic problems and their political futures, had actually reduced expenditure on defence.

He had had to contend with so many different assumptions. There was the assumption about the Warsaw Pact that, despite the enormous military increases, the Soviet intentions were basically peaceful. There was the assumption that, even if the Soviet Union did launch a massive conventional offensive, the NATO Alliance would be able to stop the Soviet advance by use of tactical nuclear weapons, and that this capability was therefore a deterrent to any Soviet attack. There were other assumptions too, not so often voiced, but no less probable. There was the assumption that the Soviet attack would be a modern Blitzkrieg, using modern chemical and biological weapons, to prepare the way for the faster, more reliable, more heavily armoured tanks supported, not by infantry on foot, but in modern armoured personnel carriers, which could keep pace with the tanks. There was finally the assumption that a major Warsaw Pact invasion of the central European sector of NATO would be initiated by large-scale, pre-emptive nuclear strikes.

There were many aspects of NATO's preparations and dispositions which positively invited the Soviet Union to strike first with nuclear weapons. His staff had given long and careful consideration to the measures which would be necessary to redress the serious imbalance of the forces on the two sides. Weapon delivery systems with more mobility and greater range were obviously required. The new generation of simple, highly accurate, small, fairly cheap surface-to-surface cruise missiles was clearly essential. Essential too was the need to arm the cruise missiles with warheads either of the 'neutron' type or of the micronuclear fission types, so that Warsaw Pact mass forces of armour and armoured carrier borne infantry could be eliminated on the NATO territory to which their initial attack would have led them, without leaving the territory of West Germany blasted, burned and radiated beyond further human use.

In the final analysis SACEUR knew that the credibility of the NATO deterrent depended on its obvious capability of preventing the winning of any war that the Warsaw Pact might start and the clear political determination of the Western Governments to resist Soviet aggression, whether it be nuclear, conventional or unconventional, whatever the cost and whatever the threat of retaliation.

SATURDAY

0001 Hours Central European Time

Greven, East Germany

On the western outskirts of the East German village of Greven, not 50 kilometres east of the great port of Hamburg, and barely 5 kilometres inside East German territory, the members of a Soviet Army rifle section stood outside the barn in which their armoured personnel carrier was hidden. This was their first night away from their barracks east of Berlin. They had arrived in the early hours of the morning and had slept, locked in the barn, until darkness fell. They were awed by the huge expanse of flickering light which blazed across the sky to the west, the night lights of Hamburg and its surrounding towns and villages, reflected off the high scudding clouds of an otherwise clear, crisp winter evening.

'Are those really only the lights of a city?' asked a soldier in wonderment. 'That's what the Corporal said,' came a voice from behind him, 'and he said not to wonder at it too much as it is just an example of the capitalists' waste of resources.'

The group of ten young soldiers huddled against the wall of the barn were all conscripts. A few of their friends and acquaintances in Russia had been able to postpone or avoid military service, but most of their contemporaries had been called up after leaving school to serve two years in the armed forces. In any case, avoidance or postponement of service had little point because they would still be liable for service until the age of fifty-five.

Military training had been part of their curriculum at school, or in the universities and institutes to which some of them had progressed. They had also had training in civil defence, which had been given even higher priority recently, when chiefs of staff of civil defence had been appointed in all the fifteen republics of the Union.

Conditions in the barn were rough and cold, but they were all hardened to the existence as life in the barracks had been without comforts too. They were paid very little, had very little free time, and what they had was filled with compulsory political lectures, and they were not allowed to mix freely with the local population, particularly in Eastern Europe. They had practically no privacy or comfort. The sudden change from life in the barracks to the virtual squalor of the barn was, in a sense, a taste of freedom.

For many though, army life was infinitely better than life in a Soviet small town or village. There they had primitive drainage, minimal piped water, an unreliable supply of electricity even for the limited uses they were allowed. Eastern Europe was a glimpse into a standard of living which many of them had never imagined, so they felt no privation.

They had other problems though. Although all members of the Union of Soviet Socialist Republics, the various races making up the Soviet Union did not always get on together. The Slavs had little time for the Central Asians, often demeaned by being put into the lowly construction units. The Ukrainians considered themselves on a par with the Slavs and were jealous of the standing of the Georgians.

The Communist Party had an absolute hold on the Army, nearly all the officers being members of the Party. The Army was an extension of the Party and the soldiers were proud that they were instruments of the Party. So despite their conditions, their morale was high, although faced with the evidence of a level of civilization which they had never dreamt of.

SATURDAY

Casteau, Belgium

At 0925 hours the officers summoned to the meeting to report on the build-up of civil riot and unrest assembled briefly in the wide passage-way outside the office of the Chief of Staff Supreme Allied Command Europe, and then moved into the large brightly lit room, and took their places round the conference table. The Chief of Staff nodded a greeting, and continued to sign a succession of documents being put before him by a senior staff officer.

At length he rose, walked round the end of his massive desk and took his place at the head of the conference table. Already seated were the Deputy Chief of Staff Operations, the Assistant Chief of Staff of the Plans and Policy Division, with two brigadiers beside him, the Assistant Chief of Staff of the Intelligence Division, with two brigadiers, behind whom sat two colonels, specialists in their fields of intelligence.

'Gentlemen,' the Chief of Staff said, 'over the last four days we have received a succession of reports which indicate that there will be a period of civil disorder at least, and perhaps serious terrorist disruption. I say perhaps serious terrorist disruption because we have had only one positive report from Berlin by a defector that such action is planned.

'You went to Berlin, saw the man and made this report,' he said to one of the Intelligence officers. 'How certain can we be that the man was genuine, that he was telling the truth?'

'I think he was genuine, General,' the officer replied, 'and he was too drugged and too frightened to be capable of lying. I think we should believe that he did have knowledge of such attacks but on what scale and when, there was no means of knowing.' In turn the Chief of Staff questioned the validity of the rest of the information gleaned during the week. At length he said, 'Right, that has cleared a few queries I had in mind. But, since there is no positive evidence and since, except for the obvious fact of the strikes already in progress, we have no documentary or other proof of the rest of the information obtained

57

this week. I am proposing only to summarize the reports in a special intelligence bulletin to be despatched today to all subordinate commands. I want you, General,' he said, turning to the Assistant Chief of Staff Intelligence, 'to draw up this bulletin for my signature. But first I want you to recapitulate briefly on the facts which you consider we should report. To begin with, of course, there is this defector's information of terrorist action.'

'Yes,' the Intelligence Chief answered, 'and then I consider we should summarize the other defector's report of the nerve and other gas weapons. After that, I think the Interpol assessment of the numbers of vehicles being taken to East Europe is significant. A contact warned of strikes and was right. She also warned that certain groups were engaged in clandestine activities, presumably in preparation for aiding the terrorists. Finally she warned that computers and communications will be hit. I think that's the full score, sir. Do you want to add any general direction as to what should be done in the light of these reports?'

'Yes I do,' the Chief of Staff answered, pausing to clear his mind so that his message would be crystal clear to the recipients, 'I want you to draft a final paragraph stressing that while it is obviously essential that nothing is done which will prejudice their ability to engage in military operations, they must nevertheless be ready to give all possible assistance to the civil authorities. Add that if there is a conflict of priorities they should, in the present instance, err on the side of assisting the civil authorities since there is no evidence that, except for preparations for their usual winter manoeuvres, the Warsaw Pact have made any warlike moves of either their land or air or sea forces. That is all, gentlemen. I want that report, with any relevant appendices, on my desk for signature at 1300 hours. And so to avoid any communication disruption I want officers detailed to take copies of it by hand today to all the force and Army group commanders in Allied Command Europe.'

The officers rose and stood momentarily as the Chief of Staff moved back to his desk. Then they picked up their papers and left the room.

Outside in the passage-way the Assistant Chief of Staff Plans and Policy gave his orders to the American Intelligence officer to deliver a copy of the bulletin to the Central Army Group and

to take another copy on to the United States Army Headquarters at Heidelberg.

SATURDAY

All Day

Western Europe

In Western Europe, Saturday was like any other Saturday. It
was a day for family shopping, especially as Christmas was only
a few days away. It was a day for family outings, and for family
reunions. It was also the day for the main sporting events.
Throughout the United Kingdom, there were the football cup
and league matches. In France and the United Kingdom, the
rugby teams were in the last lap of the run-up to the picking of
the international teams. In France, Germany, Italy and
Switzerland, in the high mountains, the winter sports season
had just started.

The countries of Eastern Europe and the Soviet Union were
taking part in all those events. Soviet football teams were either
playing in matches that day or had arrived and were in training
for matches the next day. There were Soviet football teams
training for Sunday matches in Hanover and Cologne. There
was an East German male and female athletics team competing
in the first day's events of a two-day match in Frankfurt. The
Red Army Choir was in Munich putting on daily shows over the
Christmas period. The Czechoslovak national ice-hockey team
was taking part in a tournament in Stuttgart. After its successful previous visit to Hamburg, the Dresden State Orchestra was
in Bremen for a short season.

The East European teams had usually been given encouragement by large groups of supporters who were flown in for the
main events, and the choirs and orchestras were boosted by
occasional influxes of admirers from their own countries.

SATURDAY

Britain and France

At midday, the Russian cruise liner *Alexandr Pushkin* was moving slowly up the Thames Estuary to dock at Tilbury before darkness, while the *Shota Rustaveli* had already tied up alongside the quays at Antwerp. The *Leonid Sobinov* was in the Solent, moving slowly to the ocean terminal in Southampton docks. In Le Havre special arrangements had been made to enable the passengers from the *Mikhail Lermontov* to go shopping, by keeping certain stores open after the normal closing time to give the Russians unimpeded access. In Tilbury and Southampton a dozen large coaches had been hired to take passengers to the shops which they had selected to visit.

For some years Soviet and Eastern European articulated trucks of juggernaut size had been used as wireless spy vehicles. Large container-carrying trucks, marked with the internationally recognized sign TIR, which indicated they were in transit and were therefore exempt from customs examination, carried sophisticated radio intercept equipment, used to record military wireless traffic and to detect the locations of the transmitters. By misuse of the TIR carnet system, designed to obviate the need to open up the carefully sealed containers which were destined for countries beyond the inspecting customs control, much equipment escaped examination. The vehicles had passed regularly through Scandinavia, Germany, Holland, Belgium, and France. During Friday and Saturday similar vehicles had passed the frontier crossings at Lauenberg, Helmstedt and Herlehausen. Each container was packed with high-powered radio-jamming transmitters and the crews to man them. Each was directed to a specific geographic position which had been previously surveyed by earlier vehicles of the same type. Each location was strategically placed to enable the jamming transmitters to blot out the air traffic transmitters, civil and military, on as many airfields as possible, within the radius covered by the power of the transmitters. They were going to have to be immobile on the allotted sites, so were being moved in as late as possible so that their presence would not arouse suspicion. All NATO airfields in West Germany, Holland, Belgium and Denmark were to be covered. Some of the airfields in Britain, those in East Anglia, were also to be affected by vehicles which had landed at Harwich, ostensibly in transit to Eire.

SATURDAY

1400 Hours Central European Time

Casteau, Belgium

At 1400 hours a group of senior officers gathered in the office of the Assistant Chief of Staff Plans and Policy and listened intently to a Dutch Brigadier from the Air Defence Division of the Supreme Headquarters.

The Dutch Brigadier paused for a moment and then continued, 'As I was saying, we have become increasingly concerned during the last twenty-four hours about the malfunctioning of the "hot-line" between Washington and Moscow, which is being reported to us from the Pentagon. Over a period of about a week now, a series of difficulties, none major, none very long-lasting, has been hitting the system. In the last thirty-six hours the difficulties have become more acute and the periods of severe malfunction have lasted longer.'

'Can you identify the causes at all?' the Chief of Staff asked, 'or can you determine whether the malfunctions have been deliberately caused?'

'No, sir,' the Dutchman replied, 'we have not been able to determine what has caused the malfunctions, so we can't say whether they are deliberate. We can only suspect they are, because the system is tested regularly and has given no trouble before.'

The Dutchman hesitated for a moment and then said, 'As I see it, General, there are three possibilities. First, this could be a genuine foul-up and we'll find the answer in due course. Second, this could be a bogus foul-up, which will appear to sort itself out

61

in due course and we might be conditioned to this sort of mal-functioning by a series of incidents until the real foul-up comes because the Russians don't want the system to work. Or third, this might be the start of the real foul-up and it won't come right, and we shan't be able to talk to the Russians if there is an emergency. As of now, we can't tell which it is and I don't see how we could ever distinguish.'

'Thank you, Brigadier,' the Chief of Staff said, turning to the Assistant Chief of Staff Intelligence. 'Have you anything to add, General?'

'Yes, sir,' the General replied, 'if the hot-line is being delib-erately disrupted and if, this time, it is for real, then we shall have to make sure that we keep a very close watch on the orbits of the Russian satellites which we think are killer satellites, which could be used to put out our vital communications and surveillance satellites.'

'And remember, gentlemen,' the Chief of Staff interrupted to say, 'the United States programme for killer satellites does not even reach the testing stage until mid-1981. So we have no answer for some time yet.'

'It's worse than that, sir,' the Assistant Chief Intelligence added, 'because we reckon that the Soviet killer satellites which depend on destruction by explosion are a first generation. We reckon that a much more effective method is the blinding of the solar cells of our satellites by laser beams. The Russians have already done that using ground-based lasers and have already put lasers into some of their satellites — like the one that burned up over Canada. That had a nuclear power system, unlike their earlier and our solar-cell power systems. It means that they can have killer and other satellites which will be better protected from our lasers, will be able to generate lasers in space, and will have such a huge power source that they will have much more efficient space radars.'

'It may be worse than that, sir,' the Dutch Brigadier remarked. 'We really don't know how far the Soviets have got with their particle beam weapons. We know that the United States can match the Soviets with high energy ground-based lasers, but the Soviets are probably some years ahead in the field of high energy directed ionized beams, the technique of directing the vast energy derived from nuclear explosions. If they have got beyond the test stage, not only can they destroy all our satellites by one means or another, but they would also be capable of destroying our ballistic missiles in space, before they can reach their targets.'

'That's so,' said the Chief of Staff, 'but if they have reached that stage it can only be very recently or they would not have spent the huge sums they have devoted to their extremely efficient civil defence system. Nevertheless we should all be aware that, for some years, the Soviets, in a number of respects, have a window of superiority and that we cannot rely on a situation of mutual assured destruction. We have got to be fully alert for any signs of aggression. This time it looks as if there might be a build-up towards an unconventional form of terrorist aggression. That is all, gentlemen. Be sure that the intelligence bulletin we discussed this morning and a summary of what we have heard this afternoon gets to all senior subordinate commands today — and I mean today.'

SATURDAY

1600 Hours Central European Time

The Border of West Germany

Later that afternoon a platoon of three armoured cars and two scout cars of a British armoured battalion came to a stop on a small side road leading east from the village of Bodenteich on the main road from Wolfsburg to Uelzen. Using country lanes and well worn tracks, as did all the small units of the border patrol, they had been keeping watch on a length of the Iron Curtain stretching 10 kilometres north-east from the East German village of Langen-Schmölau and 10 kilometres south. The Lieutenant and the Platoon Sergeant were old hands and had patrolled various parts of the frontier for about a year. They both climbed out of the turrets of their armoured cars, jumped to the ground and met between the cars on the rough road.

'Might as well call it a day now. We shan't be able to see much soon and the weather looks as if it is turning nasty,' the officer said.

'Last time I came this way,' replied the Sergeant, 'we had a bloody awful time getting back to the village as we left it too late and in the darkness took a side track which led nowhere. We shan't be able to see far in a few minutes.'

'You have nothing to report of any activity today, have you? It wasn't easy to see much beyond the curtain wire fence anyway. Anything we should report though?'

'No,' the Sergeant said, 'except I got an uncomfortable feeling that there were more eyes than usual peering at us today, not only from the watch towers, but from woods and some of those thick hedges on the higher banks. I can't say that I think there's anything to report. It's just a feeling.'

'Funny you should say that,' the Lieutenant answered musingly. 'I got something of the same sense of there being something unusual. But I thought it was because I seemed to detect, without any concrete evidence, that there were more troops about and they were being darned careful about being seen. Once or twice, when we were halted out of sight from the watch towers, where we could get a view from the edge of those woods further north, I thought I could see figures where I have never seen them before. Funny time of year for there to be any build-up, except that their winter manoeuvres start soon.'

'Funny time of year, yes, but they aren't very funny people, and it might just be that they are doing something because it is a funny time of year and we wouldn't be expecting anything. I'll call the other two and see what they say,' the Sergeant said and yelled for the two corporals of the platoon, who immediately ran to join the Lieutenant and the Sergeant.

'Got anything to report, you two?' the Sergeant asked.

'When we were further north,' answered one Corporal, 'and the rest of the platoon had moved off, I was still watching through my binoculars maybe three or four minutes after the rest of you had moved, and I thought I saw the top of one of those new motor-rifle infantry combat vehicles — BMPs — moving away towards the east. Mind, I said, I thought I saw that — I saw something — and that's what I thought it was — but I've never seen one in the flesh — so I could be wrong.'

'OK,' the officer said, 'but that's not really enough to make a report that there are BMPs in this area. I'll say that one was thought to have been seen — but the sighting is not positive and cannot be confirmed. That do?'

'I didn't see anything which I didn't expect to see,' reported the other Corporal. 'I've been here lots of times before and there seem to be more people about here than on other stretches. When I was in another platoon, the Sergeant said it was maybe because they use this area to train their frontier guards. I thought there was quite a lot of movement, which I couldn't really identify.' The Lieutenant summarized, 'I'll report when we get back that there was a general impression of activity seen. And of course we none of us have been able to hear anything, I imagine, because of the strong wind from west of north which would blow any noise of movement away from us.'

'In your briefing before we came out,' the Sergeant asked, 'was there any mention of us keeping a special lookout because of any other reports — air recce, satellites — you know what I mean?'

'No,' said the officer firmly, 'in fact I got the impression that HQ was sorry for us having to do the patrol at this time, in the cold, because they thought we would be wasting our time.'

'I hope we are,' said a corporal gloomily. 'This is the first time for three years I have had the wife and kids with me at Christmas. It'll be just my bloody luck if it's this Christmas as the ruddy Russians decide to spread themselves to the West.'

'Don't be so gloomy, man,' said the Sergeant. 'You should be getting a Christmas mood now — I know I am. I think we'd better go though, sir, or we'll get lost in the woods like I did last time.'

'Right,' said the officer, 'mount up and we'll move off immediately.'

After the sun set on Eastern Europe, and the black shadows spread slowly across the landscape further and further to the west armoured cars, scout cars, MICVs, BMPs, light tanks, BRDM heavy armoured reconnaissance vehicles, motorcycles nosed out of their hiding-places and moved slowly, with lights dimmed, to new locations closer to the Iron Curtain, from which they were to move back east during the manoeuvres soon to start. The forward Soviet divisions which had been positioned to act as the NATO enemy moved into their final locations and the divisions behind them stepped forward as if to be ready to

65

resist NATO invasion, both sides intent on hiding their moves and locations. All along the Iron Curtain the furtive, careful moves took place in the dark. With the prospect of hard exertion and severe conditions looming closer and closer, an air of grim commitment had enveloped all except the most senior of the front-line soldiers. Months of training were behind them, the novelty of new places had worn off, the interest of new routines had waned. All they had before them was the prospect of very hard and long hours of work, a sobering and daunting prospect to fighting men all down the ages, going into battle or into realistically simulated battle conditions.

SATURDAY

1700 Hours Central European Time

Paris, France

In Paris, the two hundred delegates attending a conference at the invitation of the French Communist Party had spent the Saturday afternoon trying to show some sort of interest in the conducted visits they had made to Versailles, the Louvre and the Bastille. The picked men and women of the Paris Spearhead Group were conscious that very soon they were to go into battle. Rehearsed as they had carefully been, trained to a pitch of alertness and enthusiasm, nevertheless they were bound to feel the same apprehension, the same fear of the unknown, as those going to a more conventional type of war. The Spearhead Groups would be operating behind the enemy lines and would rely on surprise, on the use of terror, on the inherent ability of clandestine forces to bewilder and perplex the enemy who would be attacked where attack was least expected. Their French hosts, the Support Group, had not been enchanted by the lack of visible signs of enjoyment. They had secretly been forced to wonder whether they had failed their valued guests. So much of what they had planned for over so many years depended on the outcome of the next few days. Their dreams of a Marxist millennium were close to realization, with unlimited power and position for themselves in partnership with their comrades of the

Soviet Union and other socialist states.

Like the Support Groups everywhere else, theirs had been a hard and searing decision to make — to aid and abet the actions of a foreign power in their own countries. They were all acutely aware of the precedents in history — Quisling and his followers who had helped the Nazis to take Norway — Laval and his co-conspirators who had schemed to enable the Nazis to take France. The Support Groups knew too of the fate that lay in store for them in the event of failure. They could expect retribution in their own countries and no great welcome in the Soviet Union. They knew that success was absolutely vital. Unlike the Soviet forces who could fight to return to Russia in the event of the attack failing, the Support Groups would have nowhere to go. Their actions were going to be influenced by desperation as well as determination.

SATURDAY

2000 Hours Central European Time

Detmold, Westfalen, West Germany

In the small West German town of Detmold, in Westfalia, lying at the southern end of the Teutoburger Wald, the whole population was in a festive mood. The narrow cobbled streets of the old town, virtually undamaged by the Second World War, were thronged with warmly wrapped crowds, promenading the streets until a late hour, window-shopping, stocking up with last minute purchases, or just out for an evening walk to enjoy the Christmas decorations and to meet friends. The streets and shop windows were brilliantly lit, the decorations were imaginative, cleverly designed and matching the season.

In the Detmolder Hof Hotel, the local intelligentsia, the families of the surviving great landowners of the area and of the refugees from Prussia were gathered for their sumptuous annual dinner dance. In the town hall, the Bürgermeister and the local dignitaries and business men with their families were holding the customary banquet and ball. In the bars, guest-houses, taverns, smaller hotels and in the restaurants, the well-dressed, boisterous populace of the town and farms were settling down for a long night of good food, wine and enjoyment.

The Central Officers Mess of the British Garrison was ablaze with lights and illuminations for the Christmas Ball, to which guests had been invited from British battalions at Lemgo, Hameln, Paderborn and Herford, from German battalions further north, and from the Royal Air Force squadrons at Gütersloh. The Christmas Gala Ball at the Sergeants Mess was a festive scene with guests from as far and wide as at the Officers Mess. The Corporals Clubs and the NAAFI Canteens were also in the throes of their Christmas parties — the whole barracks were a blaze of lights and a sea of sound, decorated by the presence of laughing girls, enjoying the gay scene which they were helping to enliven.

In the cavernous hangars of the tank park, the guard, huddled into its greatcoats for warmth, crowded round the blazing coke stove in the centre of their room. Outside, in pairs, the sentries followed the patrol route round the inside and outside of the hangars, the tank wash-down areas and the fuel pumps. In the distance they could hear the sounds of the festivities, the music, the laughter, the engines of the visitors' cars.

'Wish I was down in the canteen, don't you?' a trooper on guard duty asked his friend and co-sentry. 'Seems bloody silly to have to have sentries patrolling this lot at this time of year. I can't believe them Russians want to invade — certainly not at Christmas.'

'Maybe they will, maybe they won't,' answered the other sentry 'Every year it's the same though — one lot tells us that the Russians are a menace and want to conquer the world — and then another lot tell us that that's all wrong and that they are just like us and just want peace and to be left alone.'

Still conversing, the two sentries continued on their rounds. In the Sergeants Mess the Christmas draw of the prizes in the Mess Raffle was greeted by loud cheers and laughter. The NAAFI canteens reverberated to the sound of the massed male and female voices singing the top hit of the pops. In the Officers Mess the climax of the spectacular cabaret dance of the acrobat foursome dancers was greeted with clapping and cheers.

Unseen by the patrolling sentries, or by the Duty Officer and Duty Sergeant on their tour of inspection of the guard posts, the muffled, camouflaged figures of two Support Group guides lay on the crest of the hill overlooking the tank hangars. In the light cast by the high arc-lamps on the front of the buildings, they could see the sentries and watch that part of the route of their patrol.

'All the tanks of this battalion are in those hangars,' one muttered.

'Where are the trucks and scout cars?' asked the other without turning his head, still peering through night-binoculars at the scene below him.

'They are behind the hangars, on the truck park, further down the hill — near the barrack blocks. Over to the left, are the main gates of the barracks. The road from there leads down a fairly steep hill into the town.'

'And when will all these parties end? We shan't be able to complete our reconnaissance properly with these extra cars and people about. I want to be able to get some idea of what the barracks look like without these visitors. If we are to do our task properly we must be able to see the place as it usually is. Will all the visitors have gone by the morning?'

'Usually these special occasions end at about 0300 hours. But a lot of the cars will have gone by about midnight,' answered the first man. 'We shall have about an hour before dawn to look round the camp and check exactly where all the vehicles and guard positions are. There won't be any problem.'

'There'd better not be,' growled the second man. 'We don't want any silly mistake to spoil the operations.'

SATURDAY

2100 Hours Central European Time

Commandatura Headquarters, West Berlin

Some twenty-four hours after Ulrich Unterleib's intelligence report had left Frau Henschel's tiny flat in East Germany, it arrived on the desk of the British Major on duty at the Headquarters of the three Western Military Commandants in West Berlin. Attached to it was a note, unsigned, from the West

German Liaison Officer who had received it from the agent who was last in the complicated chain of informers, which had processed the progress of the report from Unterleib via Frau Henschel to its final destination in West Berlin. The note said:

'Reference the attached report about the positioning of the Soviet Assault Regiments in preparation for the winter manoeuvres in East Germany — these Assault Regiments, you will note, are equally well positioned to move west over all the border crossing points between the Baltic and Austria. This is a highly dangerous position. I strongly submit that manoeuvres to test the efficacy of the Soviet defences against such a type of attack, need not be conducted on so wide a front. Moreover, if the Assault Regiments move west, the follow-up motor-rifle divisions are ideally located 50—100 kilometres east of the border to follow in an invasion. The one and only fact that argues against this possibility is that none of the tanks of either the motor-rifle divisions or the tank divisions have left their peace-time barracks. Nevertheless I am of the definite opinion that this information should be taken very seriously and should be reported at once to the Western Commandants who should be recommended to inform immediately their Governments who should at once issue the necessary alert warnings to the whole of the North Atlantic Treaty Organization.'

The note was marked at the top and bottom of the page: 'TOP SECRET — MOST IMMEDIATE — ACTION REQUIRED AT ONCE.'

The Major, by direct secure telephone lines, immediately spoke in person to the American, British and French Commandants and received the assurance of each that they would immediately pass the contents of the message and the covering report to their Governments in Washington, London and Paris. Meanwhile the West German Duty Officer had already passed the information to his Government in Bonn with the suggestion that the Secretary General of NATO, the Military Committee and the Supreme Allied Commanders should be alerted.

It was almost one hour later — 2200 hours in Brussels — before the Secretary General of NATO had been informed by the Governments of France, Germany, the United Kingdom and the United States that each considered the report about the Soviet Assault Regiments to be of sufficient importance to

70

warrant a simultaneous approach to the remaining governments to consider whether a NATO wide alert should be issued.

It was 0200 hours Central European Time in Brussels before
the staff of the Secretary General had received acknowledge-
ments of his message from all the NATO Governments and
0400 hours before all the queries raised by individual Governments had been finally clarified and the definite decisions of
each could be expected.

By 0500 hours the NATO secretariat had received the agreement of all Governments that the intelligence report should be
accorded the maximum degree of importance and the NATO
Military Committee had been summoned to determine what
military steps should be taken. In Brussels the NATO Council
of Ministers had gathered at 0545 hours to consider the
diplomatic moves which should be recommended in advance of
or simultaneously with the military preparations which the
Military Committee might propose.

In Paris, the President called a meeting of the members of his
inner cabinet for 0600 hours, to determine whether, against the
previously stated policy of French Governments since the early
1960s, the French Armed Forces would be put under the
command of the Supreme Allied Commander of Europe and if
so, to what extent his operational orders would be acceptable to
the French Government.

SUNDAY

0700 Hours Central European Time

Creuzburg, East Germany

Before dawn on the Sunday morning, Hans Wogner rose and
dressed carefully so as not to wake the rest of the household. In
the barn, he ignored the Soviet sentry, started up his ageing
tractor to let the engine warm up before the journey to market,
and made sure that the long four-wheeled farm trailer was safely
hitched on at the back. Each Sunday he took the trailer loaded
with potatoes, swedes and beet, to the market at Eisenach,
about 12 kilometres away, just south of the autobahn, running

east in the direction of Gotha, Erfurt and Weimar. The Sunday sales of the root vegetables which formed so large a part of the East German winter diet were the family's main source of income. Whatever the circumstances he could not afford to miss a week's market. In fact he had been clearly informed by the Soviet Army Sergeant of the Russian troops who had arrived earlier in the week that he was not to deviate in any way from his normal routine at the weekend. So when the tractor was warmed up he started on his journey along the deserted roads.

At the market there was considerable speculation about what was afoot. There were farmers who knew other farmers from many kilometres north and south of the autobahn.

'I come from near Heiligenstadt, north of here,' one farmer said, 'and I have friends who come from near Worbis, and they say that right up to the subsidiary border crossing at Teisungen, which isn't open very often, there are Soviet soldiers and personnel carriers hidden away in barns, sheds, factories and so on. My friend has a friend who says that on his farm he even had to build a hollow haystack — bundles of hay fixed to a large wooden frame — and there is now a Soviet armoured car hidden in the stack. He's not very pleased because he has got to have the crew in his house.'

Another farmer chimed in to say, 'I come from near Meiningen, south of here. We've got 'em all round us too, but what they think they are doing there, I don't know. Mind you they could hide an army in our steep valleys and woods — they probably have, come to think of it.'

'There aren't any tanks around anywhere, so far as I've heard,' said another farmer. 'I can't see how there's going to be anything big in the way of manoeuvres if there aren't any tanks. They've got to have tanks if they're going to practice a Blitzkrieg attack. No tanks, no proper attack, is what I say. Anyone seen any tanks?'

'Seen a lot of armoured cars,' said another voice.

'And a lot of these new anti-aircraft missile things. But I haven't seen any tanks. And you could hardly miss them, could you?'

'No, you couldn't miss a tank. I hear these new T72 tanks are as big as the old Panther — not as big as the Tiger. Anyone remember them, back in 1945? Now if we had had enough

Panthers and Tigers then, the Russians wouldn't have been able to push us back from the east — nor could the Western powers have pushed us back from the west. No, if there aren't any tanks around — and we've agreed that there aren't — then I think this is another of their manoeuvres.'

'If you ask me,' said another farmer, 'it's my opinion they've got to have all these manoeuvres to keep their soldiers out of mischief — to give them something to do.'

Hans Wogner listened carefully to all the sage opinions from the much older men around him and went home to tell his family not to worry, because no one had seen any tanks, and everyone knew that without tanks there could not be an attack — not a proper Blitzkrieg attack.

SUNDAY

0800 Eastern European Time
0700 Central European Time

Bulgaria and Hungary

About an hour before it was dawn in East Germany, the sun had already risen on Bulgaria. In the small towns and villages bordering the main north-south road from Sofia to the Greek frontier at the Rupel Pass, reconnaissance units of Soviet divisions had moved in during the previous few days and were hidden away, as in East Germany and Czechoslovakia, in preparation for a repeat of the large-scale manoeuvres of two years previously, when Soviet troops had been brought across the Black Sea in special landing craft. In Petrich, Melnik, Vrach, Krupnik and Blagoevgrad, the life of the population had been considerably disrupted by the arrival of so many vehicles and troops which had to be carefully hidden. In these poor country areas families had been put to a great deal of inconvenience. Unlike the relatively richer areas of East Germany, Czechoslovakia and Hungary, the Bulgarian countryside and built up areas had fewer suitable buildings, and the houses and farm buildings were small and cramped. The Soviet troops were well hidden by each dawn and the locals went about their hard-working lives, with little time to give much thought or attention to the intruders.

The situation was the same in the area north of the Bulgarian frontier with Turkey. On the roads leading across the frontier to Edirne, Babeaski and on to Istanbul, the small Bulgarian towns and villages had also been filled with Soviet troops. Not only were they in Svilengrad, Kharmanli and Khaskovo on the main highway from Sofia, but they were also in Elkhovo, Tevrel, Yambol and Sliven on the main highway from Bucharest in Rumania and the furthest south-western provinces of the Soviet Union, not 300 kilometres away from Northern Turkey.

In Hungary too on the roads leading west from Budapest, at Szentgotthard, Kormend, Vasvar and Sumeg, by dawn on Sunday Soviet units had moved into position and were hidden. On the northern part of the frontier with Austria, the Soviet troops had not moved further west than Gyor on the road to Vienna.

But nowhere had the heavy tanks been moved closer to the frontiers, and so it was generally accepted that the planned exercises were to be manoeuvres for the Warsaw Pact light covering forces to practise their tactics in meeting a NATO invasion.

SUNDAY

0750 Hours Central European Time

Detmold, Westfalen, West Germany

On the next morning, Sunday, Detmold, tucked away in its valley on the east flank of the Teutoburger Wald, was shrouded in a wintry mist, when the sun rose at 0750 hours. In the sleepy town streets and in the barracks, there was little sign of life. The roads were clear of traffic, it was too early and too cold for the children to be out. Only a few dogs barked. In the cities, towns and villages across Western Europe, the scene was much the same. Peace and goodwill reigned, the peace of a morning after a late night and of a morning before the real festivities of the holiday began, and the goodwill of the festival which was, to the

Western world as a whole, a time of friendliness, kindness, humour and enjoyment.

Just before the first light of the still unrisen sun had spread a thin luminousness across the hilltop overlooking the tank hangars, the support group reconnaissance patrol had quickly moved back to their vehicle, hidden in a nearby lane.

'That was a very useful patrol,' said the leader. 'We saw all we needed to see. Are you sure that the guards on the hangars are only armed with revolvers and that each guard only carries a few rounds of ammunition?'

'I am quite sure,' answered the other German, 'and the guards at the main barrack gates are no better armed. All the rest of the ammunition is in the bunker we saw. All the tank ammunition is locked in there too. When we have fired the locks they will not be able to get into the bunker without a great deal of work.'

'So we should have little trouble in disposing of the guards,' the leader replied. 'Then we can move to eliminate the officers. We will take their families — and the older children who can travel without causing us difficulty. The younger children and the babies must be disposed of. We do not want them to complicate the move. You understand?'

In the darkness, the two Germans nodded to each other, fully aware, both of them, of the degree of ruthlessness that they would need to use in furthering their ends.

'Speed will be the most important element of the success of our task. We do not want to give time for a recovery from the first shock of our attack. And we do not want to be delayed by having to make any special arrangements. The very young, the old and the sick must be got rid of.'

'Now,' said the other German, 'we had better get back to the car before we meet too many people. Then we can sleep for some hours, before we need to stand by for the signal for action.'

SUNDAY

Paris, France

As the morning mists cleared from the Champs-Elysées in Paris, and the first of the sun's rays to penetrate the low clouds shone palely on the glistening wet leaves of the trees, a small group of figures left a side entrance of the Elysée Palace, and walked briskly towards the Place de la Concorde.

The President of France, often unpredictable, with his immediate staff, walked quickly across the Place and on towards the Cathedral of Notre-Dame. As they walked, the President said, 'We shall just have time for the service. The arguments about our decision not to put the French forces under NATO command can wait until we return. The Soviet invasion has not started yet.'

Fifty yards behind the President and his staff, moving carelessly to give no appearance of following the group in front, a nondescript figure managed never to lose sight of them. As he shambled along the pavements he mumbled and coughed and occasionally laughed out loud. He appeared to be slightly drunk or drugged or a little lunatic, unlikely to cause any harm or disturbance.

Fixed into the dirty scarf which he wore round his neck, the ends tucked loosely into his baggy overcoat, there was a small microphone, connected to a portable transmitter hidden in one of his bulging pockets. His coughs, cackles and mumbles were picked up and broadcast to his collaborators, hidden in an attic flat on the hill of Montmartre, overlooking the city.

'They're walking to la Concorde — hee hee hee — cough — I can just about keep up with them without looking too obvious — cough cough — I believe they're going to Notre-Dame — will confirm in a few minutes — ha ha ha — cough — I'll sing a little ditty to pass the time — no I won't, I'll just hum and laugh.'

Some minutes later he broadcast again. 'Yes, they're going into the Cathedral — I'll hang about outside, pretend to be dozing off, where I can see them when they come out. Going off the air now until I have something further to report. Out.'

SUNDAY

Morning and Afternoon

United Kingdom

After a late breakfast on board, most of the passengers and crew members of the *Leonid Sobinov* disembarked to take their places in coaches lined up along the dockside at Southampton to go on short tours of southern England. The passengers and crew members were indistinguishable from each other, but all easily identifiable as from Russia or Eastern Europe by their clothes and mannerisms. They were dressed in warm, heavy coats and a variety of fur caps. They carried similar neat picnic hampers and large vacuum flasks, slung over one shoulder with plastic straps. The customs men glanced cursorily at most of the Russians, asked to see the contents of a few of the hampers, ignored the vacuum flasks, and generally conveyed an air of benevolent goodwill. The Russians were not over demonstrative in response, but were not unduly taciturn, though one to two of the men and women were clearly under some strain.

Overnight each coach load, numbering about forty men and women, had been briefed by men and women from all over the United Kingdom, who had volunteered to give aid and advice to the Spearhead Groups of the Soviet Union. Detailed plans had been drawn up of the headquarters, barracks, airfields and other key sites which were to be attacked. The location of guard rooms, the strength of each guard, the layout of the key points in each target, had been carefully pin-pointed, and the best tactical routes plotted out. Support Group collaborators pretending to be tradesmen, insurance agents, women's make-up experts, canvassers for charities, recruiters for religions, had been able to penetrate most locations, or had been able to make inquiries from other innocent delivery men, repair men or post-men who had filled in gaps in the information.

The groups of Russian men and women, determined, well trained, well briefed about their targets, and well led, were to be formidable assault groups at each location. The guards at the target points, on a Sunday afternoon before the Christmas holiday, were unlikely to be at their most alert. In most cases they would be nearing the end of a twenty-four hour watch, marked by tedium and boredom. It would be unlikely that they would be able to offer any great resistance, even if they were fully alert.

The sight-seeing tours for the coach loads had been carefully prepared, so that there was to be a genuine tourist attraction to visit, close to Southampton, and other tours had been booked for the following two days. For their purposes, they were within easy distance of the Armoured Corps Depot; the Headquarters of the United Kingdom Land Forces; the School of Infantry; barracks of infantry and tank battalions; the School of Artillery; naval establishments and dockyards; RAF airfields; the Headquarters of the Special Air Services Regiment; the Government Communications Centre; Heathrow Airport; Gatwick Airport; and within a two hours' drive to Central London.

As well as the main targets to which each coach load would be directed, there were secondary targets which would be dealt with after the main targets had been hit. Television transmitter masts, Post Office telephone transmitters, Home Defence Regional Centres, ammunition supplies, military and air repair depots and others.

The aim of the groups was to deal first with the places where resistance might be expected, and then, when they could expect their surprise to have been blown, to go on to the unprotected, but still vital targets. They were to hit hard at each place, ruthlessly killing where there was any sort of opposition, both to achieve their ends rapidly and to spread fear and alarm as far as possible.

After dealing with their primary and secondary targets they were to occupy previously selected strong points, where wireless and telephone communications to the Soviet Embassy complex in Kensington Gardens in London had been installed, separate from the normal civil telephone system, with the help of trained telephone engineers recruited in London. There the groups would await further orders.

The Groups which were to come ashore from the *Alexandr Pushkin* at Tilbury would also travel in coaches in teams and would spread out to deal with the British and United States airfields over a vast circle round Cambridge. These Spearhead

Groups also had subsidiary targets and they would concentrate at pre-selected strong points after completing their main and secondary tasks.

The large Spearhead Group in the Soviet cruise liner, *Mikhail Kalinin,* which had docked the previous evening in the Clyde, so that its tourists could visit the Castle of Inverary, Loch Lomond, the Highlands and other tourist attractions, would be within easy reach of the British and American Polaris ballistic missile armed nuclear submarine bases at the Gare and Holy Lochs, as well as Renfrew Airport and air force bases further distant.

SUNDAY

0800 Hours Central European Time

Casteau, Belgium

Two officers, one British, one German, of the Intelligence Division of SHAPE sat in their office discussing the build-up of evidence of various kinds of unusual activity.

'Any sign of the Soviet Navy moving out of its ports? Or any indication that their tank forces or their tactical air armies are being moved westwards?' the German Colonel asked.

'No sign at all of any of the major indicators,' his British counterpart answered. 'What about their civil defence organization? Is there any sign that the civilian population is being moved to shelters? If they are going to move any vast number of people they would have to start in good time. Any change in the orbits of their satellites?'

'No,' the German Colonel answered. 'The usual checks show no change in the situation. All we can assume is that we are getting early warning signs of action which may not take place for some days. But there have been some fairly startling events in the last twenty-four hours which you won't have heard of. I won't try to list them in sequence.

'You remember the German police killed a suspected terrorist three days ago? From documents found on him, they discovered a terrorist hide-out, complete with arms, ammunition, medical

79

kits and wireless sets. In the flat, they found details of two other addresses, which they raided the next night. One, a suburban house, was empty, with plenty of evidence to show that the occupants had left hurriedly pretty recently. The other was a flat at the top of a tall block. There they surprised two occupants, a man and a woman, who were both killed in the shoot-out which followed. Both were making preparations of some kind for terrorist action. They were sorting arms and ammunition, had diagrams of locations which were unidentifiable, and were equipped with very sophisticated, new, Soviet portable wireless sets.'

'That may all mean nothing more, of course, than another spate of terrorist actions over the Christmas period — except for the wireless set. That's a new aspect, isn't it? And maybe a significant one,' the British Officer asked.

'That's so,' the German answered, 'but wait till I tell you more. During last night, the Dutch police raided a house in Eindhoven, on a tip-off, and found and killed four men who were making the same sort of final preparations as those in Germany.'

'That's interesting, very interesting,' the other said, 'but it doesn't add up to an imminent major threat to Western Europe.'

'But wait,' the German replied. 'The Belgian police have reported directly here that they will be raiding two suspected terrorist hide-outs in the Namur area later this morning. They report that the criminal underground in the country is alarmed at the scale of violence and mayhem which is said to be being planned.'

'Well, that doesn't get us much further either,' the British Colonel answered, frustrated that the picture which was emerging still had so little definition.

'The last piece of news is perhaps the most significant,' the German interposed. 'Early yesterday evening a small van ran off the autobahn near Bielefeld crashing and killing the four occupants. From the papers on the bodies, the German police tried, throughout the night, to contact relatives or friends or neighbours. By early this morning, it became clear that all the papers were false, that the van was one which was last recorded, before yesterday, as having passed through the frontier post at

Helmstedt, going into East Germany. None of the bodies carried any weapons. But what is a vehicle from East Germany carrying passengers with false papers doing?'

'Now that does put a different complexion on things,' the other said thoughtfully. 'They could be an assassination squad or some such, and if they are, how many more of them are there? Maybe there is to be a wave of assassinations by a terrorist group which may not approve of the improving relations between the East and the West. There is still not enough to be sure on. Report everything — sure — but we can't say that these incidents by themselves add anything to the alert situation already being discussed.'

From mid morning onwards reports started to come in of the disruption to public life and communications, caused by the widespread strikes, which had been threatened earlier. Telephone and telex links became more and more interrupted, though still not so disrupted that urgent messages could not eventually be got through. Some of the more sophisticated, and vitally important, computer links began to show faults and to be out of action for short periods. Power supplies in some areas had to be rationed by voltage reductions, as power men failed to report for duty and some installations had to be run at reduced capacity.

The raids carried out by the Belgian police on the hide-outs they had been told of, produced more evidence of terrorist preparations. By early afternoon, Interpol, from its headquarters in Paris, was issuing frequent warnings of an apparently concerted and widespread campaign of minor acts of sabotage to telephone lines and telex links.

SUNDAY

0830 Hours Central European Time

Fulda, Germany

At Division 12 headquarters near Fulda, 35 kilometres from the East German border, short, laconic wireless messages of the day's first light mobile patrols were coming in. A visiting Intelligence Officer from Central Army Group Headquarters wondered why he had bothered to make such an early and uneventful visit to the frontier. The next message was more interesting:

'Three five. Two families of East Germans have come through the Iron Curtain at first light this morning. They are unhurt and their vehicle has suffered only superficial damage. Both families are from Suhl, due south of Gotha. They are being held in custody by the police at Mellachstadt. Out.'

The Central Group Officer immediately asked to be taken to see the refugees and was flown at once to the town's football field, from which a short drive in a police car brought him to the small police station. Both East German families were elated at their escape, which they had been planning for a long time. The visiting officer was intrigued to know how they had succeeded and asked the interpreter to find out the details.

'They say,' the interpreter replied after questioning the two families at length, 'that it was sheer luck and they can't explain the circumstances. One of these two men has a friend who works regularly on the Iron Curtain equipment — the ditches, mines, fences, barbed wire and so on. This friend happened to remark a few weeks ago that considerable savings were being made at a number of places, including the minor border crossing point near Henneberg, by replacing live mines, booby-traps and electric fences with dummy equipment.'

'Did you ask how he knew this?' the CENTAG officer asked the interpreter, who, after questioning the two East German families in further detail, turned back saying: 'It's all a bit mysterious. The friend found out quite by mistake. He and another man dropped a box of detonators which they expected to explode. But it didn't. They decided not to ask too many questions, but made surreptitious inquiries among the other workers, some of whom had also discovered by mistake dummy detonators and explosives, especially on the verges of the narrower roads leading to the minor crossing points along the East German border.'

'Ask him how he got out, will you?' said the visitor, 'I mean find out whether he just drove down the road or whether he drove along the verge.'

82

'They drove along the verge,' the interpreter replied after further questioning. 'He says that he could not drive along the road as the fixed and locked obstacles were in position. These are strong and would have damaged his vehicle. But he calculated that, without mines and booby-traps, the verges would be safe and he could force his truck through the fence and barbed wire. So that's what he did and only barely damaged his truck.'

'Thank you very much,' the CENTAG visitor answered thoughfully, totally mystified.

The West German police were not very interested, the Grenzschutz — the West German frontier force—could offer no explanation, the staff at the Headquarters of the United States Division 12 could only hazard vague guesses.

It was only when they were airborne on the way back to CENTAG that the officer suddenly realized that only if the Warsaw Pact intended that there should be unimpeded progress for a number of vehicles would it ensure that the road verges were no hazard.

On landing he telephoned SHAPE.

SUNDAY

1000 Hours Central European Time

Brussels, Belgium

By mid morning the Secretary General of NATO had co-ordinated the views of the Allied Governments and had agreed that a limited alert should be issued to senior civilian and military staff, pending a decision early in the afternoon, by the Military Committee as to the military and logistic preparations to be ordered.

In order to reach its decision the Military Committee had ordered an urgent evaluation of the latest intelligence reports regarding the dispositions of the Soviet and Warsaw Pact Forces — particularly to determine whether naval, air and tank forces had been moved.

During the morning they received the various reports.

From the Supreme Allied Command Atlantic (SACLANT)

they heard on a linked telephone conversation, 'There is no evidence that either Soviet or Warsaw Pact naval and mercantile ships have been moving out of their ports in greater numbers than usual. The outgoing naval underwater and surface vessels have been roughly balanced in numbers and type by the ingoing vessels. There is no satellite evidence that preparations in the home ports are at an unusual level of activity. Soviet cruise liners and container ships have been trading at an increasing level over a number of years. Soviet and Warsaw Pact fishing, whaling and factory-ships are sailing the seas in no greater numbers than could be reasonably expected. Nothing further to report.'

From the Supreme Allied Commander Europe (SACEUR) they received an operational telex stating, 'Situation report at 0930 hours Central European Time — two hours after first light and after evaluation of early day cover by aircraft and satellite reconnaissance and of operational wireless traffic of Warsaw Pact land and air forces. No further movement seen of light forces already reported and notified by Warsaw Pact in connection with winter manoeuvres due to start shortly. No movement seen of these light forces being redeployed for aggressive action westwards. But no significant redeployment would be necessary from present positions if aggressive action was planned. Soviet and Warsaw Pact main forces further east are generally on a line about 50—100 kilometres from the frontiers, apparently in defensive positions, without main battle tanks, which have not moved from normal locations. No movement seen of Soviet and Warsaw Pact tank divisions. No movement seen of tactical air armies, nor preparations on forward airfields. Summary — in present locations Pact light forces could operate westwards in sudden attack and could be supported some time later by main forces when tank units have been moved forward to take part in standard main assault battle tactics on specific sectors. No such concentration has yet taken place. Natural that NATO commandants in Berlin feel vulnerable. Suggest all headquarters in Allied Command Europe down to brigade level should be alerted to evaluate all intelligence reports, but that no specific mobilization moves be made at present. Reconnaissance will be increased throughout daylight hours and a further evaluation will be made as a result of last light reports to determine what action should be taken during the night in case of first light or daytime attack tomorrow. Message ends.'

The Military Committee passed both reports, with their own recommendation to take no further action until after last light reports had been evaluated, to the NATO Council which met briefly at 1200 hours to decide on its policy. All Allied Governments were notified of the Council's decision by 1330 hours, that it concurred with the recommendation of the Military Committee.

Meanwhile at all levels of headquarters in Allied Command Europe down to brigade level, in the headquarters of the Western Commandants in Berlin, in the sector headquarters of the frontier patrol force, and in the Allied tactical air forces, the latest intelligence information was evaluated and re-evaluated. Elsewhere, in the ministries concerned with external affairs, it was noted that there had been no indication of a change in the gradual improvement of relations between East and West, which had occurred over the previous months. Anxiety was voiced in some ministries concerned with internal affairs about the evidence of a possible increase in terrorist activities, designed, it was assumed, to take advantage of a possible reduction in the alertness of the security forces over the Christmas and New Year holidays.

Detailed investigation of all the facts which might indicate the intentions of the Warsaw Pact continued during the afternoon.

SUNDAY

1200 Hours Moscow Time
1000 Hours Central European Time

The Kremlin, Moscow

At midday Moscow time, the chiefs of the Soviet intelligence agencies met to determine whether there were any last minute changes required in the plans as a result of alterations in their previously assessed strengths of the NATO forces. A senior staff officer, using a large wall map illustrating the NATO force layout, summarized the known information.

'The current strength and disposition of the enemy forces is as follows: in Norway there are only the Norwegian forces of one brigade group, with three infantry battalions. They have some independent tank companies and infantry battalions — and about one hundred tanks. Across the country they have eleven militia type regimental combat teams with about five thousand men in each. No great forces as you can see, and reinforcement by the rest of NATO takes about a week.

'Next — Denmark — has two mechanized divisions — about 350 tanks. Both divisions are located in dispersed locations throughout the country. All the Danish forces are therefore far back from the demarcation line between East and West. The Danes do not allow either foreign forces or nuclear weapons to be stationed on their territory.

'Between the demarcation line and the Danish frontier there is a West German mechanized division, with two combat air wings, stationed in Schleswig-Holstein, covering the whole width of the front between the Baltic and the River Elbe — not a large force for such a large area.

'South of the Elbe down to the area of Göttingen, there is the NATO Northern Army Group with four West German divisions, four British divisions, two Dutch divisions, one Belgian division and a United States brigade — all supported by the Second Allied Tactical Air Force. The Belgian and Dutch divisions are mainly located within their own countries — 400 kilometres west of the demarcation line. The other NATO divisions are located in barracks situated at distances between 50 and 100 kilometres west of the frontiers.

'In the southern half of Germany, under the NATO Central Army Group, there are six United States divisions, seven West German divisions and a Canadian Battle group, supported by the Fourth Allied Tactical Air Force. Some of the Americans and German forces are located within 50 kilometres of the demarcation line, but the majority are further west. Just east of the Rhine in south-western Germany, there are two French mechanized divisions — but neither is under the immediate command of NATO. The French have a further six divisions just west of the Rhine in France — again not under NATO command.

'Italy has allotted eight divisions under NATO command, all located on the northern part of the country, but none within 50 kilometres of the northern and eastern frontiers.

'Greece has allotted thirteen divisions under NATO command, about six of which are stationed in Northern Greece along the whole length of the frontiers with Albania, Jugoslavia, Bulgaria and even with her ally Turkey. These divisions are thinly stretched over such a long distance.

'Turkey has placed twenty-two divisions under NATO command, the majority being in Eastern Turkey close to the frontier with the Soviet Union. On the Bulgarian and Greek frontiers, within the area of Turkey in Europe north of Istanbul, there are only four divisions.

'Our latest information is that all the NATO land, sea and air forces are still located in their peace-time locations in barracks where they have been clearly identified and where what defences exist are well known.

'There are light NATO forces patrolling the borders by day and the West German frontier force in small isolated positions close to the frontiers both by day and by night.

'Finally the information available up to forty-five minutes ago from sources in Western Europe does not indicate that, as yet, any measures of general alert have been instituted.'

SUNDAY

1500 Hours Greenwich Mean Time
1600 Hours Central European Time

Windsor Castle, England

The two teams of four members of the special group which had been detailed to kidnap the British Royal Family mingled with the tourist crowds thronging the State Apartments. Each team consisted of three men and a girl. Two men in each team carried elaborate camera equipment, and bulky leather cases slung over their shoulders for the special lenses, filters and flash equipment. The girl and other man in each team carried camera tripod parts as well as large multi-coloured umbrellas, in case of rain

87

while they were filming outdoors. Their looks and their clothes were unremarkable. They mixed quietly with the queuing crowds and seemed to be making for nowhere in particular.

'I think we're edging towards the right place,' said a man in his late twenties. 'I have picked up three of the guide points marked on the plan of directions. There don't seem to be many officials about. How do you feel?'

'I'm all right,' the girl answered. 'I started off feeling a bit tense. Now I can't wait to get on with the job. Do you think there will be any problem?'

'I don't think so,' said a short, fair man. 'Keep a really close look out on the route we're following because remember we've got to get out this way.' He paused and then in the same tone of voice said, to the girl's initial surprise, 'We shall probably be able to get much better pictures outside where the crowds are less — oh, I beg your pardon, I hope I didn't shove you too hard.'

A man and wife with two small children glared at him as they passed, the woman saying, 'Who do they think they are blocking the way like that. Suppose they think they're royalty or something.'

'That was close,' the girl said to the fair short man, 'you don't suppose they heard anything we were saying, do you?'

'No,' the man answered. 'I saw them coming in time and blocked their way deliberately. But we were being pretty careful about what we said. Seen anything of the other lot?' he inquired, turning to survey the queue behind.

'Yes, they're not far away — still in that last large room we came through. When we get through the next main room and the rest of the crowd starts coming back in the other direction, that's when we have got to find our way. I'll lead. Make sure the others follow and see where we go.'

SUNDAY

1600 Hours Central European Time

Brussels, Belgium

For the first time for some days the Belgian Prime Minister had a free afternoon to spend as he wished. He had a standing invitation from friends who lived just outside Brussels on the road to Louvain to visit whenever he could. He had been able to foresee a free day, during the previous week, and his wife had telephoned to ask if they could accept the invitation to lunch on Sunday, and had been gratified to be told that they would be more than welcome.

Her phone call, made from the hairdressers, where she had gone for her usual weekly appointment, had been overheard by the girl on the staff, who had been planted in the establishment for just such a chance piece of information. The Special Group assigned to deal with the Prime Minister were promptly alerted, and, as he lunched with his friends, he was closely observed from a nearby house, whose owners had gone away for the Christmas holiday.

'Everything OK?' asked a small, wiry man with thinning light ginger-coloured hair, peering through binoculars at the house nearby.

'Yes,' the other man answered. 'The cars are ready, and the crews are alerted.'

Two streets away, parked in the entrance of the garage closed since midday, other members of the Special Group waited attentively in a minibus caravanette, with the curtains drawn except for the driving-cab, where the driver and his girlfriend sat reading magazines, talking animatedly, smoking cigarettes, listening to a blaring transistor wireless set on the seat between them.

Inside, four other members of the Group sat waiting for the signal that the Prime Minister was leaving. A blonde girl, with her hair done in Afro-style ringlets, sat with headphones clamped over her ears, intently waiting for the signal to be transmitted over the small transmitter-receiver wireless set propped against the seat back.

89

SUNDAY

Belfast, Northern Ireland

The tourist passengers and some of the crew of the small Russian cruise liner the *Baltika*, which had docked in Belfast late on Saturday afternoon, had been taken into the open countryside in coaches to see the beauty of the scenery and to judge for themselves whether the counties were totally engulfed in civil war. Prior to the visit, which had been well publicized, both the Provisional Irish Republican Army and the Irish National Liberation Army had stated that they would in no way hinder or endanger the welcome visitors from the Soviet Union.

In a dilapidated house, with boarded up windows, in one of the meaner and more decrepit streets of the Ardoyne, the Commander of the Support Group provided by the Provisional IRA sat listening intently to the earphones of a wireless set, hidden in a suitcase, on the small coffee-table in front of him.

'Hello, Rory One,' a voice could be heard saying over the crackling atmospherics of a low-powered transmitter, 'they have finished their tour of the countryside and are just going through the dock gates now, over.'

'Hello, Rory One,' the Commander replied, 'your message received and understood. How long will it be before their operation starts? Over.'

'Hello, Rory One. I don't know exactly, but I would guess that it would be an hour. They have to embark, collect their kit, muster in their groups and come ashore to form up, before they can start anything. I will give you good warning as I shall see them coming ashore. Over.'

'That's good, Rory One,' the Commander answered. 'We will wait to hear from you, but meantime we will also get to our positions. Out to you. Hello all stations Rory, you will have heard all that. Move now to your positions. Over.'

The outstations answered in numerical sequence, 'Rory Two. Will do. Out.' 'Rory Three. Will do. Out,' and so on to the last group.

The Support Group Commander turned to a young girl standing beside him and said, 'Right, girl, You heard that? Now nip along to the telephone cell and make sure that all the groups connected by phone know that we are moving into positions. Off you go.'

Operations in Belfast in support of the Soviet Spearhead Group were to be the reverse of those in other places. As there were so many British troops in the Province at a high state of readiness, as well as being battle-hardened, the tactics to be employed had had to be carefully thought out. The British troops were deployed in support of the civil power in a defensive role — they were politically precluded from taking offensive action, except in the most exceptional circumstances. Their battle expertise had therefore developed in the defensive roles to which they had usually been tied. They had few offensive weapons in their armouries and those they had they had seldom been able to use.

The plan in Belfast was therefore to seize the docks with the strong Spearhead Group from the liner, to receive immediate IRA Support Group reinforcements before the British armed forces were aware of what was happening, and immediately to set up strong points using all available resources to create well defended positions.

The IRA Support Groups, apart from those inside the docks with the Spearhead Groups, were then to position themselves so that the British troops moving to the dock area, or indeed any-where within Northern Ireland, would be harassed by mines, booby-traps, and direct attack by small arms fire and by mortars. The liner *Baltika* had taken on board a large supply of weapons for use in the impending battle, but the Soviet Spearhead Group was also equipped with deadlier and more instantly lethal weapons.

SUNDAY

1620 Hours Central European Time

Autobahn from Berlin to West Germany

Gunther Kleber was driving fast, heading west, on the

autobahn from his home in Berlin to the checkpoint at Helmstedt, on his way to a business appointment in Hanover, early on the Monday morning.

Ahead of him lay a day or so of lucrative work, then the holiday with his family back in Berlin, then the arrival of his parents and sister and her family who were due to stay for Christmas. Christmas Day was to be followed by a holiday for the rest of the week. He debated whether he would take his wife and the girls skiing to the Harz mountains.

He had passed over the motorway bridge, rearing up into the night sky to cross the black, fast-flowing waters of the Elbe. He had glanced to his left and made out the lights, dim by West German standards, of the sprawl of Magdeburg. He slowed as he saw ahead of him the lights of several bright torches being waved at him, and then pulled off the road to his right, on to an open clearing at the edge of a belt of pine-trees, where he could make out the dim shapes of a dozen or more cars and vans.

It was 1630 hours, Central European Time. At 1645 hours, Central European Time, Gunther Kleber was dead, shot through the head from the back of the neck by the 7.62mm bullet of a silenced Soviet-made Tokarev pistol held flat against the top of his spine. His almost naked body, wrapped in a length of oil-stained canvas, was deposited among the pine-trees.

When he had braked his car to a halt, the driver's door had been snatched open, the seat belt had been unfastened, and while two men had dragged him, falling head first on to the ground out of the car, another hand had reached in and switched off the lights, and taken out his brief-case.

'Stand up and come over here. Move fast — faster,' a voice behind one of the torches had barked at Kleber.

Bewildered at the suddenness of what had happened, not a little frightened, and winded by the fall and the rough handling, Kleber could only gasp, 'What are you doing? What do you want?'

'What is your name?' barked the voice.

'Kleber,' said Kleber, 'Gunther.'

'Well, is your name Kleber or Gunther? Make up your mind.' The voice rasped, impatient and exasperated.

'Gunther Kleber,' replied Kleber.

'Where do you live?' he was asked next. 'Full address.'

'Herrenhausen 12, Berlin. Why do you ask?'

'Give me your wallet.'

A black-gloved hand reached forward below the torch beam and snatched Kleber's wallet, which he had taken from his inside pocket. In the reflected light of the torch Kleber could see three faces bent over his wallet examining the contents.

'Who are these?' barked the voice again, holding out a snapshot of Kleber's wife and daughters.

'My family,' answered Kleber still shaken and wondering, and now shivering with the cold of the biting wind.

'Good,' said the voice, and added, 'very good,' with an inflexion of the voice which made Kleber jerk with an apprehension which he could not identify, but which was aggravated by a snigger from one of the other two figures behind the torch beam.

'You have been driving too fast, Kleber. You should not have exceeded the speed limit of 50 kph and you would not then have got here at such an inconvenient moment. But since you are here we shall use your car, your clothes and your documents. Come this way and undress.'

Kleber hesitated. He wondered whether the drivers of the vehicles he could see close by would come to his rescue. He shouted 'Help' once, at the top of his voice. He was promptly silenced by a blow to the back of his head with a heavy truncheon, wielded by another man standing behind him.

He was dragged unconscious to the edge of the wood, laid on a piece of canvas, undressed quickly but carefully so that his clothes remained clean and unmarked, rolled over onto his face, shot in the back of the neck, and his body bundled into the canvas and dumped in the wood.

SUNDAY

1630 Hours Central European Time

Farm in East Germany

From the upstairs window of a bleak farmhouse on the west edge of the village of Morsleben, four pairs of eyes gazed south towards the autobahn. They had watched a succession of car lights pull off the road and then be switched off. Heinz and Gudrun Stellman, with their son and daughter-in-law, were upstairs in their own home because the downstairs, their brand new hay barn and the cattle byre had been taken over by soldiers of the Russian Army, with their troop carrier and reconnaissance vehicle.

'I don't like this,' Heinz muttered. 'First we have these Russians in our house. Then we have these lights stopped where the *Volkspolizei* never allow any vehicles to pull off. Next we shall have them setting fire to our wood on the edge of the road.'

Gudrun Stellman nodded owlishly. The Russian soldiers had moved in on the Wednesday night. Since then she had been unable to call her house her own. She and Heinz had had a difficult time controlling their headstrong son Helmut, whose opinion of the German Democratic Republic and their overlords, the Russians, was born of intense loathing and frustration against regimentation.

Behind Heinz Stellman's worried mutter there was fear, real fear, that once again in his lifetime there was going to be upheaval and turmoil. As a young boy he had had to work hard to make the farm pay, when his father had been killed in the Kaiser's war. He had had to produce more and more during Hitler's war and particularly in the last dreadful year after the Allies had landed in France, until the German surrender in 1945. His farm had been pillaged by the hordes of displaced persons and the escaping Allied prisoners of war. His land had been cut up and his buildings and fences ruined in the Allied advance to the Elbe. And it had not stopped there. No sooner, it seemed, had they advanced 3 kilometres to the east than they had returned and gone 10 kilometres west again, back to the final frontier between East and West Germany. Then the Russian Army had occupied his farm. He remembered that as a time of disaster and horror. He was not married then and had been shocked at those young German girls who had willingly given themselves to the Russian soldiers, and appalled at the treatment of other young girls and women who had been dragged, screaming and protesting, into his farmhouse to be abused and raped until their minds or their bodies broke, and they were driven out of the house to fend for themselves.

And here were the Russian soldiers back again, as the friends

94

and allies of his country.

'I said there was more to it when they gave us the new barn,' muttered Helmut. 'They don't give anybody anything for nothing. And ours isn't the only new barn, as I told you.' His father nodded absently, remembering the arguments since the spring when the builders had arrived to build the barn, and to repair the cow byre and enlarge the doorway.

Downstairs the Russian soldiers cleaned their weapons, looked at books and magazines, and listened to the Stellmans' wireless set while they waited for their next orders.

SUNDAY

1645 Hours Central European Time

Autobahn in East Germany

Kleber's car still stood where it had stopped, but the driver's seat was now occupied by a Soviet agent and his passengers were four members of a Spearhead Group.

There was unhurried movement along the line of cars, vans and minibuses. Well trained and rehearsed crews climbed into their seats and, one by one, the vehicles switched on their engines and lights and moved out on to the road and headed west to the border, up to the wire and minefields of the Iron Curtain.

Along the length of the East German and Czechoslovakian frontiers with West Germany, at all the border crossing points, similar convoys of all kinds of vehicles moved out of their various assembly points and towards the border posts. There was nothing remarkable about each collection of cars, vans and trucks. They appeared to be small parts of the million strong mass of vehicles which each month crossed the borders, going east and west, between the two parts of Europe. They might have been, and were meant to look like, tourists, business men, whole families. In twos and threes they joined in with the normal flow of traffic and became part of the rush back to homes and families.

In a minibus seating six, the driver settled behind the wheel, switched on the engine, then the lights and moved to his place in the queue. Beside him a woman member of the Spearhead Group settled into the fur collar of her thick coat, and stared straight ahead.

The four passengers in the rear seats, in unaccustomed new clothes of West German cut and manufacture, tried to look relaxed and as if they were looking forward to the holiday ahead. Their thick civilian overcoats and their fur-lined hats hid their identity for the imminent border inspections.

In the north at the Schlutup crossing point, east of Lübeck, some of the vehicles had crew members who were Danes, picked for their part in the scheme of things that was to take place in Denmark. At the crossing point at Lauenburg, south-east of Hamburg, there were, among the Germans, also Dutch and Belgians. At the Helmstedt crossing point, east of Braunschweig, among the German crews, there were British and French crews. Further south, at Herleshausen and at Henneberg, among the German and French crews, there were American speaking Cubans, Puerto Ricans, Mexicans and others from the Americas. And at the crossing-points even further south, from Czechoslovakia into West Germany, at Schiernding, Waidhaus, Furth, Eisenstein and Philipreuth, there were more American speaking crews among the Germans.

Most crews of the smaller vehicles had one or more girls — whether large or small, pretty or not, all with an unfeminine stony intensity about them which marked them as being as determined fighters as the men.

In the larger vehicles, the vans, the high-sided lorries and in some giant articulated container-carrying juggernauts, the visible crew in the cab was only a small part of the total. In the containers on the juggernauts, sealed with chains and padlocks and marked with the TIR carnet showing goods in transit, thirty East Germans sat on improvised seats, gasping for the thin flow of fresh air coming through the small disguised ventilation holes on the top and sides.

In the sixty minutes between 1630 and 1730 hours that evening, a large number of squads of men and women of many nationalities moved across the frontiers into West Germany. By the last light of the pale sun dropping behind the horizon, some crews, averaging, with short stops, a speed of about 60 kilometres an hour, had easily reached their appointed destinations in Western Europe, there to do the damage and create the alarm and terror which was their task.

At their destinations they were met by local collaborators, and guided by them to the key installations and sites which were their immediate targets.

The acquisition of the vehicles and the assembly of the crews had been a long, major operation, though surreptitious, clandestine and imperceptible. Over many months the vehicles had either been stolen or purchased, throughout Western Europe, and then openly driven to East Germany. For the stolen vehicles, forged documents had been provided — for the vehicles that had been purchased, genuine documents had been easily obtained. Spread over a large part of the year, the flow had been unremarkable, insufficient in itself to indicate at all that there had been a deliberate campaign to obtain vehicles or even to obtain special types of vehicles. The operation had been the simpler because almost any type or vintage of vehicle would meet the need. Some of the juggernauts had been hired ostensibly to carry special loads just before Christmas — not an unusual arrangement and therefore not liable to draw suspicion.

The crews, who had first obtained the vehicles and who had then delivered them to East Germany, had been more of a problem. After delivering the vehicles they had had to be returned to their home countries. Most of them had been unemployed or were petty thieves of one sort or another. The deal to them had been no more than a quick way of earning some money. They did not mind where or how they travelled, as long as they were not required to pay. They had been led to understand that there was a brisk trade in the vehicles. Some had been returned direct from East Germany as undesirable visitors to the Republic of the Democratic East Germany. Some had been landed in the seaports of the Baltic, Mediterranean and Atlantic coasts.

The terrorist crews for the final journey now in progress had been transferred from their own countries to Eastern Europe by way of Algeria, Libya, Iraq and the Lebanon. They had met up, and been given their battle orders and special equipment in the barracks of the East German Army.

97

SUNDAY

North Norway

To comply with the demand of the peremptory Soviet note delivered the previous Friday, the Norwegian Garrison Commander had left his headquarters at Kirkenes and had arrived at the border outpost building in time for his 1700 hours meeting with the Soviet Border Commissioner. Promptly at 1650 hours Central European Time, the arc lights which illuminated the Soviet frontier barrier gates had been switched on. Three large Soviet camouflaged staff cars, one more than was usual, the Norwegian Garrison Commander noted, drove slowly along the 400 metres of bumpy road, passing through the belt of no-man's land which had been kept clear of undergrowth and planted with mines. The small Soviet convoy had stopped briefly at the high electrified wire fence, while a man go out of the leading car and unlocked the padlocks on the gates which he then swung back to either side.

The meeting had started exactly on time and had dragged on for almost thirty minutes. The Norwegian Commander had had enough experience of meetings with the Russians to know that he could not hurry the proceedings. But it was not at all clear why the Russians had called the special meeting as nothing they raised was of special significance. Apart from the three Soviet staff car drivers, who sat stolidly in an outer office by themselves, the conference was between nine Russians of various ranks, the most senior being a colonel, to match the rank of his Norwegian opposite number, and six Norwegians. The two sides sat facing each other across a long length of narrow tables placed end to end and covered with a dark green baize cloth. There were ashtrays at intervals down the tables and a few rough glasses and two jugs of water. On a side table, behind the Norwegians, were the glasses, drinks and snacks, ready for the usual ceremony of a party of sorts which followed each of the meetings, whether on Norwegian or Russian soil.

As the meeting progressed slowly, the Russian Colonel glanced more frequently at his wristwatch, so frequently in fact that it appeared to be more of a nervous twitch than a conscious act of looking at the time. All the while he and the other Russians were either toying with their pens or pretending to take notes on the pads in front of them.

At 1730 hours exactly to the second, the Russian Colonel tapped the table in front of him twice, with his left hand. As he did so he dropped the pen in his right hand and, reaching inside his uniform jacket, he drew out a small silenced automatic. The other Russians copied his moves. Simultaneously the six Russians exactly opposite the six Norwegians, reached out their hands across the table, to the total surprise of the Norwegians, and at the same moment each Russian fired two shots into the face of the Norwegian opposite. As they did so, they and the three remaining Russians roughly pushed their chairs back on the bare wodden boards, making as much noise as possible.

The commotion made by the chairs and the Russian voices, all speaking at once, covered the sounds of the heavy falls of the six dead Norwegians as they slumped across the tables, before collapsing on the floor. The Russians stood back from the six corpses in front of them, still talking to make the scene sound natural from outside the room.

'Wait one more minute,' said the Colonel, 'and then we shall be sure if those outside suspect anything. Levitin, go to the door and make sure that no one comes in just yet. Chernov, be ready to go out to the drivers and to see where the rest of the Norwegian soldiers are. There are usually not more than a dozen in this building, especially when we meet at this time of day.'

Chernov left the conference room. In the outer office the three staff car drivers got to their feet as he entered.

'Where are the other Norwegians?' he asked abruptly. 'You have noted which rooms they are in, as you were ordered to do?'

'Yes, there are three men in a small kitchen just down the corridor, preparing hot drinks and some food,' said one driver.

'There are four men in the main office across the entrance hall,' said another driver, 'and they are manning two wireless sets and sit near the telephones.'

'And just inside the main entrance, there are three men who are in charge of vetting the passes of anyone who comes into the building,' said the third driver.

Chernov went back into the conference. 'No alarm outside —

the other Norwegians are in three separate small groups in different rooms,' he reported.

'In that case,' said the Colonel, 'the four of you detailed to deal with the communications room go now. We shall wait in the corridor outside until you have completed the elimination in there. If the occupants of any of the other rooms appear, they must be dealt with immediately.'

Four Soviet officers, with their silenced automatics held ready, moved quietly to the door of the communications room, opened it, walked calmly in, levelled their guns at the four occupants, fired two shots each, and watched in silence as their victims' bodies slumped in their chairs, then collapsed to the floor and lay still, with small pools of blood oozing from their wounds onto the clean wooden floor.

Immediately their task was done, they moved across the corridor into the small kitchen. They repeated the earlier action, killing the three surprised cooks, who collapsed to the floor, dropping the utensils they were using, the clattering noise bringing the three door attendants crowding to the entrance of their small room.

As they stood in surprise at seeing the Russian officers crowded into the corridor, the three Norwegians were shot and fell back into the room where they had been seated.

Pointing at the Russian officer nearest the main entrance, the Colonel ordered, 'Look outside and see if there are any of the enemy about — and you four, put on the caps and overcoats of the Norwegians nearest to your size. When we move across to those other buildings, we must look as if we are going as welcome guests.'

SUNDAY

1830 Hours Eastern European Time
1730 Hours Central European Time

North Turkey

On the southbound carriageway of the main road into Turkey from Svilengrad in Bulgaria, four large Russian trucks drew up to the Turkish border and customs post north-west of Edirne. At about the same time four other Russian trucks pulled up at the Turkish post, north of Edirne, on the road from Elkhovo in Bulgaria, on the main road south from Bucharest in Rumania.

The driver of each truck stayed at the wheel, while the front passenger and ten men climbed out. The crews of two trucks moved at a leisurely pace towards the frontier guard and customs offices on the southbound carriageway, while the men of the other two trucks went to the offices on the northbound carriageway. The dozen Turkish officials in each office were sitting at the desks and counters inside, drinking coffee, reading papers, listening to the wireless blaring music from the studios in Istanbul, and paying the minumum of attention as the traffic late in the evening was always less, and in less of a hurry.

They barely had time to look up or alert themselves before they found they were surrounded by the thickly wrapped men who had pushed their way in through the swing doors, bringing a gust of cold December wind with them. It only took a few minutes for the men from the trucks to kill off the staff of the two posts and then to move outside to deal with other officials in the buildings nearby.

By 1740 hours, the two crossings from Bulgaria into North Turkey were securely in the hands of the Pact forces and the communications systems by which warning might have been passed to Edirne and on to Istanbul and Ankara, had either been put out of action or was being guarded by Turkish collaborators who could answer inquires.

SUNDAY

1730 Hours Central European Time

Casteau, Belgium

A group of fifty West European trade unionists were visiting SHAPE in the course of a tightly packed programme of lectures and seminars on international current affairs which only had the Sunday free for a visit to SHAPE. The visit was part of a series of instructional tours for trade union study groups arranged by the Adult Education Commission of the International Labour Organization. All the details of the day's schedule of events were arranged with SHAPE from an office with a good address in Geneva on apparently impeccably authentic notepaper and coded in the correct wording and terminology.

It had long been the custom for both the NATO political headquarters in Brussels and the military headquarters at Casteau to welcome visits by study groups of adults and schoolchildren to inform them of NATO's political, economic and military problems and to give them some idea and reassurance as to the measures being taken to guard Europe against the growing threat by the Warsaw Pact.

The Union study group was entertained to lunch in the SHAPE restaurant and, as was usual on such occasions, the senior military staff who were to lecture and answer questions lunched with the guests. As he was free to take part on the day, the Chief of Staff joined the three members of the Education Commission at lunch, together with the Deputy Chief of Staff Operations and the Assistant Chief of Staff Plans and Policy Division. Four less senior members of the SHAPE staff sat at the tables occupied by the trade union students.

After lunch the hosts and visitors moved to the lecture hall situated close to the restaurant at the back of the headquarters building, separated from the office and Operations Centre complex and the main entrance by swing doors, carefully guarded by two military policemen.

At the rear of the headquarters building, there were, apart from the restaurant and lecture hall, a shop, a post office, men's and ladies' hairdressers, and a library both to provide for the needs of the staff of the headquarters and for their relations and friends. Access to these more public facilities was through the same main gates which led, in one direction, to the front, official entrance, and also round the side of the complex to the public car parks at the side and rear and to the separate entrances which families, friends and other visitors, were allowed to use.

Lunch was a lengthy meal lasting, with coffee and liqueurs, until 1430 hours. There was a short period for relaxation and for the guests to assemble in the lecture hall before the first presentation, by the Chief of Staff, started at 1500 hours. His was followed by those of the Deputy Chief and the Assistant Chief, which, with questions, lasted until 1615 hours. Tea was taken then until 1630 hours, followed by discussion in five syndicates each chaired by a SHAPE officer.

At 1715 hours drinks were served in the lecture hall and the SHAPE officers and the three members of the Adult Education Commission mingled with the student unionists.

Just before 1730 hours a group of the students moved to the hall exit and into the corridor outside leading to the guarded swing doors, giving access to the offices and to the Operations Centre. As they reached the two military policemen, the three men in the lead drew from their suit pockets pen-sized nerve gas weapons with which the two guards were killed instantly.

The group then ran down the main corridor, into a side corridor and, pausing only to kill the guard at the entrance to the Operations Centre, the leader, using the guard's key, opened the door to the Centre and he and his followers crowded in, killing the occupants.

At the main entrance, in the lecture hall, in the main corridor, the military staff, the members of the Education Commission and those students not forming part of the Spearhead Group, were also killed.

In the Operations Centre, surrounded by the dead and dying NATO staff, the terrorists suddenly became quiet. Determined as they were, violent and revolting death on the scale that was all round them sickened at least a few of them and silenced the remainder.

From the main Operations Centre, some then moved to the other occupied offices and a small kitchen. They knew exactly where to go and what to do. The wireless and telephone links which might have to be answered were manned. The logs of action taken already that evening, and action still to be taken, were carefully examined. The bodies were dragged out of a side door, to be laid in rows on the grass outside. Two men dressed themselves in military police uniforms and stood guard at the main entrance. As a special weekend arrangement the next shift of duty was due to take over at 2100 hours. The Spearhead Group would be ready for them when they arrived to go on duty.

Two officers of the staff of the Operations Centre had just ended their allotted short break from duty, which they had used for a short walk in the fresh air, had made their way slowly,

103

thoughtfully, and therefore quietly, back to the entrance of the Operations Centre, down a long side corridor of the headquarters complex. Ahead of them the door of the entrance of the Centre was slightly ajar. From the less brightly illuminated corridor, they had a good, clear, though limited view, into the brightly lit interior. Their attention to the crack in the door had been drawn by the sounds of considerable commotion coming from beyond the entrance. Their attention was further riveted when the sounds abruptly ceased, and, even through the narrow gap, they could make out that a number of men and women, not uniformed, had become still and silent, and that the two or three of uniformed military staff they could see had fallen in convulsions to the floor.

Warned by a sixth sense not to investigate but rather to make good their escape, the two men turned quickly, ran hurriedly back the way they had come, turned a corner into a connecting side corridor and, as they heard voices behind them, went into a darkened office, shutting the door swiftly and silently behind them.

While his companion listened at the door, one officer moved to the desk, picked up the telephone, made sure that there was a dialling tone, and tried to get through to the switchboard. He had no clear idea as to whom he would ring, but was desperate to pass the warning through to other members of the Headquarters, and through them, if possible, to other NATO establishments.

It dawned on him eventually that he would get no reply from the switchboard, which had also been taken over. As a last chance he dialled to connect to the civilian lines, got through and remembering no other number, dialled that of a friend's house. To his relief his call was answered.

'Willi — Bill here — maximum alert — we've been —' his voice ended abruptly as he turned at a sound behind him and received a full one-second shot of nerve gas.

At the same time as the attack took place on the main headquarters building, a smaller Spearhead Group managed to gain access to the SHAPE Operations bunker, some miles away, took it over too, killing the skeleton staff who were on duty and piling the bodies into an unlit deserted tunnel, abandoned after the building of the bunker had been completed.

104

SUNDAY

The Kremlin, Moscow

While most of the Western world was still going about its business and pleasures in the normal way, the Soviet Council of Ministers, with key officers and officials in attendance, met in the Kremlin. The members of the Defence Council assembled on the rostrum at one end of the room. In the other body of the hall ministers gathered. The attendant experts, officials and staff stood behind the seats in the balcony at the other end of the hall. Maps marked with a myriad of small coloured flags and tapes were on one side wall. It was a solemn occasion and nobody sat until the President and Commander-in-Chief of the Soviet Union took his place. He arranged his papers carefully on the table, and looking over the tops of his glasses as was his habit, he opened the meeting.

'Comrades, you have been summoned here now so that you can be informed of the details of the preparatory moves for the attack on NATO.

'The Head of the KGB will first summarize the operations for which he is responsible as he must then leave to deal with other important matters.'

The General at the head of the KGB moved to the dais and said, 'I will be brief, Comrades, because to go into all the detail of the operations in which we are engaged would take many hours. I should first say that our preparations have been in progress over many years. It has had to be a very gradual process to replace men and women in the embassies, consulates, trade missions and so on, with specially trained operatives properly instructed in every detail of their tasks. We have been fortunate in some cases, where illness has necessitated a change. We have been not so fortunate in others where an existing staff member, who should have stayed, or a new staff member who had recently been installed, has been uncovered by NATO counter-espionage and had to be withdrawn. On the other hand, in other cases we have used this process to our advantage, by allowing a

105

staff member to be uncovered in spying activities, to have that member expelled so that we could send in the replacement we wanted. It has been a slow business, and has had to be handled with great care so as not to indicate that there was a concerted master plan which could be suspected of being a part of something bigger. We have been at war virtually for this time, manoeuvring to get our forces into position, winning a battle here, losing another battle, having some undecided battles. But it has been a war with no holds barred. We have had losses — so have the enemy. But we have been the more determined as we had a deadline at which to aim.

'We have of course continued with our normal duties of espionage and subversion. On top of these we have undertaken seven other tasks. First to enable the special units of the International Terrorists to remove the heads of state and prominent personalities, we have had to maintain constant watch on all these people. By careful collation of the details of their habits and timetables, we have been able to advise the best time and place to strike. Second, we have had to forge the closest links with the special terrorist units so that we can be sure that they are fully trained and briefed. To this end we have trained the training staff of the PFLP so that they could teach the special groups. Third we have had to locate the targets for the Spearhead Groups — the headquarters, the communications centres, the nuclear warhead stores, the ammunition dumps and so on. Fourth we have had to help to organize the Spearhead Groups and their operations. Fifth we have had to recruit the Support Groups to meet the Spearhead Groups, especially those which have had to move in early into attack positions. We have had to find secure accommodation for them, supply them with food, obtain extra transport, get maps and diagrams of the targets they are to strike. We have also made the needed arrangements for the operations of the Spearhead Groups which have moved into war positions disguised as tourists from cruise liners, the bulb growers, the team supporters, the orchestra admirers and so on. Sixth we have made very careful contact with the terrorist groups within each country, who insist on acting on their own, but whose exploits must not hinder the efficient execution of the primary tasks. We have had to tell them which targets they must at all costs avoid interfering with, and we have suggested alternative targets which will either directly help our operations or which, by being hit, will confuse the enemy's security forces as they will not be relevant to our operations. And finally, seventh, we have kept in contact with the more reliable members of the Communist Parties of the Western democracies. They will not necessarily be of much use to our purposes but, through their connections, they might get some wind of impending events and need to be told just enough to be sure that they keep quiet.

'Unfortunately some of these groups are not as reliable as others and have taken it into their own hands to take premature action on the information we provided.

'Of course, throughout this time we have not neglected the counter-espionage aspects of our work. Fortunately for us, and with some help from our supporters, whether deliberate or inadvertent, both the CIA and FBI in America came under close scrutiny and had certain of their vital operations curtailed or cancelled. This was a bonus that we could not possibly have planned on, but, when it came, it removed very considerable pressures from us, since it also affected the British, German and French Intelligence services. It has enabled us to install and keep agents in certain very sensitive and highly important positions. I will answer questions if there are any.' There were no questions so the head of the KGB left to supervise the operations for which he was responsible.

'I shall next ask the Foreign Minister to give his considered opinions about the enemy's likely reaction to our operations,' the President announced.

The Foreign Minister moved to the dais, and placed his notes before him. 'Comrades, what I have to report is that the Western countries still believe that, like them, the Soviet Union wants peace. This basic fact is the one which helps all our purposes, political, military, economic. We have never wanted peace with capitalism, until it is destroyed. We only wanted *détente* to enable the Soviet Union to pursue its objectives unhindered. We are not prepared to accept nuclear parity and adopt the American vision of a peace ensured by the threat of mutual assured destruction as the result of an acceptance of parity. We have pursued our aims with determination.

'The Western countries, including America, have lost the

107

political will to keep pace with our increasing strength and the political resilience to meet our expanding moves. The strategic balance no longer exists. The acts of the Soviet Union to protect socialism anywhere in the world cannot be resisted.

'In Europe in particular, there has been an erosion of the will and determination to resist the advance of communism. The forces which are ready to spring to the side of a victorious communist advance are strong and growing stronger. That, Comrades, is the position as I see it.'

The Foreign Minister gathered his notes together and went back to his seat. The President rose from his seat and moved to the dais. He disdained notes and the pointer. He looked serious and alert and there was a note of confidence and controlled excitement in his voice when he spoke.

'Comrades, Marshals, Admirals, Fighters for Freedom, a great day for communism and the far-sighted wisdom of Marx and Lenin is about to dawn. This will be another giant stride forward for the march of socialism in the ceaseless war we are fighting against capitalism and fascism. For we are not going to war again, but rather we are launching another campaign in a ceaseless war. We have lost some battles. We have won many others. These are all incidents in our war against imperialist aggression and suppression to open the way to victory for communism.

'Since the setback to our plans in 1962, when we were prevented from siting missiles in Cuba because of the superior strength of the United States Navy and their intercontinental ballistic missile numbers, we have advanced on every important front. There have been a few failures. China has refused our offers of peaceful co-operation. The reactionary forces of fascism overthrew the progressive socialist state of Allende in Chile. Otherwise we have had success almost everywhere. First and foremost the strength of communism was displayed in Vietnam, Kampuchea, Laos, Ethiopia, Mozambique, Angola and Afghanistan. We have strong allies in the Middle East. In Africa there are other governments who are actively aiding and in sympathy with the Soviet Union. In Europe the Communist Parties in Italy and France have remained strong forces.

'Militarily we have also advanced very far. The forces of the Warsaw Pact are the most powerful armies and air forces in the world. The Soviet Navy is now so strong that it can gain superiority in any part of the seas which we wish to dominate.

'We have been able to exploit the loop-holes in the SALT Agreements with respect to heavy missiles and we have provided significant improvements in quality. The whole Soviet strategic offensive force has undergone a programme of modernization which had resulted in greater accuracy, flexibility and invulnerability. We are in a position to undertake action knowing that it will not necessarily result in mutual assured destruction of the Soviet Union and the United States. Our civil defence measures have been completed.

'We are now at a point where we either take every advantage of our superiority or we miss the opportunity which may not occur again for a long time. To reach this level of superiority, both militarily and politically throughout the world, we have had to take certain risks. The Soviet economy is not as strong as we would like, because we have had to put large resources towards the production of war equipment. Our agriculture is not as flourishing as is necessary, because we have not been able to provide it with enough resources or manpower.

'But, with the help of the West, we have so far been able to overcome these difficulties. The Soviet Union and the communist countries of East Europe have been able to obtain huge financial aid from the West. We have also been able to gain valuable technological help by inviting Western countries to install factories in the Soviet Union.

'As far as our agricultural needs are concerned, where we have had inevitable shortages because of the emphasis on military preparations, we have been able to obtain the grain and fats we needed from North America and the European Economic Community.

'But the time has now come when we can no longer borrow more money — indeed we shall soon have to start repaying massive sums, and we shall then not so easily be able to buy to meet our agricultural needs. Nor is the West now so willing to provide the advanced technology we want.

'So we must get what we want by the occupation of Western Europe. By this means we can cancel our debts. We can obtain the technology and the advanced factories we need. And we can occupy the agricultural lands to provide our requirements of

109

grain and fats and other commodities.

'When this has been achieved and we move to secure the sea routes through the Red Sea, by the occupation of Egypt and the Sudan, from our bases in Ethiopia and South Yemen, we can then get all the oil we shall need from Arabia. By occupying Greece and Western Turkey, we shall have a totally secure sea route to the Black Sea ports.'

The President resumed his seat and motioned to the Commander-in-Chief of the Soviet Navy who moved to the dais, 'The main task of the Soviet Navy,' he said, 'has been to continue to operate in such a way that NATO Intelligence has not built up any picture of ship movements which would indicate our intentions. The ships now at sea are carrying extra emergency provisions of warlike and non-warlike stores such as food and water. So the first task of the Soviet Navy has been successfully accomplished — it has given no indication of our preparations.

'The Soviet Navy has helped to provide Spearhead support in those areas not accessible or easily reached over land.

'Soviet Navy personnel, together with reservists who have been called up for service, as well as MVD Security Troops, have been specially trained. These forces have been embarked in cruise liners, factory-ships, fishing vessels and various merchant ships. These ships have entered selected NATO ports in the last few days for a variety of purposes.

'In order to give NATO no indication of impending operations, the fleet disposition of ships including the Naval Strategic Nuclear Force of submarines which have separate strategic responsibilities has been unchanged. The Northern Fleet has 110 submarines of all types and 50 major surface combat ships. The Baltic Fleet has 35 submarines and 50 major surface combat ships. Both fleets have their necessary quota of submarine chasers for inshore patrols, and fast patrol boats armed with surface to surface guided missiles. The Baltic Fleet has a high number of motor torpedo-boats. Both fleets have sufficient amphibious ships and landing craft. And both fleets will have the full support of oiling ships, supply ships, depot ships and repair ships. The intelligence collection vessels are already on station, where NATO would expect them to be.

'The major part of the Naval Air Force will be ready to operate on the Norwegian Front as operations in the Baltic and the Black Sea, where other naval forces will be employed, can be adequately supported by the Soviet Tactical Air Armies on those fronts.'

The Commander-in-Chief ended his presentation and at a nod from the President resumed his seat, his place being taken by the Chief of Staff of the Soviet Army.

'Ostensibly in preparation for winter manoeuvres about which we have given NATO due notice,' he started, 'we have moved light reconnaissance assault forces close up to the frontiers with NATO in Europe. These forces can be used for deep penetration operations. Further east we have pre-positioned motor-rifle divisions, apparently in defensive positions for the manoeuvres to counter the light reconnaissance forces. We have not moved any of the tanks of these divisions from their barracks. We have not moved any elements at all of the tank divisions. We have not moved any aircraft of the Tactical Air Armies. Our airborne divisions have not been moved from their peace-time locations.

'Nevertheless we are ready to exploit the expected success of the attacks of the special and Spearhead Groups about which you have already been told.'

The Chief of Staff ended by saying, 'NATO military forces have not moved from their barracks except for the standard light border patrols. It is therefore apparent that, even if they have detected any of our preparations they have not yet suspected the scale of our preparations.'

The President rose and left the hall as the meeting ended.

SUNDAY

1730 Hours Central European Time

At the winter solstice, when the sun is at its furthest point south of the equator, the time of sunset in Central Europe is 1555 hours. Sunrise the following morning is at 0800 hours. After the sun sets and before the sun rises there is a period of half-light lasting for about thirty minutes. Last light in the evening is therefore at about 1630 hours and first light at 0730 hours — some fifteen hours of darkness. For their strategic purposes, in order to achieve the greatest possible results during the hours of complete darkness and then to establish strongly defended positions on their objectives, the Warsaw Pact needed to have the maximum possible time of darkness. However if they were to attack the most important front, Central Europe, at 1630 hours, it would already be 1830 hours in Bulgaria — two hours after last light. On the other hand the areas which were to be covered by the Pact forces in Northern Greece and European Turkey, were smaller than those in Central Europe, and therefore delay on the two eastern fronts was acceptable.

But 1630 hours Central European Time was 1530 hours Greenwich Mean Time, still thirty minutes before sunset and sixty minutes before last light, the optimum time for the Special and Spearhead Groups to attack their targets. Since communications throughout Western Europe were so technically advanced, it was clear that, without special measures, an attack on one front would be known about, within a short time, on other fronts. A simultaneous attack, ignoring the differences of suntime, in the various time zones, would better ensure an element of surprise for all the attacks.

Another vital consideration was that 1630 hours Central European Time, the optimum time for attacks to start on the Central Front, would be 1030 hours Eastern Standard Time in Washington, a time of day which would give the United States about six hours of daylight in which to mount their initial responses. It was considered vitally important to reduce this available time as much as possible by delaying the time of the start of operations. On the other hand a really significant reduction of about four hours would drastically affect the time available to secure the objectives in Western Europe.

It was concluded that the first essential was the successful capture of Western Europe and that for this the attacking forces should have all the time possible. It was most important that the Special and Spearhead Groups, to have the maximum chances of success, should have the best condition for their surprise attacks — darkness. Except in Dublin and Belfast — and Reykjavik in Iceland even further to the west — last light would not be before 1630 hours Greenwich Mean Time, 1730 hours Central European Time in Germany, when it would have been dark for sixty minutes.

The Soviet High Command decided to set zero hour at 1730 hours Central European Time, forgoing one hour of darkness, but affording to most of the Special and Spearhead Groups the essential ingredient of darkness for the success of the operations. The time selected then left the Soviet Union with the uncomfortable knowledge that the moment of the synchronized attacks would be 1130 hours Eastern Standard Time in Washington when, even on a Sunday just before Christmas, the defence and security agencies could be expected to be on the alert. The High Command therefore decided that other measures would have to be adopted to try to obtain the degree of surprise needed.

SUNDAY

1730 Hours Central European Time

Helmstedt, West Germany

There were the usual number of travellers waiting for their possessions and documents to be examined at the customs and frontier post offices on both the westbound and eastbound carriageways of the autobahn at Helmstedt. A queue of about a dozen cars and trucks had built up on the eastbound carriageway, as the leading car's driver was having great difficulty in finding the correct papers, and the details on his customs declaration form required close scrutiny of his vehicle. Only a skeleton staff was on duty as it was a Sunday evening, and the delay caused the line of waiting vehicles to grow. The drivers and passengers of the waiting vehicles crowded into the frontier offices.

On the westbound carriageway, a group of about twenty vehicles arrived almost together, not an unusual circumstance in itself and not therefore noticed by the frontier guards, who were unaware that beyond the East German frontier post, down a small hill to the east, and round the last bend of the autobahn from Berlin, all traffic had been under the strict control of the

113

Soviet Army for the last hour, since darkness fell at 1630 hours. In the West German Frontier post on the westbound carriageway there were therefore only the vehicles of the Spearhead Group designated to take over the post.

In the offices on the eastbound carriageway, there were only genuine travellers, but the Spearhead Group allotted to its takeover were ready, poised to act, in the vehicles halted across the central reservation area in the westbound carriageway.

In both frontier posts, as the minute hand of the main electric clock above the entrance flicked to the half-hour point, the Spearhead Groups went into action. On the westbound carriageway, men and women armed with automatics and machine-pistols, fitted with silencers, moved into the offices close to their vehicles. Without undue haste, which might have caused the alarm to be raised elsewhere in the frontier post, others moved across the central traffic area and into the offices on the eastbound carriageway. It was a matter of seconds only before the majority of the customs, police and frontier guard men lay dead on the floor. Some of both the Spearhead Groups had leapt the counter to deal with the staff behind it, while others had pushed their way into the back offices and the communications centre and had killed the startled West Germans at their desks and switchboards. In the eastbound carriageway frontier post, the few terrified genuine travellers, men, women and children, were similarly slaughtered.

Only then were any words said by the Commanders of the two Spearhead Groups.

'Take the bodies outside and pile them away from the buildings. Remove the documents of each of the staff here whom you are going to replace temporarily. We can gain a few more hours of surprise if we can pretend, in answer to any inquiries on the wireless or telephone, that nothing has happened here. Sound a bit sleepy or bored, to disguise your voices. The relief shift is not due here until 0700 hours tomorrow, so we should not be troubled.'

SUNDAY

Border Crossings, Western Europe

As soon as the clearance operations were completed and after cars and trucks blocking the autobahn had been moved out of the way, a signal was flashed by hand torch to the watching sentries at the East German frontier post, 400 metres to the east across the strip of no-man's-land. In the darkness the long lines of the vehicles of the Soviet Assault Regiments had closed right up to the East German frontier during the previous hour.

From their hiding-places in the barns and sheds and false haystacks on the farms, from the warehouses, factories, halls and railway engine sheds in the small towns and in the cities, and from the wooded valleys of the countryside, the motorcycles, scout cars, armoured cars and armoured personnel carriers had moved to their allotted positions on the autobahn.

Just east of the East German frontier post at Helmstedt all four carriageways, the two normally eastbound and the two westbound, were packed with Soviet vehicles, parked nose-to-tail, with their engines switched off, silent except for the muted sounds of the crackle of wireless sets, the operators intently bent over the lighted dials, listening out for emergency messages.

Up to that time and for as long as possible afterwards, the moves of the Pact Forces were to be in wireless silence — all wireless operators alert to receive messages, but no transmissions being made unless and until it became urgently necessary. Only the normal wireless traffic was to take place, simulated by ghost sets specially deputed to the task, so that the NATO signal intelligence units would not be alerted either by a sudden increase in wireless messages or an unexplained sudden reduction in routine traffic.

On receipt of the light signal, engines roared into life, the frontier barrier gates were lifted and four lanes of traffic, the leading scout cars in line abreast, their bright headlights gleaming, moved up the slight hill to the West German frontier.

Just beyond the frontier the vehicles in the two westbound

lanes would continue west on the autobahn, past Braunschweig, and Hanover, north of the Ruhr to the Rhine crossings. The vehicles in the two normally eastbound lanes were to swing off the autobahn just west of the frontier post on to the road leading to the south of Braunschweig and on to Hildesheim, Hameln, Paderborn, south of the Ruhr to other Rhine crossings.

At every frontier crossing of the Iron Curtain in Europe the fast, deep penetration Assault Forces of the Warsaw Pact Armies crossed into the territories of the countries of the NATO Alliance, unexpected, unseen, unheard, unhindered and unhurried.

SUNDAY

1735 Hours Central European Time

Tarvisio, Italy

At the time ordered by coded message the Spearhead Group selected from the Red Brigades, having previously moved the few miles from Tarvisio, seized both the Italian and Austrian frontier posts at Coccau. Using the special Soviet light automatic weapons each fitted with a silencer, which had been smuggled to them via the displomatic bags of the Eastern Bloc Embassies in Rome, it was only a matter of moments, as at the other frontier posts astride the Iron Curtain, for the guards and customs staff to be killed.

After the initial attacks, which had been carried out by small groups of specially picked men and women, larger reinforcements from the Red Brigades were called forward to the frontier and to the important road and rail installations south of Tarvisio, leading to Udine, and to the North Italian Plain and the major cities of the north.

'You will have to be alert and have all your wits about you to deal with any attempts to dislodge us,' the leader said to each group taking up positions to hold their key points and to repel attacks.

'The Soviet forces directed on Italy crossed into Austria from Hungary five minutes ago. The leading scout and armoured cars have 280 kilometres to cover before they reach us here to help if we are attacked. Travelling at an average speed of 50 kilometres per hour, they cannot be here in under five and a half hours. We should allow for some delays and they are bound to have some stops to change drivers and to check their vehicles. It would be realistic not to expect them here in any strength in under six and a half hours and probably nearer seven hours. So you must be organized to deal with any opposition at least until midnight and probably until 0100 hours. Have you any questions?'

At a few of the posts he was asked, 'What action do we take against ordinary travellers?'

'You must regard all travellers as enemies. They must be killed instantly. We cannot hold prisoners — they would be inconvenient to guard. In any case we shall have to assume that anyone who is not of the Red Brigades is a potential enemy, however innocent a traveller they may be.'

'What happens when we have used up the ammunition for the silenced guns?' was the next question.

'When you have used that ammunition then, and not till then, use your Skorpion machine-pistols and your Walthers. But the longer we can keep our attacks as silent as possible, the longer we can confuse the enemy because they will not be able to know where we are and how many of us there are. Silent, secret, ruthless action will cause much greater terror than a noisy battle which they will expect.'

SUNDAY

1745 Hours Central European Time

Brussels, Belgium

A few minutes before 1745 hours, the front door of the house at which the Belgian Prime Minister and his wife had spent the afternoon opened and they could be seen in the brightly lit hallway, saying good-bye to their hosts.

In his observation post in the house across the road, one man watched intently through his binoculars and ordered another to alert the car and its occupants in the garage below, and the group in the caravanette two streets away. In the driveway, before the front door, up a short curving drive with two entrances from the street, was the Prime Minister's official car, the uniformed chauffeur holding open the back door of the long black Citroën limousine. Drawn up close behind the Prime Minister's car was a smaller dark green Renault, the driver sitting behind the wheel, and, in view of the cold of the winter's evening, the two detective bodyguards sitting in the warmed interior at the back.

As the Prime Minister and his wife left the front door and walked, still chatting animatedly to their hosts, to the waiting car, the leader gave the order to act.

Into the small microphone of the portable transmitter receiver he held in his hands, his companion said, 'Go now. PM One and Two are just getting to the car, PM Three is holding the door open, PM Four is at the wheel of the second car, and PM Five and Six are in the back seats of the second car. PM One and Two must be taken alive if possible. Out.'

As he stopped speaking he heard below him the clang of the metal up-and-over door being hoisted open, and a moment later the blast of the exhaust of the car as it was driven fast out of the garage, the tyres squeaking as they gripped the smooth cobble of the driveway and squealing again as the car was swerved abruptly left and then sharply right to get into the entrance of the house opposite, and to pull up in front of the President's limousine, blocking its exit.

At the same time, from its waiting post two streets away, the caravanette came careering down the road, to pull into the other entrance and to stop behind the car in which the detective body-guards were beginning to bestir themselves and to look for the door catches to get out to protect the Prime Minister.

From the back of the caravanette, three men sprang out, ran to the car in front from which the driver and the two guards were just emerging. Three shots from their silenced automatic weapons killed the three men, who slumped back into the car. Without waiting to see the full effects of their attack, the three men ran on to kill the host and his wife and then to go on into the house to deal with the servants and any other occupants.

Meanwhile, two men and a girl jumped from the car blocking

118

the Prime Minister's car, one man going straight for the uniformed chauffeur with his automatic, the other man and the girl grabbing the Prime Minister and his wife. As the chauffeur fell to the ground, the man who had attacked him grabbed his uniform cap and put it on his own head. The Prime Minister and his wife stood dazed and uncomprehending, until he was led round the back of the limousine to be settled in through the further car door, while the girl pushed and shoved his wife into the near-door. The two were finally pushed and turned in the back seats so that it appeared that they were sitting naturally.

The new driver, cap pulled down over his eyes, got into the driving sat and started the engine. As he did so the three men who had run into the house came running out again, indicating that they had killed four inside the house. They stooped to pick up the dead bodies of the host and hostess, and dragged them by the heels into the brightly lit hall, and shut the front door behind them as they emerged. They then got into the dark green Renault and settled themselves so that they appeared to be the escort car with its correct occupants.

Meantime the leader of the group and his companion had quickly tidied the room from which they had kept watch, one had closed the garage door, and had run across the street into the back of the car still parked blocking the drive, the other into the front of the Prime Minister's car.

As soon as they were in, the car backed into the street. The Prime Minister's car and the escort car drove slowly out of the gateway, and turned towards Brussels. Behind them, at a distance, the caravanette followed and, behind it, when it had turned, the last car joined the small cavalcade, far enough behind not to draw attention.

Inside the still brightly lit house, nothing stirred.

At the Laeken Palace, north of Brussels, two British made Range Rovers with a shooting-party of six men in each vehicle, drove up to the domestic back entrance to the Palace. When a palace official went out do inquire what the visitors wanted, he was told that the two parties had had an extremely good day's hare shooting and wished to offer half a dozen to the King and Queen. Such a civil gesture seemed so appropriate to the season that the official invited the party to take their presents in to the kitchens, while he went to inform the personal staff to their Majesties of the gift which had been brought. Three men from each Range Rover took the game into the kitchen, killed the few members of staff who were just coming on duty to prepare dinner, and then followed the first palace official, at a distance, up the long flights of stairs and down the corridors to the private quarters.

They knew their way exactly and also knew where they were likely to meet members of the official and private staff. In the event they came across nobody until they arrived, close behind the official who had met them, as he reached the door to the private quarters. There he was killed, as was the equerry who came towards them when they had entered. In a small sitting-room they found the King and Queen, with members of their families. All were ordered to make themselves ready to leave, and were then led through the Palace corridors to the back entrance, to be driven away in the two Range Rovers, and a small dark red van which had arrived while the Group was in the Palace.

The Defence Minister and his wife staying with friends in Antwerp, were taken to one of two cars which had arrived at the front door unannounced, and from which a man and two girls had got out, dressed for a dinner-party. They had rung the bell at the front door, which had been opened by an elderly maid-servant, who was instantly killed and her body laid in a small alcove off the hall. The three had then gone straight into the main room of the house where the Minister and his wife were having drinks with their hosts and some friends. Before any of the startled party could even rise from the settees and armchairs in which they were seated, the Minister and his wife had been bundled out of the room and the others shot. The dazed couple were led out to the waiting cars, which immediately drove off.

In other parts of Belgium, the Foreign Minister, the Finance Minister and others were similarly kidnapped.

SUNDAY

Southern England

Throughout the day the coach loads of Russian tourist visitors from the cruise liner *Leonid Sobinov*, berthed at Southampton, had visited the various tourist attractions in Southern England.

One coach load had driven first to Salisbury and after visiting the Cathedral and the historic buildings of the City had gone on to see the house and treasures of the Earl of Pembroke at Wilton. Eventually the visitors had boarded their coach to return to their ship at Southampton.

Outside the gates of the Park, the guide, who had travelled all day with the coach, a member of the Red-Black Group and the member of the Support Group allotted to help that particular team of the *Sobinov* Spearhead Group, turned to the coach driver and said, 'Right, chum, now you do what you are told or I will kill you.'

The startled driver, after nearly running in to the hedgerow, slowed the coach down, and turned to the guide saying, 'Lay off, brother, a joke's a joke but there's a proper time and place for one. I've got to get this lot back to Southampton, and then I've got to get the coach back to the garage — so, come on now, just let me get on with the driving.'

'I'm not joking, mate,' said the guide. 'You do what you are told from here on, or I'll kill you and drive the coach myself — and I mean it.'

The driver could see from the look in his face and from the tone of his voice that he did mean it. 'OK,' he said, 'where do you want me to go?'

'That's better. Now we understand each other. Do you know the way to the barracks outside the town? You do? Good. And when we get there, don't try anything brave like trying to alert the guard, or anything. Understand?'

The driver nodded and drove on. In the seats behind him the members of the Spearhead Group prepared themselves for

121

impending action. From the inside of their bogus vacuum flasks and picnic hampers they took out small automatic weapons. They checked these weapons and placed them in pockets where they would be easily accessible. They broke down the large umbrellas and special walking-sticks and assmebled their nerve gas weapons ready for use. They dismantled their cameras and camera equipment and assembled other weapons disguised as camera parts.

The coach stopped at the closed barrack gates. The guide got out and, peering at his map by the light of a hand torch, walked over to the sentry on the gate. One of the Russians took his place by the driver ready to prevent him from trying to make a sudden move.

'Can you tell me where we are, mate?' the guide said. 'We seem to be lost and we have got to get back to Southampton.' He had been joined by two of the Russians, who stood slightly behind him.

'I'm on duty here and I can't give you the directions,' the sentry said. 'You'd better come in at the side gate and have a word with the Corporal of the Guard. This way, but just the three of you. You others will have to stay out here.'

As the guide and two Russians walked through the side gate to the guard-room, a fourth Russian detached himself from the crowd, stepped forward to the sentry, shot him, and caught the twitching body as it fell. The guide knocked on the guard-room door, which was opened by a bored soldier in full uniform.

'I'm sorry to bother you,' the guide said, 'but I have a coach load of foreign tourists outside, who have got to get back to their ship at Southampton, and we've lost the way. Can you give me some directions?'

'Got a map?' said the Corporal, who had moved to the door.

'Yes,' said the guide, 'but it's not very easy to see it by torch light. Can we come in for a minute?'

'OK,' said the Corporal, 'but mind, only a few of you.'

Inside the guard-room, seated round a rough wooden barrack table, the rest of the guard members looked up in a tired manner, showing only slight interest in the surprise break in the boredom. As they did so, four more Russians pushed their way in through the door, without saying a word.

'This won't do,' the Corporal said, and as it began to dawn on him that all was not what it seemed, he added, 'who did you say these tourists were?'

'I didn't say,' the guide answered, motioning the Russians further into the room. As he spoke the Corporal and the remainder of the guard were killed by the Russians, one of whom had found the key to the main gate, which he immediately went out to open.

The coach was driven through the main gates which were closed behind it. Inside the barracks, the lit windows of the offices of the duty staff clearly indicated the target to the Spearhead Group. In the next thirty minutes, the entire staff was killed, the vital communications systems taken over and the remainder of the Spearhead Group left the barracks, closing the main gates behind them. Silently, secretly, the Group had eliminated a vital link in the chain of command of the defence forces of the United Kingdom, leaving six men to answer the telephones. Its immediate task completed, the remainder of the Group went to deal with its next target and then to go on to the stronghold it was to occupy until given further orders.

Across Southern England similar tasks were being completed by the Spearhead Groups from both the *Leonid Sobinov*, berthed in Southampton, and the *Alexandr Pushkin*, berthed in Tilbury. From the latter the Spearhead Groups had spread out over East Anglia and the East Midlands. Strategic airfields of both the squadrons of the Royal Air Force and of the United States Air Force were attacked, the control towers captured, the key duty staff killed, and where possible, the aircraft sabotaged.

In every attack the emphasis had been on speed and silence, and the ruthless killing of every individual encountered. For as long as possible during the vital hours of darkness of the Sunday night, the population at large was to be kept unaware that, in their midst, the defences of the country, the leading personalities, the vital links of command and control, and even of communication to the outside world were being destroyed or removed.

Here and there, innocent, unsuspecting members of the public were involved. A courting couple, whose car was parked in a lay-by near the entrance to an airfield in Norfolk, were shot where they sat, the bodies left propped in the seats of the car, as if they were still alive and talking. A village policemen, on the last round of his beat near an important defence establishment, who happened to arrive on the scene to see the gates being opened when he knew the premises were closed for the holiday, and who stopped to make inquiries, was immediately shot, his body and his bicycle being pitched over a hedge.

After completing their tasks outside London, the coaches of the combined Spearhead Groups, carrying several thousand determined, ruthless killers and saboteurs, joined the thinning stream of holiday traffic entering the London area from all directions, unnoticed and unremarked. Ahead of them, the Support Groups were already in position, prepared to receive the Spearhead Groups into the strongholds.

SUNDAY

1745 Central European Time

Western Europe

In Le Havre, in France, where the *Mikhail Lermontov* had ducked the previous night, the Spearhead Groups landed immediately after breakfast. In their case, the main targets being all in the Paris area, or within a short distance beyond the city's outskirts, the coach loads were directed on Paris with the pretence of visiting other tourist attractions, except for Rouen and Versailles, on the way. The pattern for them was the same — main targets to be hit first, then secondary targets where resistance was unlikely and finally the seizure and holding of preselected strongholds both in the city and outside it.

The passengers and crew of the *Shota Rustaveli*, which had docked at Antwerp, had dealt with NATO Headquarters in Brussels and Supreme Headquarters at Casteau as well as the Belgian Government departments in Brussels and had seized the port of Antwerp.

The Ukrainian bulbgrowers, visiting the Dutch tulip growers, had been accommodated in The Hague, in preparation for their actions there and in Rotterdam and Amsterdam.

Sunday had been a day of more general sight-seeing in small groups, travelling in minibuses, guided by members of the Red Help. The thirty Spearhead Groups had been directed on the Government ministries and agencies. Their position was different from that of the Spearhead Groups in the United Kingdom and in north-western France. They expected to make contact much sooner with the reinforcements coming directly from East Germany. Their role was therefore more flexible and widely disruptive without the need to secure strongpoints. If the worst came to the worst, they could fight their way east to join up with other Communist forces.

In Holland the Dutch police were on the alert in case of action by either the Red Help or the South Moluccans. The Spearhead Group which attacked the docks at Rotterdam met with strong resistance. The Dutch security forces were well positioned in strongly protected buildings and were able to inflict very severe casualties. At length the Spearhead Group, making use of two cross-bow launched nerve gas canisters, were able to gas the occupants of two key defence positions, so enabling the Group to move further into the dock area to their objectives.

In Germany, two plane loads of Russian football supporters had been flown to the Hanover—Langenhagen airport and to Cologne—Bonn—Wahn, for the afternoon match. In each case the Soviet team had flown in two days earlier to prepare for the games. The four hundred supporters at each airport had been picked up in coaches to be taken to the matches. After the matches the Groups had moved into action.

Here, as in Holland, the German security forces were on the alert against re-formed terrorist groups and to guard against persistent IRA and INLA attacks on British barracks and installations. At the Hanover—Langenhagen airport the Spearhead Group section attacking the control tower were surprised by the fact that the take-over and hand-over times of the security guard had been altered so that the attack met with the resistance of two full guards at full alert. The whole Spearhead Group section was wiped out by a hail of well-aimed automatic fire in a few seconds. The noise of the shooting however alerted other sections attacking others parts of the airport. These moved quickly into position so that when, ten minutes later, the security guards ventured out of the control tower they were

125

overwhelmed by the greater numbers of the attackers, rushing swiftly and silently out of the surrounding darkness.

Two plane loads of East Germans had been flown to the airport of Frankfurt-Rhein/Main to watch the indoor athletics match in Frankfurt between an East German and a West German team. The four hundred spectators had been taken to the stadium in a fleet of coaches. Their targets, in the immediate vicinity, had been hit as planned, after the match ended.

Czechoslovak supporters of the National Ice Hockey team had travelled from Czechoslovakia in their own coaches, arriving the day before to be in good time for the final series of matches on the Sunday at Stuttgart. They left after the final to make their way back through Southern Germany, their route taking them to their target objectives.

The Red Army Choir, in Munich for a series of concerts over the Christmas holiday, had taken with them spare singers, their own small orchestra for their practice sessions, the costume manager and other assistants, making a total party of three hundred and fifty men and woman. At the end of the afternoon concert the Group had taken over the airport and key military installations nearby. The premises of Radio Free Europe were more heavily guarded than the Group had expected. The German security guards were only eliminated after they had killed more than half of the Group section attacking them.

In Iceland, where the weather had worsened over the previous two days to a force ten storm, a Russian factory-ship and four whalers had needed no other excuse to take shelter in the harbour of Reykjavik, where the sympathetic Icelandic Government had provided warmly heated coaches for a tour of the Island, to include a sight of the United States base, from which the ocean surveillance aircraft flew to keep their watch on the Denmark Strait between Iceland and Greenland.

The six hundred Russians, hidden in the cavernous holds of the ocean fish factory-ship which had docked the previous day in Cherbourg, had had to contain themselves with patience for some further hours and to make the best of their uncomfortable quarters. At zero hour they had seized the port, the naval installations, a number of ships and, soon afterwards, were in full control of the town.

The same applied to ninety Russians, locked away in the

126

container ship which had entered Cork in Eire on the Saturday afternoon. They had been more relaxed as they had not expected their operation to be difficult or dangerous. A swift take-over of the port facilities to enable it to be used by Soviet ships needing resupply after long days at sea, had not been the simple operation the Group expected. The Garda and the Irish Army and security forces had many years of experience of operations against the terrorists. Their intelligence network had become more and more efficient and sophisticated over the years, and there were those in the IRA and INLA who could not resist boasting. The Irish security forces were therefore in prepared positions on the quayside to prevent the Soviet forces disembarking. They had not however reckoned on the strength of the IRA forces deployed to support the Spearhead Group and were surrounded in their positions and eventually overwhelmed by attacks from behind and by the Spearhead Group which had disembarked unseen into barges on the seaward side of their ship.

One of the most important Spearhead Groups was that of the Soviet Winter Sports Team, with its French Support Group members, which carried out a series of visits, the one on the Sunday taking them to the French strategic ground-to-ground missile sites on the Albion Plateau which the group captured with little opposition. The Spearhead Groups, provided from the augmented crews of three Soviet Navy ships on a goodwill visit to Brest, again with their French Support Group members, also carried out an operation of key importance. Their social visits, on the Sunday, took them near to the French ballistic missile-armed nuclear submarine base at L'Ile Longue, where two of the five French submarines were being prepared for sea trials and where one of the other operational ships was being overhauled. All three French ships were captured without a shot being fired by either side.

SUNDAY

Detmold, West Germany

On the hilltop, overlooking the tank hangars of one of the British tank battalions, the Spearhead Group had moved into position as soon as it was dark enough, at 1630 hours, to ensure its movements were hidden. By 1700 hours the whole Group had got itself into positions where it could overlook the buildings and the concrete apron in front of them, brightly illuminated by the arc-lamps high up above the tall doors of the hangars. From his position the leader could see, and hear by the noise clearly audible across the open expanse of field, that, although the double sentries could have easily been attacked as they walked their beat round the buildings, there were also, in the tree-lined areas round the canteens and clubs, just behind the hangars, in the main part of the barracks, a great many people making their way to and from the afternoon children's parties, which were just breaking up, and the adult evening parties which were just starting. Any attempt to use the routes behind the hangars as a means of creeping up, unnoticed, on the sentries, was clearly not going to succeed. Equally any attempt to reach the sentries across the open ground of the airfield, with the light from the arc-lamps spreading out across almost the full distance of the 300 yard stretch which separated them from their objective, would risk detection and a loud challenge from the sentries. The leader decided that there was only one course open to him.

'Get two cross-bows ready. We shall have to kill the sentries with long-range shots before we can get near the hangar. You will take the taller of the two sentries when I give the word. You will take the other. You must make sure that you hit them first time in the face. Anywhere else on the body, and the nerve gas will not kill instantly. If you miss them altogether, and the bolt hits the hangars, we can expect that the noise will alert not only the sentries but the guard commander, who may well sound the alarm. Your accurate shooting is vital.'

The two markmen assembled the cross-bows from the parts

128

carried by the Group, fixed the telescopic infrared sights, adjusted the attachable fin stabilizers to the shaft of the bolts and took up their positions, sitting on the ground to give maximum control of the weapons.

'Wait till the sentries reach that far corner,' the leader said. 'They seem to be in the habit of stopping there on each of their rounds. The moment they both face this way, shoot — and be sure to hit.'

As the two men paused at the corner and turned to face the hilltop, the high-pitched twang of the two cross-bow thongs sounded almost simultaneously. The Group held their breaths for the few seconds that elapsed before the two sentries fell to the ground.

The Spearhead Group ran forward and killed the rest of the tank-park guard in the guard-room. From there, walking in small groups as if they were some of the usual occupants of the barracks, they went first to the main gates. They killed the sentries and the other members of the guard before moving on to the main switchboard room of the barracks where they disposed of the three men on night duty. They then, with Support Group guides leading the way, went in independent groups to the main targets in the barracks. They killed the bachelor officers, in the Officers Mess building and in the nearby quarters. They shot the Commanding Officer, the Second in Command, the Adjutant, the Quartermaster, and their families and the few servants in the houses, as well as the Adjutant's dog, which had barked in frenzy at the sight of so many strangers.

They killed all officers and senior non-commissioned officers who might otherwise have organized resistance. The more junior men of the battalion in the barracks and the families remained unaware that anything had happened and of what lay in store for them.

SUNDAY

1800 Hours Central European Time

Western Europe

Throughout West Germany, France, the Netherlands and

129

Belgium, the specially pre-positioned Spearhead Groups, guided and aided by the locals in the Support Groups, moved silently and swiftly into action. American, British, Canadian and German battalions closest to the Iron Curtain were dealt with first. Then, leaving cadres to guide other Pact Forces when they arrived, the Spearhead Groups moved west to link up with further Support Groups, to deal death and disruption to the battalions further to the rear.

Similarly, as at Supreme Headquarters in Belgium, the operations staffs of the subordinate headquarters of Allied Forces Central Europe in Holland and of the Northern Army Group and Central Army Group in Germany and the major NATO Tactical Airforces' airfields were attacked and put out of commission. In Norway and in Italy the Headquarters of Allied Forces North and Allied Forces South were neutralized.

By 2100 hours Central European Time the main headquarters throughout Allied Command Europe were dealt with and all communications between them, to NATO, to the Allied Governments and to the outside world were cut. The key personnel of the fighting ground units and the control centres of the fighting air units were disposed of.

Here and there, one or two individuals, some connected with the defence establishments, some with the police, some with the various organizations, became aware that individuals they wished to contact, or buildings which they needed to enter, telephone or telex lines which they wanted to use, were not available to them. At that hour they merely felt annoyance at the inconvenience and mostly went back to their other pursuits without making further investigations.

Some individuals in each country tried to find out what was happening but, what with the all pervading holiday spirit, the skeleton holiday duty staffs, the unavailability of senior staff, who might have taken more positive steps to untangle what was already clearly a chaotic situation, all efforts to clarify what had happened were abortive. Some gave up the effort in disgust, others, more determined or more alarmist, tried even harder to find someone to make some sense of the situation, and failed.

To the ordinary man in the street all seemed normal. It was Christmas time and the last thing they could expect was that others should be on duty if they were not.

SUNDAY

Windsor, England

In the next main room of their tour of the State Apartments at Windsor, the leading team of the Special Group detailed to kidnap the British Royal Family turned down a small side corridor and into a small store-room, filled with household cleaning materials and spare furniture. The main tourist crowds, intent on not missing any item of interest, turned in towards the centre of the room, to examine more closely a magnificent display cabinet of jade and ivory trinkets. Moments later the first team was joined by the second team. There was just room for the eight men and girls, though in the limited space and among the dust cloths, mops and cleaning liquids, the air soon become heavy and hot.

'Stand still everybody,' whispered the leader. 'We've got to wait about thirty minutes before we hit. Until then the last of the tourist public will still be making its way out and the servants of the Royal Household might still be taking away the afternoon tea things. So keep still and breathe calmly. In a few minutes I think it will be safe to leave the door slightly open.'

It was a tedious and trying wait, with tensions and the temperature mounting each minute. One man slightly opened the door, which helped the situation until, about five minutes before they were due to emerge, someone passing outside slammed the door shut. The Special Group held their breaths, wondering if suspicions had been aroused and whether they would be discovered. But nothing happened, so it was clear that an efficient Palace official was merely making a final check of the rooms after the last of the tourists left.

At 1730 hours the leader said, 'Right. We go now. Pretend for as long as we can that we are wandering, lost, tourists. We'll only break our cover when we really have to. But don't talk, because we don't want to attract attention if we can avoid it.'

He opened the door wider, moved to the end of the short

corridor, glanced in both directions into the main room, and beckoned the others to follow. They turned right and went through a double door leading into a long gallery. They knew that the last but one door of five in the wall on their right was the room for which they were making. When they were only twenty paces short of the door, an equerry emerged, not looking in their direction, closed the door behind him and started to walk down the gallery in the opposite direction. Half a dozen paces further on, some instinct made him turn, to see the Group behind him just moving forward.

'You've missed your way, I'm afraid,' he said, walking towards them, smiling. 'Let me show you where you should go.'

'Thank you very much,' the leader said, aiming a shot of nerve gas into his face and catching, with another man's help, the body as it fell. They placed it behind heavy, crimson velvet curtains hanging in front of a seat in a bay window, where it was completely hidden.

One man opened the door to the sitting-room where the Royal Family were gathered and the Special Group crowded in behind him. In seconds all the occupants of the room were hauled to their feet to stand motionless, waiting to see what would happen next.

'OK,' the leader said, 'collect them by the door. I will lead the way, just to make sure we are not headed off. If we get separated, remember that we are making for the small turret staircase down to the Inner Courtyard, where the coach will be waiting.'

Earlier that afternoon a coach carrying partially handicapped children was given special permission to enter the Inner Courtyard to set down its load, who were then able to make their way to the State Apartments by a special short route. Later in the afternoon, when the time came for the children to leave, it was impossible to get the coach started. Eventually the children were taken away in another coach, provided at short notice. The first coach was still in the Courtyard, the driver, and a mechanic sent by the owners, working to try to get it started, but with no success up to then.

As the group arrived at the foot of the turret staircase into the Courtyard, the driver and mechanic hurriedly closed the engine covers and put away the tools. A girl in the lead shot the

Palace Grounds warden, who had been keeping watch over their efforts, and two men propped his body against the walls of the Castle. The Special Group shepherded its charges into the coach. When the last was finally in and the Speical Group had joined them, the driver started the engine and drove slowly towards the main Castle gates. The Guards sentry gave the vehicle only a cursory glance as it passed and noted nothing unusual as he had been previously warned to expect the coach to leave when the engine could be started.

Outside the Castle gates, the coach turned right, down the steep hill in the town, over the narrow High Street bridge, past the school at Eton and on towards the M4 motorway and Heathrow Airport.

SUNDAY

1800 Hours Central European Time

Western Europe

In Paris, the President and leading members of the French Government were taken away south in a variety of vehicles, which had been used by the Special Groups, to Orly Airport.

The same occurred in The Hague in Holland, in Oslo in Norway, in Copenhagen in Denmark and also in Luxemburg. Without exception, the preparatory investigations by the KGB agents, the subsequent further careful liaison with the Special Group agents fresh from their intensive training in the PFLP camps in the Lebanon and Aden, and, in some cases, special information provided by Communist spies well placed in Government offices and agencies, all led to immaculately conceived and conducted terrorist snatches of key individuals. Success was also due, to a considerable extent, to the widespread efficient use of the silent nerve gas and silenced automatic weapons, so that the operations not only achieved surprise, but were executed with considerable speed because of the certainty of the killing capacities of the weapons used at close quarters. But above all the near total silence with which each killing or kidnap was conducted ensured secrecy for a particular

133

operation and a greater degree of probable success for those which were to follow.

The Special and Spearhead Groups suffered some casualties. In Oslo, a sudden gust of Arctic wind, swirling down a narrow street where one Government Minister was being kidnapped, blew light powdery snow into the face of one of the attackers, who was shot by the Minister's bodyguard who in turn was shot by a second attacker. In The Hague, as two shots from a silenced automatic were fired into the face of the Foreign Minister, the shock of the shots caused an involuntary spasm to the trigger finger of the assailant's companion, standing just behind the attacker, the burst of three shots entering his heart and lungs through his back. The wounded assailant, dying and incapable of movement, would have been such a hindrance to the further operations of the Group that the leader had no alternative but to kill him and to leave his body with those of the Dutch bodyguards, and that of the Minister. Careless handling of some of the nerve gas weapons resulted in more than a dozen deaths, during the night, of members of Special, Spearhead and Support Groups. There were a few cases too, where, in attempting to kill at too long a range for the automatic hand weapon in use, the attackers made themselves sitting targets for bodyguards who, thus alerted, were able to take cover and retaliate with heavier weapons, more accurate and more lethal at the longer range.

In London, where precautions against potential IRA attacks had not been relaxed, the Special and Spearhead Groups had the unexpected shape and size of their weapons to thank for being able to take police and special guards by surprise. The Defence Minister and his wife were killed with their bodyguards, who crowded so closely round their charges when the Special Group moved forward to attack, that the shots from the small hand automatics killed the intended victims as well as the bodyguards before the latter were able to draw their weapons in defence.

In Bonn, and in the German cities and towns to which the Government Minister had dispersed for the holiday, the security police were particularly alert. The security guards of one Minister, whose car was stopped on a heavily wooded mountain road, were able to fire their heavier automatics before the

134

attackers moved in close enough for their lighter weapons to take full effect. But fired in surprised confusion, the bodyguards' shots had been sprayed wildly into the air, missing the attacking Special Group. To investigators, from the village in the valley below, who arrived on the believed scene of the incident some time later, the shots were a mystery. The Special Group pitched their victims back into their vehicles, and drove them away. There were no signs of an armed attack on the road, and on the verges there were only signs that vehicles had stopped and the occupants had walked or fallen in the thick snow.

SUNDAY

1700 Hours Greenwich Mean Time
1800 Hours Central European Time

Belfast, Northern Ireland

Darkness gradually shrouded the dock areas of Belfast. A cloudless sky, lit by the red orb of the sinking sun until it finally disappeared below the horizon, meant that the pale pink afterglow provided too much light for safe movement by the Spearhead Groups waiting to disembark from the Soviet cruise liner *Baltika*.

When it was eventually completely dark, the gangway exits were ostentatiously roped and the lights switched off. The dock police and the few dockers still about decided that the ship was shut for the night and retired to their offices and rest huts.

When the wharves were deserted, the Russians moved silently down the gangways and took up their positions from which to defend the dock area against the British garrison when it finally received information about widespread terrorist attacks and moved to secure the dock area.

SUNDAY

Northern Italy

As night settled over Italy, the Red Brigades, backed by highly trained killers of the Special Groups, and guided by KGB experts from the Soviet Embassy in Rome, moved into action to spread death and terror on a wider scale throughout Italy than they had ever previously attempted.

Police posts, army posts, telephone exchanges and key crossroads and road junctions were seized. In the main northern towns of Venice, Padua, Bologna, Verona, Parma, Brescia, Milan and Turin, and at the port of Genoa, the Red Brigades emerged from their strongholds in the highly industrialized suburbs, and, using their new, silenced, automatic weapons, killed all certain and even likely opposition, on a scale which was to appal and terrify whole communities when they discovered, the following day, what had happened.

In a wave of slaughter, in which the Red Brigades' pent up furies and frustrations vented themselves, every occupant of police stations, police barracks, army barracks, prison staff quarters and Italian Army Headquarters throughout north Italy was gunned down, the dead bodies being left to litter the rooms in which they had been caught unawares.

In places, with psychotic humour, the bodies were arranged in simulated life-like tableaux, to depict drunken and sordid scenes denigrating members of the forces of law and order. The wild rampage led some Red Brigade members into the churches, where whole congregations were killed, the bodies removed and hidden in the dark corners of the churchyards outside, so that despairing relatives, who came later to look for the worshippers, went away having found no traces.

The swiftness and the silence of the attacks, in stark and surprising contrast to the previous Red Brigade's attacks which had been marked by noisy holocausts of bullets and shattering explosions, combined to spread a deeper degree of terror, because of the unexpectedness of the silence and of the impossibility of knowing where the killings had taken place.

By midnight, those of the populace of north Italy not safely at home were bewildered and frightened.

SUNDAY

1800 Hours Central European Time

Vardö, North Norway

Flying just above sea level at a speed of 250 kilometres an hour, ten MI-6 Soviet helicopters, each carrying 65 fully armed men, directed on the installations on the Vardö Islands and on the Norwegian coast 5 kilometres to the west, came sweeping in from the east. They had assembled during the previous two days on the north coast of the Rybachly Peninsula, north of the main Soviet fleet base at Murmansk and barely 100 kilometres from Vardö. Having first flown due north in order to come in on Vardö from a less expected direction, their speed brought them in sight of their objectives within thirty minutes of taking off. Ahead of them, acting as Landfall Finders, three of the smaller Soviet MI-8 helicopters, each carrying twenty fully armed men and special marker lights, flew in at sea level from the south and crossed the Norwegian coast between the two small fishing communities of Langbunes and Kramvik. From there they flew up the valley of the frozen Langvikelva stream, heading slightly east to cross over the frozen lake Oksoyvatnet, to land from the west close to the coastal installations and those on the Vardö Islands.

The duty Norwegian operators, warm and snug, and shielded both from the outside temperatures and outside noise by the thick, very efficient double walled and double glassed insulation of their posts, were taken completely by surprise. Without time to grab their racked weapons, they were gunned down at their posts and their bodies were dragged outside to be pitched into the deep snow banks lining the path to the door.

At the same time other men were installing the special marker lights to guide in the MI-6 helicopters. Within thirty minutes the strategic communications and installations were captured and were being manned by Norwegian speaking opera-

137

tors, who were able to continue, for a period at least, the normal wireless traffic to the main Norwegian Headquarters at Bodö, without giving any hint that the vital radars and links had been captured.

On other targets throughout North Norway, which were objectives of helicopter-borne attackers, the process was the same. Small Landfall Finder marker forces were landed from MI-8 helicopters flying ahead of the main force, which followed in MI-6 helicopters. All targets were well within the range of both the Soviet helicopters, the MI-8s having a range of 475 kilometres and the MI-6s with a range of 650 kilometres.

Any Norwegians who happened to be out or on the objectives, were gunned down. The Soviet attackers had been told firmly, 'It's the country we need, with its ports and installations. We do not need extra people.'

SUNDAY

1800 Hours Central European Time

Kirkenes, North Norway

At Storskog and at Skafferhullet, where unmade local country roads on the Soviet side crossed the Norwegian border to join the east-west Norwegian road 5 kilometres south of Kirkenes, Soviet assault forces, led by tracked armoured personnel carriers, crossed at 1730 hours, killing any Norwegian frontier guards who had survived or evaded the attack by the Soviet Border Commissioner at Storskog. A small force moved east from Storskog to Tarnet, to link with Soviet troops which, having crossed the frontier at Bjornstad, 35 kilometres to the east, were moving west on the cross-country route marked out for the Norwegian 'snowmobil' tractors. The rest of the Storskog force and the troops which crossed at Skafferhullet, moved on to Kirkenes and the airfield at Hoybuktmoen, about 15 kilometres away. A few startled inhabitants of Kirkenes, hearing the unaccustomed noise in the streets, ventured out from their houses, to be gunned down in the streets or as they stood at their open doors, the interior lights of their houses silhouetting them and making them perfect targets. No mercy was shown by the Soviet gunners manning the machine-guns fixed to the mountings on top of each armoured personnel carrier.

At the airfield, the startled duty staff, who had seen to the last incoming flight hours before, and were expecting no other traffic until the next day, were shot at their posts, in the warm insulated control building.

Driving past the turning to the airfield, the Soviet forces headed west for other objectives.

Throughout Norway, it was to be a night of shock and sudden death to many who thought they were well away from any immediate danger, and whose thoughts were fixed on Christmas. Some were to be gunned down in the course of their duties at airfields or telephone switchboards, or in police stations and army barracks. Some were to lose their lives haphazardly because they happened to be in the way of the Soviet troops and could not get away before being killed. Later in the night some were to die in their own homes, or after being dragged outside, because the house happened to suit a Soviet commander as his headquarters. Some of the elderly died of the shock that the country was to be yet again under foreign domination.

SUNDAY

1800 Hours Central European Time

Schlutup, West Germany

In concert with the attacks on all the other frontier posts on the Iron Curtain in Europe, the West German post at Schlutup, 5 kilometres east of Lübeck on the Baltic, was attacked by an East German Spearhead Group. The staff at the post, and the few civilians who happened to be nearby, were killed secretly, silently and with the surgical certainty that the silenced automatic hand weapons ensured. When the frontier barriers were lifted, motor-cycles, armoured cars and BMP combat vehicles of the deep penetration assault forces poured over the border, side by side until the route diverged north of Lübeck, taking one

Group due north to Kiel, and the other due west to Neumünster.

In a BMP combat vehicle of the assault group leading the advance to Neumünster, a Soviet Corporal, who had been briefed about the scope of the operation only moments before the advance started, laid his map out on his knees and by the light of the light bulbs on the bulkheads, supplemented by his own hand torch, explained the plan to his section.

'Our platoon of three BMPs is the leading platoon of our company, which is the leading company of the battalion, leading the regiment on this route. Got that? We have crossed into West Germany here — at Schlutup — see it on the map? We will advance on this road to Neumünster, then north to Rendsburg to capture the crossing over the Kiel canal, then over to the west coast to Husum and into Denmark at Tönder. Then we go all the way up the west coast of Jutland to as far north as we can go. From there we shall be taken by amphibious ships to Oslo, in Norway. Understand that? Any questions? No?

'Right. When we are going up the west coast another battalion, which you can can see on our right now, will be going first to Kiel and then to Flensburg and into Denmark just north of there, and on to Aarhus and Randers. Both battalions will keep in contact up the centre of Schleswig-Holstein and in Denmark. Got that? Now ahead of us there may be other Soviet forces — I lost track of all the details we were being given. So when we get up there, keep a good look-out for them and don't go shooting them up. Other forces will land at Copenhagen, over here on the map. See it?

'Right — now what's next? Oh, yes — behind the battalion on our right, another battalion will be following. It will move north only as far as the crossings to Fyn Island and then on to Zealand, to Copenhagen. With it will go the KGB and the MVD troops to take over the security policing of the country and to set up and run any corrective or concentration camps which will be necessary.

'We may have succeeded in achieving total surprise against the two Danish divisions and the one West German division which are the NATO defence of Denmark. We may have very little fighting to do as, ahead of us, Spearhead Groups will have killed key officers and staff and Special Groups will have dealt with the Royal Family and the Government ministers and senior officers.

'But if we have to fight, or if civilian crowds get in our way, there is only one thing to do, as you have been taught and trained — kill as quickly, efficiently and completely as you can.'

SUNDAY

1800 Hours Central European Time

The Iron Curtain

Where the Warsaw Pact Forces crossed the frontier posts which were in use for twenty-four hours every day, there was only a short delay while the Spearhead Groups dealt with the customs staffs and the few members of the West German frontier forces, the Grenzschutz, who were on duty in and around the offices.

At the smaller frontier crossing points, usually only used at special times of the day or even only on special days, the barriers were down and locked at both frontiers — the East and West German ends of the no-man's-land strip dividing them. At these points, the East Germans made special arrangements to enable the Pact Forces to achieve a swift passage across the frontier. To one side or the other, and in some cases on both sides, of their own frontier post they had gone through an elaborate charade of strengthening the high wire screen, replacing the anti-personnel devices, and relaying the anti-personnel and anti-vehicle land mines.

Under cover of this activity, they created safe lanes through the Iron Curtain by fitting dummy devices and mines, so that after darkness fell on the Sunday evening, and prior to zero hour, specially trained fighting patrols of the Assault Regiments were able to cross into West Germany and to move silently to encircle the billets of the Grenzschutz, a few hundred metres back from the frontier posts. At zero hour, some members of the patrols moved swiftly in to gun down the West German frontier forces, while others made their way quickly to the West German frontier post and barriers, there, by the use of small plastic explosive charges, to blow open a cleared passage,

141

first for the civilian type vehicles of the Spearhead Groups, followed by the motor-cyclists and combat vehicles of the Assault Regiment on the route.

SUNDAY

1200 Hours Eastern Standard Time
1800 Hours Central European Time

Washington, USA

In the Combined Operations Centre of the Pentagon in Washington, part of the shift of communications technical experts and some of the staff officers, who had started duty four hours earlier, were being replaced by the early afternoon shift who had come from eating the special Christmas lunch in the canteen. One of the newcomers commented, 'Say — that screen is playing a few tricks isn't it? Oh sure — you go ahead and get your meal — I'll get down to this set and see what's wrong with it.'

His predecessor was in a hurry to leave. He reckoned that, if he was quick, he could have the Christmas lunch and still have time to get out to his home and see his children before he would have to be back in the Pentagon for his next shift of duty.

The Colonel in charge of the communications terminals of the Operations Centre was not very happy about handing over to his replacement. 'We've had stupid problems for the last six hours. Sometimes we can get MOD London, then it fades. We had no trouble with SHAPE in Belgium earlier, but now keep getting all this background noise. The Moscow 'hot-line' has been OK but now we are getting intermittent interruptions and the guy on the other end says he can't hear me well and maybe I can get someone who speaks Russian. Maybe I can — maybe I can't — when he hears me OK there's no problem. You'll have to watch it, the whole set-up seems to be going wrong.'

His successor was no happier to be taking over any problems. As with the rest of the staff, both coming on duty and going off, Christmas roster was a chore he could have done without. He

142

could have put up with a quiet time, a few hours for reading and maybe a TV show later on. But the last thing he could stand was for the wires and sets to act up.

'Goddam,' he said to no one in particular, 'what in hell's got into this set-up today? The land lines are screwy, the wireless links are messed up, and the satellite terminals are all sick with white spots. Come on now, all of you, let's get this lot sorted out.'

Try as they did, the faults persisted. Not willing to admit failure, each operator and supervising staff officer redoubled his efforts to rectify the faults. An atmosphere of desperation pervaded the Operations Centre. The technical faults were clearly too complicated to be put right without the technical engineering experts, of whom there was only a skeleton staff. No sooner was one fault put right and the engineer moved on to another piece of equipment than the same or a similar fault would recur.

At 1300 hours, the Colonel in charge reported that he was having trouble with all the communications and that NORAD, SACLANT, SAC and all other command headquarters in the United States were experiencing difficulties with their command and control links. Nor was the problem limited to the United States. It was increasingly difficult to make certain contact with Europe and world-wide links were at best distorted.

The Colonel was told to report again after thirty minutes if the situation had not improved.

SUNDAY

1700 Hours Greenwich Mean Time
1800 Hours Central European Time

Whitehall, London, UK

Under the bright street lamps lining the wide expanse of Whitehall, the pavements were deserted, there were few cars, and only the occasional late double-decker bus passed towards Parliament Square in one direction, and towards Trafalgar Square in the other. At Westminster there were more people, mostly making their way to and from the Abbey to the underground train station opposite the illuminated clock tower of Big Ben at the Houses of Parliament.

Half-way up Whitehall, overlooking the blaze of lights reflected in the dark waters of the Thames, the high Ministry of Defence building appeared alive and alert. Certainly the fluorescent tube lights of the offices on the upper floors indicated that staff were on duty and watching over the nation's defence.

Inside the locked doors on the ground floor, the scene was different. A Spearhead Group, dressed as office cleaners, knocked on the back door at the south end of the building, demanding to be allowed in. An unwary Defence Department doorkeeper opened the door and was killed. His body was dumped in the cupboard containing the trolleys used for delivering mail throughout the building, and his place was taken by one of the Group dressed in the dead man's uniform.

In twos and threes, the Group then went through the building, killing the duty staff and taking over their posts to answer calls from within the UK, from Europe and the United States, in such a way as to hide the fact that the vital command links had been taken over.

Elsewhere ministers, senior civil servants and the service chiefs, who might have been in contact with the Defence Ministry and might have suspected that the situation was not right, were the targets of Special Groups.

The Chief of the Defence Staff and the Chiefs of Staff of the three armed services were early victims. The Special Groups assigned to their elimination kept close contact with these targets throughout Sunday and completed their tasks very soon after zero hour.

The Permanent Under-Secretary survived longer as he went early to church to attend a baptismal service, stayed on for the evening service and was therefore safe until the service ended. The Special Groups diverted his car down a quiet side street and killed him and his wife with nerve gas when he opened his car window to inquire about the diversion.

Other senior military staff, both serving at the Ministry of Defence and at naval, military and air establishments throughout the country were killed in their homes, or where these were in securely protected areas, when they were enticed

144

out of their homes and away from protection by various subterfuges.

The Special Groups eliminated all their targets by 2100 hours, except for a few of the less important and those who were on trains or aircraft or in other places where they were obviously not going to get in touch with a military headquarters.

SUNDAY

1830 Hours Central European Time

Helmstedt, West Germany

By 1830 hours the leading reconnaissance scout car of the first Assault Regiment advancing west on the autobahn from the frontier crossing point at Helmstedt, was about 70 kilometres inside West Germany at a point 20 kilometres east of Hanover. Ahead of the scout car, the motor-cyclists of the Assault Regiment were clearing all German civilian traffic off the route by the simple expedient of forcing it down access roads or onto the verges or down embankments, wherever the autobahn crossed a valley. There were few German vehicles as most of the population were already at home.

On the regiment's left another Assault Regiment started alongside in the normally eastbound carriageway of the autobahn. Just west of the frontier post, this regiment branched left on to the main road which took it through the small town of Helmstedt, through the even smaller town of Konigslutte and, by 1830 hours, it reached the road and rail-crossing about 10 kilometres east of Hildesheim.

With full headlights blazing and having the advantage of the use of the normal excellent lighting of the autobahns and the intersections, the Regiment which skirted north of Braunschweig met with no delays at all. The night, though clear, was only dimly lit by the last of the final quarter of the moon, just sufficient to show in vague outline the country on each side of the passing vehicles.

In Helmstedt the scene was different. A Spearhead Group killed the police at their posts and disconnected the telephone

145

lines. All exit routes were blocked by motor-cyclists of the Assault Regiment behind the Spearhead Group with strict orders to shoot any wandering Germans. The railway too was blocked so that all physical exits and communications links from the town were disrupted. All links which might have served to pass a warning were cut. The same pattern was being repeated in every town and village on every route. It was realized that a complete blanket on all warnings was impossible after a time, but if a silence could be clamped on all towns within about 100 kilometres of the frontier which could be reached within the first two hours, any warnings passed after that would be too late and might then occasion more panic that effective reaction. Later in the night, the sheer volume of disclosures of an attack caused just the confusion which the Pact commanders aimed to use to their advantage.

SUNDAY

2000 Hours Central European Time

Near Dinant, Belgium

The Supreme Allied Commander Europe and his wife had spent Sunday with Belgian friends in their château on the banks of the River Meuse close to the French frontier south of Dinant in Southern Belgium, as they had often done during the past year.

At about 1830 hours an aide accompanying the Supreme Allied Commander made a routine telephone call to SHAPE both to report again the location of the Commander and to receive a situation report from the Operations Centre. Over the previous months since his appointment he had come to know most of his usual contacts in the Operations Centre and could recognize their voices and verbal mannerisms. On this occasion his telephone contact was a stranger, which surprised him.

'Say, do I know you? What is your name?' he inquired after being told that there was nothing untoward to report.

'Name's Holderness, Captain, You won't know me. I am only filling in a duty over this week-end to let some of the other guys have time at home before Christmas. There are a few of us here

146

today — doing the same thing.'

The aide felt a sense of unease despite the glib explanation, and became even more worried when another strange voice answered his routine call an hour later. He asked to speak to a number of officers whom he knew by name and was told that they were not available. He questioned his informant about more details of the situation and, though he could not fault the information he was given nor the format in which it was put, he was left with a feeling that he was talking to complete strangers, who had not the small talk nor turn of phrase that he thought instinctively he would expect them to have. He reported his worries to the Allied Commander.

'General. I can't put my finger on what worries me, but I just have a gut feeling that something isn't right at the Operations Centre.'

'Well, we are due to leave here soon, Captain,' the General replied. 'We'll go now and we'll call in at the Centre on the way home. You rustle up the cars and the escort and we'll be off as soon as I can drag my wife away.'

The small convoy left about thirty minutes later — the car carrying the military police escort leading the way, followed by the Supreme Allied Commander's staff car, with the car carrying the aide and the emergency wireless set and its operator at the rear.

An hour later as the short convoy crossed a bridge over a small tributary of the River Sambre, a massive explosion ripped out the centre arch, taking with it the Supreme Commander's car. The military police car, leading the convoy, was hurled forward over the parapet of the bridge to fall on to the jagged rocks on the edge of the stream below. The car carrying the aide and wireless set was propelled by its own forward motion headlong into the gap caused by the explosion, to fall upside-down into the stream before being covered by the falling debris of the blasted bridge and broken bits of the General's car. It was over half an hour before local residents, searching to find out what had caused the explosion, came on the scene of the destroyed bridge and were gunned down by the Special Group, lying in wait, to prevent news of what had happened to the Supreme Allied Comander reaching his headquarters.

SUNDAY

Washington, USA

The Colonel in charge of the Operations Centre reported, as instructed, at 1330 hours that the situation with all communications had not improved and indeed though no links had actually failed, reception and transmission of information and messages had become more and more confused.

At 1400 hours he received an urgent telephone call from North American Air Defence Headquarters that tracking stations throughout the missile early warning system positively confirmed, and were eventually able to transmit messages which were at least partially intelligible, showing that a number of Soviet satellites, long regarded as potential killer satellites, had moved out of their standard orbits.

The Colonel called further experts from within the Pentagon and together they reported that it was apparent that most of the killer satellites were capable of effectively neutralizing key NATO satellites without being moved any further out of their standard orbits as they were probably equipped with very high-power nuclear energy systems, capable of producing lethal laser beams at long range.

The general alert was therefore promulgated, with the proviso that, though it was clear that the Soviet Union was in a position to disrupt surveillance and communications at any time, there was no evidence as yet of any reason why they should want to do so or of anything which had already happened which they would want to hide.

SUNDAY

West Berlin

When it was eight o'clock in the evening and still there had been no telephone call from her husband to tell her, as he always did, that he had arrived safely in West Germany, Heidi Kleber and her two daughters became really worried. They knew that, as he had left Berlin in the early afternoon, even allowing for delays at the checkpoints, he should have reached the West German border before about five o'clock and Hanover well before eight o'clock when he would certainly have called them by phone unless there had been some unforeseen delay or an accident — or worse — as he was going through East Germany.

'We must tell the police, *Mutti*,' said Inge, the older and calmer twin. 'He must have had an accident and the police will know. Even if they don't they are the ones who will be able to find out where he is.'

'Yes, darling,' said Heidi Kleber, unwilling to admit to herself that anything might have happened, still hoping against hope that they would get a phone call. Erika, the more emotional, younger twin sat hunched in a chair, her hands clenched together on her lap. There was a hint of tears in her eyes and a sob in her voice, as she said, 'Inge, there's nothing wrong. Don't even think that there is. He's all right, I'm sure he is.'

'Darling Erika,' said Inge, 'I am sure he is, but he may just be somewhere he can't get in touch with us. All I want to do is to tell the police so that they can be on the look-out for any message about him and so that they know where to telephone us about what has happened.'

'Yes, you do that, Inge,' said Heidi Kleber, at last making up her mind that to telephone the police would not be to admit, even to herself, that there had been an accident, or worse.

149

SUNDAY

North Norway

The scope of Soviet intentions had been so well camouflaged that only small groups of men throughout NATO were able to put up even a token resistance. In a sense, the assured belief within NATO that it would be possible to obtain some small indication of Soviet intentions, and that therefore there would certainly be time to issue the warning orders for war preparation, had contributed to the disaster. It would have been better if the assumption had been that there would be no clear warning. The warning signs had not been clear enough to be fully acted on, so attacks, when they came, achieved surprise.

Although having the smallest total of armed forces of any of the nations of NATO, Norway was more capable of fighting an invasion, with no warning, than other nations with far larger standing armed forces. Like Turkey at the other extremity of the Allied front, Norway's common frontier with the Soviet Union in North Norway was an added incentive to vigilance. That, and the knowledge that routes across North Finland had been improved by the Soviet Union, enabling it to mount an attack on more than one front and with a considerable weight of men and machines. The Norwegian Army was fully prepared to open fire on any Russian incursion across the frontier. While the commanders of other NATO forces were duty-bound to refer to their Governments before an open act of war could be taken, every Norwegian soldier already had his orders, in the form of a Royal Decree, to defend his country if it was attacked.

In addition, and again unlike the other nations in NATO, the Norwegian reserves who had completed their conscript service, were organized into eleven Regimental Combat Teams, each of about five thousand men. To reinforce both the regular armed forces and the Reserve combat teams, a Home Guard of eighty thousand men could be mobilized within four hours.

For these reasons the Soviet High Command decided to take special measures for the attacks on Norway. But, when the helicopter-borne attackers appeared out of the night sky and were immediately directed by small Spearhead and Support Groups to eliminate the Regular Norwegian forces in their barracks and bases, the fighting did not stop there. Reservists and the Home Guard, who kept their weapons and some ammunition at home, promptly took it into their own hands to try to resist the invaders. But in the small far north communities the numbers of individual armed men were small and their efforts at resistance were no more than token and were, from the start, hopeless.

Gundar Elkson had been visiting a sick friend, to take to him the small presents which his workmates had collected, when he heard the sound of machine-pistol fire from the direction of the airfield at Barak, outside the town of Lakselv. His own house was on the edge of the small town, about half a mile ahead of him. All around the houses were shut and shuttered against the cold. In front of him he could see the last street light and, as he looked, he could make out the dark shapes of about a dozen darting figures, weaving their way from shadow to shadow. Down a small alley between two houses, close by where he stood, he knew there was the side door to the house of another friend.

Inside the warm living-room, he blurted out, 'There's shooting at the airfield and about twelve men advancing down the main street from that direction. Get your rifle and ammunition and we'll round up a few more men and see what we can do.'

Within minutes, from houses nearby, they had recruited three more armed men and had obtained from the wife of a fourth man who was out of the house a rifle and ammunition for Gundar Elkson.

They had meanwhile heard further shooting from the direction of the main square, close to which was the small headquarters room of the local platoon of a combat team. The firing had been in intermittent short bursts and had been followed by complete silence. Gundar, having heard the first shooting and being responsible for calling out the others, had assumed command of the small group.

'We'll go down to the platoon room and see if we can deal with whoever is there and recapture it.'

151

The others followed without argument. When they reached the edge of the square, from where they could see the lights in the platoon room, one said, 'Suppose they have all got machine-pistols — we won't have a hope with just five rifles.'

'Well we can't wait to find out,' Gundar answered. 'We need to know who this lot are so that we can raise the alarm if necessary. Maybe there are others we don't know about too — but we can't just hang about. Perhaps we can deal with this group and capture their machine-pistols. What we'll do is this.' He then proceeded to explain his plan of attack of the platoon room. They were to approach it from both sides, two of them from each flank, while one man took up a position opposite the door, to give covering fire if needed. They moved quickly to their positions each side of the door, and when Gundar was sure that the man covering them had picked out that they were in position to attack, he led the four men to the door.

They never had a hope. From dark doorways each side of the one man, on the opposite side of the square where they had been hidden with a field of fire to the platoon room, three men moved out into the square, firing their machine-pistols from the hip as they advanced, two shooting down the four Norwegians across the square, while the third gunned down the other man before he could fire a shot from his rifle.

Apart from the overland attack on Kirkenes, the attacks on the Vardö Islands and the airfields at Barak, Bukta and Hammerfest, and on Tromsö had all followed the same pattern. First had come the smaller M1-8 helicopters, each carrying the Landfall Marker groups who had set flares at the airfield boundaries. Following them had come the much larger M1-6 helicopters.

From the airfields the attackers had moved in small groups into the towns, guided by the small Special and Support Groups, which had already done what they could to disrupt telephone and wireless communications.

Except where the attackers took over police stations, barracks, airfields and telephone exchanges, the rest of the population, snug and warm in their locked, thickly insulated houses, were totally unaware of what was happening around them.

Most attacks achieved success by surprise, very few shots having to be fired. Stealth and silence ensured that the relatively few attackers were firmly in control of key installations

before more than a few Norwegians realized what had overtaken
them.

SUNDAY

2000 Hours Central European Time

Bonn, West Germany

A member of the specially picked anti-terrorist, para-military
unit GSG9, was returning to the billet he shared with two others
of the unit. His route took him past the Defence Ministry. He
passed the main door at the moment the Spearhead Group shot
the door-keeper and caught his falling body. For a second
Helmut was not sure if it was an optical illusion, the whole incident having taken place so quickly. Afterwards there was
nothing to show that anything had occurred. Within a few
moments a uniformed door-keeper was in position again.

Helmut realized that if, as he suspected, a terrorist group had
taken over the building, there was nothing that he could achieve
on his own. On the other hand he was not sufficiently convinced
that he had witnessed an attack to raise a general alarm. Nor did
he feel confident enough to go immediately to his superiors to
report a serious incident, when there might have been an innocent explanation. The more he thought about it, the more he
decided that, as it was Christmas time, the duty staff might
have had friendly visitors. But the doubt remained. He hurried
back to his billet, explained what he had seen to the other two
men, and together, after arming themselves with their automatics, which they kept near them at all times, they went back
to the Defence Ministry building.

'We'll just go up to the main entrance and say that we are
reporting for duty. If the door-keeper is genuine, he will know
what checks have to be made, and will ring through to the appropriate authority. If he is not genuine, we should be able to tell
instantly, when you two, just behind me, can draw your automatics and kill him.'

They walked up to the main door, which was opened by the
door-keeper. 'What do you want?' he asked.

153

'We have come early to go on duty,' Helmut answered.

'Wait here,' the door-keeper said, which indicated neither fault nor innocence and left the three GSG9 men in two minds as to what to do.

Behind the door-keeper the door to a small interview-room opened and two men came forward. They approached with their hands in the side pockets of their jackets. They stopped in front of the three Germans, firing their automatics without taking their hands out of their pockets, killing the three men instantly. The bodies were dragged into the interview room. The door-keeper returned to his post.

SUNDAY

1915 Hours Greenwich Mean Time
2015 Hours Central European Time

Belfast, Northern Ireland

The Commander of the British infantry battalion near the dock area, received a very garbled message from a civilian source that there was something going on at the docks, where the Soviet cruise liner was docked, that he could not say what it was but, in any case, he didn't like it, whatever it was. Reluctantly the Commanding Officer sent for the Commander of the duty company.

'You had better take three full strength fighting patrols, one for each of the main dock entrances, and go inside and see what's happening. We can't risk an incident with that Soviet ship in port. Keep it quiet if you can. Report back when you have dealt with whatever it is.'

Quietly, efficiently, intent on not raising any alarm when probably none would turn out to be necessary, the three fighting patrols were briefed and moved out. Before leaving they had synchronized watches and been given the time when the three patrols would enter the docks simultaneously. At the docks, without further orders the three patrols moved to the gates, the company Commander with his small command group following the patrol at the centre gate.

At each open gate the patrols found that the way in had been blocked with a succession of large packing cases, arranged so that it was just possible for a man to squeeze between them. Each patrol leader passed the word back to spread out and each man to take a different alleyway through the cases.

As each man on his own path reached a certain point in the maze, from a gap to one side, he was hit by a shot of nerve gas and his body pulled out of the way. The entire three patrols, of about twenty men each, disappeared in silence, as did the company Commander and his group.

At Battalion headquarters, the Commander waited for news and went on waiting, with increasing anxiety, the conviction growing that something had gone wrong, but certain that no further investigation could be realistically made until daylight.

SUNDAY

1930 Hours Greenwich Mean Time
2030 Hours Central European Time

Gare Loch, Scotland

The Soviet cruise liner *Mikhail Kalinin*, at 4,700 tons the smallest of the Atlantic cruise fleet, had docked at Port Glasgow late on Saturday evening. With a touring itinerary which was to take in Loch Lomond and Inverary Castle in the day, the passengers and crew who were going on the outing had breakfasted and disembarked by 0900 hours on the Sunday morning. The six large coaches taking them had left the docks at 0930 hours. They had first gone into Glasgow to get a passing view of the great shipyards of Clydebank. From there they had turned back on the north bank of the Clyde to pass through Dumbarton and Balloch and get their first view of Loch Lomond. They had stopped at the hotel at the mouth of Glen Douglas, south-west of the highest point of Ben Lomond, for a buffet lunch and the chance to photograph the scenery. The hotel staff were impressed by the good, quiet behaviour of the visitors, though less happy about their dour, unappreciative attitude to the meal and the service.

Soon after 1300 hours, the coaches left to travel via Tarbet, Arrochar and Cairndow to Inverary and on to the Castle. Two hours later, after seeing all the tourist attractions and having photographed the items of particular interest, the visitors left to got back to Inverary and a typical Scottish high-tea. At 1800 hours they were on the road again, to Port Glasgow and their ship.

The course of the three leading coaches had, for an hour or more, been unremarkable. But just north of Garelochhead the leading coach had been stopped by a man, standing at the road-side, waving a torch. The coach guide got out, and was joined by the guides from the next two coaches. After a quick, agitated consultation at the side of the road, the guides climbed into the coaches again and told the drivers to continue. Two minutes later the guide in the first coach said to the driver, 'Now listen carefully, for your own good. From here on you take your orders from me and you'd better be sure to do just what you are told. First off — take this right fork in the road here and go on till you are stopped again by someone waving a torch. No arguments. These tourists are a Soviet Spearhead Group whose orders are to take over the British Polaris base at Faslane Bay. We were to go straight there, but the stupid bastards have laid on a surprise children's party and, at the moment, the place is crawling with kids and their mums and dads. So we will have to wait across the Loch until we get a signal that the coast is clear. If you do not do as you are ordered you will be killed and I shall drive the bus — and that's not a boast because I have been trained.'

When the guide had finished speaking the Russian inter-preter gave a quick summary of the information to the coach passengers. Moments later the three coaches were directed into a turning in a clump of trees, where they came to a stop and the engines and lights were switched off. There they waited in dark-ness and silence.

As the first of the other three coaches approached Cairndow the guides in each revealed to the drivers who their passengers were and that they were directed to the American Polaris base at Holy Loch, north of Dunoon. The same threats were made about any failure to obey orders and the journey continued without incident until the leading coach had almost reached a road fork north-west of Dunoon, where a man waving a torch stopped the vehicle, climbed in and quickly outlined what had happened.

'The British base at Faslane has invited a lot of the children of the staff and crews based here to a surprise Christmas party. Earlier in the afternoon four boat loads left from here and will be coming back when the party is over. It's been decided that neither base will be attacked until both are clear of the children and parents, in case there is a wireless link between the two bases, which we don't know about. So we're going to a hiding-place in some woods near here until we get word that the four boat loads have returned and the passengers have been dispersed home. We may well have a few hours to wait.'

A few minutes after 2100 hours, the quiet of the small minor road in the woods in which the last three coaches had been hidden was disturbed by the high-pitched stuttering whine of a motor-cycle being driven at speed. It slid to a skidding stop at the entrance to the woods, the driver switched off the engine and called out in a hoarse whisper, 'OK, you lot. Get ready to get started. Both attacks are to go in at 2200 hours. The kids are just getting to the dockyard here and Faslane has been quiet for over an hour. We can't afford to delay the attacks any later or we shan't be able to hit our other targets before daylight.'

At 2200 hours a coach with no sign inside of the passengers, who were huddled on the floor, drew up at the dock gates at Faslane Bay, at the same time as another drew up at Holy Loch. An apparently fed up co-driver got down from each and approached the sentry on the gates.

'We had a breakdown further back. We're here to take some of the kids home. Can we come in to the dockyard?'

'All the kids have gone home,' the sentry at each place answered and then slumped to the ground, jerking in the throes of death, as the nerve gas shot directed at the face took immediate effect.

As each sentry fell, the Spearhead Group members jumped from the open coach door and silently made their way to the guard room. The startled, unprepared inmates were quickly killed and the main gates immediately opened for the coaches to enter and for the passengers to assemble quietly in the attack groups already designated for the main installations of the bases and the ballistic missile submarines, tied to the quays, manned only by skeleton crews.

SUNDAY

1930 Hours Greenwich Mean Time
2030 Hours Central European Time

London Airport

A coach joined the thinning line of traffic turning off the M4 motorway on to the London Airport entrance road. All day the stream of cars and coaches carrying travellers flying out of England to the winter sports resorts and the sunshine coasts of Europe and North Africa had jammed the access road and filled the car parks. As the day ended, the traffic had got thinner, so the coach had no difficulty in making its way to the VIP lounge. It stopped and a man got out and went to the main entrance. He demanded to see the airport manager, who had left for home some time earlier. He demanded to see the deputy and was asked by the airport attendant for his credentials and the reasons for his demand.

'My credentials and my reasons are one and the same. You had better come and see for yourself.'

He led the way to the coach and ushered the airport attendant up the steps ahead of him. At the top he said to the driver, 'OK Jim, switch on the lights.'

The interior lights were flicked on to reveal to the astonished official the rows of seats occupied by the members of the Royal Family, and three men and a woman standing in the central aisle between the seats.

'Those are my credentials and the reasons why I want the VIP lounge. Now get moving and tell the deputy manager to get here double-quick.'

He escorted the official to a phone in the entrance hall way and stood by him as the still shattered man said, 'You must come down here at once, sir. I can't tell you what it's all about — but don't call anyone else and don't raise any alarm — or you'll be very sorry that you did. Take my word for it, sir, and just

158

come to the main entrance quick.'

The two men waited for the deputy manager, who, on arrival, was led straight to the coach, without a word. The attendant climbed in first followed by the deputy manager. As they reached the top the first man turned with a helpless gesture and a look of shock still on his face. Behind them the man said. 'You see who they are. Now I'll tell you what I want you to do. First I will tell you what happens if you don't follow my instructions to the letter. If we have any trouble those people will be killed instantly. So this is what you will do, when we get to your office and you can use your phone. You will first order the control tower staff to let in the forty men and women who are waiting in the coach which is parked now outside the security doors. And you will tell them of the serious consequences if they raise any alarm or pass any warning messages. Second, you will arrange for the VIP lounge to be opened to receive this coach load and any others which will be arriving. Third, you will arrange, in the best way you know how, for two airliners already refuelled for a transatlantic trip and ready for take-off, to be moved to a quiet corner of the airport where the VIP passengers will be able to board undisturbed. And fourth, you will send for whoever is in charge of security arrangements at the airport to come to your office where he will take all his further orders from me. And finally, let me repeat that any failure to carry out these orders or to abide by the obvious intentions of the orders will be on pain of death of the whole of your Royal Family. Do you understand?'

The deputy airport manager had nothing to say and the two men went to his office where the orders were issued. By 2330 hours the VIP lounge and an adjoining room were filled with men and women who had been kidnapped from palaces, homes and offices. Shortly afterwards they were herded into airport buses which had been drawn up at the tarmac exit to the building. They were driven to the two airliners and were led to their seats, the mobile stairways were moved away, the engines were started and the two planes took off, wheeling away into the night, out of sight of the Special and Spearhead Group members who turned their thoughts to their next tasks. First the airport staff who had been witnesses to the events were hustled into the VIP lounge and killed *en masse*, and the bodies left sprawled over the tables and couches round the room.

SUNDAY

The Capital Cities Of Western Europe

At Orly Airport in France, at Schipol Airport in Holland and at Brussels Airport in Belgium, the sequence of events was very similar. The royal and presidential families and high officers of state and their wives, families and relations in some cases, congregated at the airports from wherever in the country they had been kidnapped. The control towers were taken over and air traffic allowed to proceed normally, if it suited the attackers' purposes, or stopped if there was an operational need. The passengers in the terminals were aware of some disruption but no more. Inquisitive staff who pursued their investigations of anything unusual with too much diligence were killed when they entered the parts of the buildings controlled by the Special and Spearhead Groups. The necessary aircraft were commandeered, the prisoners flown out, and the inadvertent witnesses were silently killed.

In Portugal, Spain, Italy and Greece the pattern of events was similar. Throughout Western Europe a massive operation was in train to ensure that as many as possible of the key personalities of each country were captured and removed.

At Orly Airport the President of France and many ministers and their families were hidden carefully in the terminal buildings until enough aircraft had been assembled to fly them out. The VIP and passenger lounges were not used so that the general public and most airport workers were unaware of what was happening. The VIPs had a long and cold wait in a cargo hangar.

At Madrid Airport the operation was delayed by an attack on the passenger terminal carried out by Basque separatists, unaware of the more massive operations being carried out by the Soviet Union and its allies. The explosion of the bomb, the arrival of police and ambulances, and, later, military reinforcements, hindered the transfer of the captives from the cargo sheds, in which they were being held, to the aircraft being assembled on the tarmac. The Spearhead and Special Groups were forced to delay the final evacuation until the initial turmoil had subsided.

In Greece there was a temporary disruption of the attackers' plans as the coaches and cars carrying the captives were blocked into an Athens side street by a long column of torch-bearing demonstrators marching through the city.

By 2100 hours the governments of Western Europe had been dismembered.

SUNDAY

2100 Hours Central European Time

Oslo, Norway, and Copenhagen, Denmark

At Oslo Airport and at Copenhagen Airport, the course of events had been different. At 1730 hours two Boeing 707s, each on special charter to almost two hundred assorted tourists, the first from Sofia, Bulgaria, the other from Budafest, Hungary, had landed at Oslo and Copenhagen respectively, and had discharged the passengers through immigration and customs controls. The passengers were informed over the loudspeakers that their onward journey to their hotels had been unavoidably delayed, as the coaches which were due to pick them up had not yet returned from a previous assignment. The passengers had been philosophical about the delay and had stacked their hand luggage and wandered over the airport terminal building.

At 1900 hours at Copenhagen and at 2000 hours at Oslo, the passengers had positioned themselves near the key points in the terminals and had moved in and taken over. At both airports, the result had been inevitable. The resistance had been minimal from a staff which was starting to be depleted by the departure of those whose duty had ended and who were not being replaced at so late an hour. Where there had been any hesitation to obey orders, death had been quick and the bodies removed to leave no sign of the attack. The telephone and telex links were guarded to monitor the traffic. The airport control staff were ordered to ignore their previous instructions, to divert all normal traffic to airports in Germany, and to ensure that the incoming flights

161

were able to land without delay or hindrance.

A long stream of civil and military aircraft had landed at each airport, disgorged the cargoes of heavily armed men and then promptly taxied to take off, and disappeared into the night sky again. While they came it seemed endless to the few passengers and airport staff who stared with obvious terror at the scale of the attack. Heavy Antonov 22s, Tupolevs, Ilyushins and the smaller Antonovs came in out of the night sky to the south, were silhouetted momentarily against the landing lights, taxied to a stop near the perimeter exits, were silent for a time and then started up their engines again and were gone.

Outside the airports the armed men seized any vehicle that was conveniently available. Other groups of men were formed into marching order and disappeared to their predetermined targets. Later and through the night, there were short bursts of automatic machine-gun firing, but by then it was too late.

During the arrival of the aircraft at both airports, unnoticed by all but a few of the terrified onlookers, members of the Royal Family, the Government, the NATO staffs, senior service and civil officers were herded to aircraft and flown out.

By midnight both Copenhagen and Oslo were firmly in the hands of the Soviet troops. South of Copenhagen, on the Jutland peninsula, and north of Oslo, in the small towns of the deep-sided fjords of the far north Arctic shores, other Soviet troops had taken over large areas of the two countries.

SUNDAY

2130 Hours Central European Time

Luneburg Heath, West Germany

The sudden, totally unpredicted arrival of the Soviet Spearhead Groups, followed closely by the Assault Regiments caught the forward German, American and British troops totally by surprise. It had been clearly understood throughout NATO that at least some warning would be received. Even a few hours' warning was absolutely essential to enable the forward troops to ready themselves at all for battle.

Because of previous terrorist attacks, and the threat of even more attacks, on the barracks of the German, American and British troops, arms and ammunition, tanks, guns and vehicles were carefully stored away and locked safely in case of sabotage or theft. It was therefore impossible for any troops to stand instantly to arms and be ready to fight the enemy. Late in the evening and at a week-end it took some time to muster officers, NCOs and men as fighting platoons and companies. It took even more time for them to draw their equipment and weapons from store — and still more time to collect their own ammunition and to load the reserve supplies of ammunition and fuel onto tanks and vehicles. The stowing of heavy and bulky ammunition into the turrets of the heavy tanks was in itself a slow process, and entailed first the carrying of the sealed ammunition boxes from the bunkers and the tedious process of breaking open the boxes.

Information had also to be obtained about the size, nature and exact location of the enemy threat, plans had to be made, orders issued, platoons and companies assembled and briefed as to their tasks, before a battalion could move against the enemy.

Without orders from the Bridgade and Divisional Head-quarters above, and unable to obtain clear information about other NATO battlions in the immediate neighbourhood, the battalions were engulfed in the fog of war, not knowing whether, if they moved to engage what they believed to be the enemy, they would be fighting against their own friends and allies.

Most battalions had lost their officers and senior NCOs in attacks by Spearhead Groups and Soviet assault forces. Some junior NCOs decided to ready their troops on defensible ground close to their barracks — the barracks themselves and the quarters nearby, in every case, being unsuitable ground on which to fight a battle apart from having non-combatant men, women and children, inevitably interfering with the necessary freedom to move and shoot.

Others, especially those closest to the main routes on which Pact Forces were moving, could estimate more clearly what and where the threat lay and could move to do battle with more certainty and fewer detailed orders. But, inevitably, these NATO troops went into battle uncoordinated and in small groups as

163

they arrived within range of the Pact forces. And, inevitably too, the small groups were picked off one by one, as they closed with the fully alerted Pact troops, who could be absolutely certain about where their own troops were and that any shooting coming from the darkness by the main routes was not from their own troops and so could be dealt with swiftly and ruthlessly.

Nevertheless, some of the NATO forces were able to inflict death and damage. Advancing north from their barracks six tanks of a West German battalion moved into a battle position overlooking the Hamburg-Hanover autobahn south and east of Soltau. Looking north-west they could see a long line of head-lights moving south. In the darkness, without landmarks clearly visible, it was very difficult to estimate the range to the target, and after their annual overhaul, the range-finders had not been fully calibrated. Intent on not wasting the chance to hit at the enemy, the German Commander ordered all his tanks to take up a battle position in line to engage the enemy simultaneously.

'All tanks — as soon as any tank has found the exact range to the target, give the range on the wireless so that we can all engage effectively. Out.'

Inevitably, with six tanks shooting together at an ill-defined target, there was initial confusion. Some tank commanders had overestimated the range, and tracers of their shots could be seen flying well over the top of the enemy column of vehicles. Others had underestimated the range and there was the resultant confusion of explosive bursts well short of the target. Gradually, over a period of some minutes, the shooting became more and more accurate, until eventually a direct hit was registered on the Pact vehicles and the range was declared to be 1370 metres.

At about the same time, adding further confusion to the battle, explosive bursts were seen by the German tank commanders to be falling again between them and their target. The confusion was only relieved by a wireless message from the German commander of a scout car behind the German battle line urgently announcing. 'All stations on this wireless net — there are shots being fired at you from vehicles moving towards us from behind — moving towards us from the outskirts of Munster. Out.'

Though damage had been done to the Pact column on the

164

autobahn, where vehicles on fire and ammunition exploding from them showed that the German tanks had found the range, the battle was soon brought to an end. The small group of German tanks were surrounded by Soviet vehicles. From behind and to the sides of the German battle line, Soviet anti-tank rockets and missiles, mounted on armoured cars and BMP vehicles, were able to penetrate the thinner rear and side armour of the German tanks which were set on fire, and their crews machine-gunned down as they leapt from their burning vehicles and were silhouetted against the flames.

SUNDAY

2130 Hours Central European Time

West Berlin

The owner of a house in the northern suburbs of West Berlin heard a loud knocking on the front door and a continuous pealing of the bell. Surprised at such an interruption at so late an hour he opened the door.

When he did so, he was grabbed and pushed roughly back into the hallway by three men who barged their way into the house — fully armed, uniformed men — followed closely by another group who had detached themselves from a larger body of men gathered round two military vehicles in the street outside.

In a tree-lined avenue of good-sized houses, within one mile of the north boundary of the city limits and the East German territory surrounding the city, the house was in an ideally quiet but convenient setting for the family. But the same location made it ideal for the headquarters of the East German Commander, whose troops had crossed into West Berlin across the whole length of the north boundary, less than an hour earlier.

The Warsaw Pact High Command had had a difficult problem deciding the time at which to move into West Berlin. Although the attacks on Western Europe had been planned to take place at 1730 hours, for a number of reasons the same time was not suitable for the attack on West Berlin. One of the main

165

planks of the attack plans was that, for as long as possible, the NATO forces and civilian population should not became fully aware of what was happening. It was therefore seen by the High Command as risking the best success of the attacks by entering West Berlin too early and running the risk that somehow, somewhere in the City, someone might be able to pass a message to West Germany warning of the attack, before such a warning might otherwise be passed to those in authority.

But it was also clearly seen that to postpone the attack on West Berlin beyond a certain time was to run the reverse risk that a warning might be passed to the West Berlin authorities somehow, from somewhere in West Germany, by someone who might have had the sense or duty to send such a warning.

The East German High Command, who had been made responsible for the take-over of West Berlin with East German troops, had been ordered to calculate the risks and plan accordingly. It therefore decided to move its Spearhead Groups into position at 1830 hours, one hour later than zero hour and to give them a clear hour to disrupt the communications and command set-up, before moving in further forces at 1930 hours. Two hours later, at about 2130 hours, the East German commander moved into the city with his own headquarters, whose orders were to find a suitable large house, well situated for access to the centre of the city. Before his arrival, while he was inspecting the progress of his front line troops, his staff moved into the house to make the necessary arrangements.

SUNDAY

2030 Hours Greenwich Mean Time
2130 Hours Central European Time

Outside London, England

Answering the phone in her office one of the secretaries at the British Prime Minister's country residence at Chequers received a message from 10 Downing Street that the Prime Minister's presence was urgently needed in London.

'Who sent that message?' the Prime Minister asked.

'I didn't recognize the voice nor the name, but he said he knew you intended to return to London this evening and thought you should make your return earlier than you had planned as there were certain urgent matters for you to deal with which had recently cropped up.'

'Well see if you can get hold of the Cabinet Secretary, and failing him, see if you can find anyone you know and get an explanation of this unusual message.'

Some minutes later the secretary returned to report that he had had no success in finding anyone he knew, that the telephone lines seemed to be in an appalling condition and that he was therefore unable to get any clarification of the earlier message.

'All right,' the Prime Minister answered, 'we will leave when we are ready. I am ready now.'

Fifteen minutes later a convoy of three cars swung out of the main gates and turned towards London. One minute later all three vehicles were blown to bits by anti-tank rockets fired from a hedge-line fifty yards back from the road. The leading vehicle had had to slow right down to be able to pass a farm tractor which had broken down almost in the middle of the road.

SUNDAY

2200 Hours Central European Time

Western Europe

Except for the intermittent squeal of the tracks of light tanks, combat vehicles and self-propelled guns, and the occasional extra surge of noise as engines were revved to take a sharp corner or to ascend a steep incline, the movement of the Pact Forces into Western Europe was remarkable for its lack of the thunder and lightning of battle, and sinister because of the relentless momentum of the long streams of vehicles pouring across the Iron Curtain. The speed of the camouflaged vehicles was not fast but they seemed unstoppable and the constant succession of blazing headlights was hypnotic.

After two fifteen minute stops and four hours of uninterrupted progress, long columns of Pact Forces' vehicles were already over 200 kilometres into West Germany and were again ready to move ahead, leaving behind them the guards for the thousands of NATO prisoners who had been taken.

The Pact Forces moving on Denmark crossed the Danish border north of Schleswig-Holstein, having overrun, on the way, the German mechanised division in its barracks and a few light Danish forces stationed on the Danish—German border. Nowhere had the Pact Forces met with any resistance.

Other Pact forces having skirted south of Hamburg, bypassed Bremen on the south and reached a point about 10 kilometres west of Bremen Airport. West German army, navy and airforce barracks and installations were taken, including, south of Bremen, large dumps of military equipment and stores belonging to the American Army.

South of them, the leading Pact light tanks and armoured cars seized the crossing over the River Hunte at Diepholz, north of Osnabruck. At this point they had passed the West German forces in their path and were not yet far enough west to make contact with any Dutch forces, mainly stationed inside Holland.

On the main east-west autobahn the Pact Forces reached a point south-east of Bielefeld and some went on ahead without a halt to the Royal Airforce airbase at Gûtersloh to capture the airfield and destroy the aircraft in their hardened shelters. NATO tank, artillery, infantry and technical battalions and headquarters of divisions in the Herford, Bielefeld, Lemgo and Detmold garrisons were surrounded.

On the route just south of the autobahn the Pact Forces had reached Bad Meinberg, on the way surrounding British battalions at Hildesheim and Hameln. On their flank at Detmold there were other British battalions which might offer resistance but which had already been attacked by Spearhead Groups and had lost senior officers and NCOs.

With a starting point on the border which was well west of those at Helmstedt, the Pact Forces which crossed at Duderstadt, east of Göttingen, were already at a point south of Lippstadt. From a crossing point at Herleshausen, also well to the West, the Pact Forces were at Kirburg, only 70 kilometres short of the West German capital, Bonn. Light fast assault sections were already in the outskirts in small numbers, having forgone all halts.

On the next route further south, after bypassing Frankfurt to the south, Pact Forces crossed the River Main, took Frankfurt-Rhein/Main Airport, and swung north of Wiesbaden for about 10 kilometres. At this point they were barely 30 kilometres in a direct line from the Rhine, though still about 60 kilometres short of the river crossing at Koblenz, moving on secondary, more winding roads which did not lead exactly in the direction they wished to go.

On a less direct route from the next frontier crossing to the south of Eisfeld, and forced to move on minor roads, the Pact reconnaissance forces were, by forgoing a halt for rest, at the crossing of the River Main at Aschaffenburg, and within one hour's drive from the Rhine.

The next crossing of the frontier further south, at Hirschberg, was the furthest east crossing point out of East Germany. By 2200 hours the Pact Forces were no further than the crossing of the River Tauber, still well short of the Rhine crossing at Worms, three hours driving time further west.

From the most northern crossing point from Czechoslovakia, at Schirnding, Pact Forces, on the route which bypassed Bayreuth and skirted Nürnberg, were at Crailsheim, making for Heilbron, the Rhine and Pirmasens on the border with France. They were still about 170 kilometres east of the Rhine.

Pact Forces on the next route, directed on Stuttgart and Karlsruhe, were at Nördlingen, having had to use minor roads south of Nürnberg. Even so they had almost managed to keep up with the forces to the north, moving on better routes.

From the frontier crossing point at Furth im Wald Pact Forces were at the crossings over the River Danube at Regensburg, Ingolstadt, Neuburg and Donauworth and armoured cars were at Dillingen, about 40 kilometres east of Ulm. They still had very nearly 200 kilometres to travel before reaching the Rhine at the French city of Strasbourg.

On the most southern crossing point out from Czechoslovakia at Bad Eisenstein, Pact Forces skirted Munich and the north shore of the Ammer See, about 100 kilometres north of the Austrian border. They still had a long way to go to the Rhine crossing at Mulhouse, some 350 kilometres to the west, which they were not expecting to reach until the early hours of the morning.

SUNDAY

2200 Hours Central European Time

Bonn Airport, West Germany

Throughout the preceding years the West German Federal Criminal Office Chief was in no doubt that West Germany's terrorists were regrouping and reorganizing. It was widely believed that some had been co-operating with the Italian Red Brigades, while others were thought to be preparing with Middle East terrorist groups for further onslaughts on Israel and on Egypt. Most had evaded capture in West Germany and in the countries whose police forces and Governments were prepared to help. Some known fringe members of the Red Army Fraction had gone underground to join the other known groups of urban guerrillas — the 2 June Movement and the Revolutionary Cells. There had been bank raids, stamped with the hallmarks of the terrorist methods, a typical means of raising funds for the training of the new recruits. The West German Authorities did not believe that any terror-free period was other than a time for concentration and regeneration of the terrorist groups. They expected more bank raids, more kidnappings, more indiscriminate terror. They had to be alert at all times. But they did not expect a concerted, mass wave of terror across Europe.

The urban guerrillas had acted often enough for each terror attack to be accepted with fatalism by the bulk of the population as yet another incident which could not be prevented. Each new attack was dreaded but not unexpected, and the security forces were always in a high state of alertness, knowing that only they could offer a line of defence and that the rest of the population had little alternative but to heed their advice to stay well clear of any new incident.

So it was that the Spearhead Group set to take over the Cologne—Bonn—Wahn Airport met with very strong resistance. The security guard at the locked entrance to the airport

170

control tower had become highly suspicious of a group of five men and two women who seemed to him to be spending a lot of their time too near to his post. He reported as much on his walkie-talkie wireless set and other guards near the buildings were immediately on the alert. As one of the two women approached the guard, calling out a question as to how to find a roof canteen, the guard slipped the safety-catch of his machine-pistol and curled his forefinger on the trigger. The first shot from the woman's automatic caused a convulsive tightening of his trigger finger and, as he staggered backwards to fall against the wall behind him, the weapon was raised involuntarily to point straight at the woman's face not six feet away from him.

From a side entrance to an adjoining building another guard opened fire with his weapon, at a range of less than 25 yards, the bullets spraying in an arc across the midriffs of the five men and the other woman, as he directed the jerking pistol's swathe of bullets at the targets so close to him. When all six bodies lay still on the ground, the blood seeping from the multiple wounds in their bodies, the guard moved closer to finish off any survivor. As he bent to look more closely at the first man's body, a single nerve gas shot from the weapon of one of the men still just alive, killed him in seconds. The remaining guards nearby, hearing no further shots nor any answer to their calls to their companion, were unable to decide what had happened and moved with extreme caution.

Meanwhile in other parts of the airport, small groups of attackers used their weapons indiscriminately to kill guards, officials, police, customs men and passegers, wherever they got in the way of the efforts to seize the key points of the airport. Some of the security men were able to kill a few attackers before they themselves died.

The control tower complex was not handed over to the survivors of the Spearhead Group until the arrival of the Special Groups with their VIP prisoners. Under the threat of a mass killing it was surrendered, airliners were commandeered, the prisoners were ushered aboard and the aircraft took off.

In the area surrounding the airport, the populace heard the noise of shooting and decided that as it was another terrorist incident they should stay at home and not get in the way of the police and security force operations.

171

At Frankfurt—Rhein/Main Airport, four airliners were taken over by the Special and Spearhead Groups to accommodate the large numbers of senior German and American officers, and some of their families, who had been kidnapped from the main NATO bases in the area.

At Stuttgart—Echterdingen Airport, as well as more senior German and American officers there was a number of French and their families.

At Dusseldorf—Lohausen, the senior allied staff and families of the Northern Army Group Headquarters at München Gladbach, and of the Allied Land Forces and Allied Air Forces Central Europe from their Headquarters at Brunssum, just across the border in the Dutch province of Limburg, were assembled and flown away.

From the Hanover—Lagenhagen Airport the senior staff and families of the British and German divisions and brigades in the surrounding area were taken away in the available airliners and smaller aircraft.

SUNDAY

2200 Hours Central European Time

West of the River Weser, West Germany

The attack by the Spearhead Group on the British tank Battalion at Detmold had succeeded in killing the officers and senior NCOs and throwing the battalion into confusion. Alerted by the German police that the attacks had been on a wide scale throughout West Germany, some of the junior NCOs had managed to crew and arm, ready for battle, about a dozen tanks. On a further warning from the German police that Warsaw Pact Forces had crossed the River Weser, these tanks moved out to engage the enemy.

Driving south from the barracks they came in sight of the Pact Forces west of Bad Meinberg. On an open stretch of the main road, the headlights of the line of vehicles were clearly visible to the British tanks as they moved into position to shoot. The ground on each side of the road was heavy with winter rain,

172

so that the first two tanks to deploy each side of the road became bogged in the soft ground and were unable to move any further. Four tanks were, however, able to bring their guns to bear on the target, as, on the road two more tanks were able to move into position, side by side, to bring their guns on to the road being used by the enemy forces.

Calling up the commanders of the two platoons of three tanks which had got into firing positions, the commander ordered, 'One and two — fire as soon as you are ready. One make sure you knock out the leading enemy vehicle you can see and cause a traffic jam behind. Two — when that happens you are to knock out the last enemy vehicle you can see. Between you, you will then deal with all the vehicles in between. If we can set them all on fire, or immobilize them, we shall have effectively blocked about 800 metres of the road. Out.'

The first shots from each of the six tanks were apparently wide of the mark. In the darkness it was not easy to see the strike of the very high velocity solid shots against non-armoured or thinly armoured vehicles, through which the armour piercing rounds passed like a hot knife through butter.

After each tank had fired another shot, the whole scene was brilliantly illuminated by the light of a star-shell fired from further east in the enemy line of vehicles.

'One — with that light I can see that the range is not what I thought — take advantage of the light while it lasts to check your range estimate. Out.'

Each tank got off another shot as soon as possible to take advantage of the illumination until the leader of the second tank platoon reported, 'Two — stop firing — stop firing — among the enemy vehicles there are a lot of civilian cars and lorries — look —. Over.'

'Two,' answered the Company Commander. 'I see them. If they put up another star shell, try to avoid shooting on the civilians — if they don't put up another — shoot to hit any vehicle — is that understood? One and Two over.'

The two platoon commanders acknowledged the order and all tanks waited a moment for another star shell. The delay was their undoing.

Unprotected by their own infantry, who would have been in a position forward of the tanks to guard against infiltration by enemy infantry moving under the cover of darkness, the six tanks were sitting targets for the Soviet Infantry, who had moved within easy range to hit with anti-tank rockets against the thinner side armour. One of the two tanks on the road managed to get off one very high velocity armour-piercing shot which hit and set on fire a Soviet BMP vehicle in the middle of the line of vehicles.

As the leading tanks burst into flames and blew up, the Soviet infantry moved along the side of the road and, one by one, picked off the other British tanks which were immobilized on the road, unable to move off on to the soft ground where they too would have become bogged.

SUNDAY

2230 Hours Central European Time

Paderborn, West Germany

While the tank action ended in disaster at Bad Meinberg, 25 kilometres south-west at Paderborn, a British Brigadier, driving his Volvo estate car, with his wife beside him and his two boys and girl asleep in the back, arrived at the crossroads in the centre of Paderborn on his way back from the winter sports resort at Winterberg to his headquarters at Herford.

He found the crossroads blocked by an ancient Opel car, dragged across the road. He got out to protest to the driver who was standing beside it, realized too late that beyond the car the three vehicles halted at the roadside were Soviet BMPs, and was shot down by the Opel's driver after he had uttered his first sentence in English.

Behind him his wife watched horrified, not daring to make a move or utter a sound and not wishing to wake the three children, who were still half-asleep and unaware of what had happened.

The Soviet Assault Regiment, aided by the Spearhead Group, continued to make sure that the route was clear for the following forces which were just clearing up a slight delay at Bad Meinberg, 25 kilometres further east.

SUNDAY

Western Europe

In the columns of camouflaged Soviet vehicles, there were, in small batches of three or four, uncamouflaged long distance coaches, town and city buses, and long distance trucks converted with rows of wooden seats.

To cope with the very large number of prisoners which the Warsaw Pact Forces expected to capture, nearly half a million reservists, in the age group between forty and forty-five, had been called back to act as guards for the prisoners. Selection had been from the unemployed and from the least efficient farm and factory workers, so that the country's economy would be disrupted as little as possible.

As the Warsaw Pact Forces moved further and further into West Germany, beyond into Belgium, Holland, Luxemburg, France, Denmark, into Austria and Italy, and elsewhere into Norway, Greece and Turkey, and more and more of the barracks, quarters, schools, airfields and headquarters were overrun, the Spearhead Groups and the Assault Regiments handed over their captures to the Prisoner Guards.

The Spearhead Groups, after carrying out their primary sabotage actions, had moved into barracks, headquarters and airbases to kill, and in a few cases to capture, the less senior officers and the senior NCOs, who might have organized resistance or led a counter attack. They had then, wherever possible, rounded up as many of the junior NCOs and men, as well as their families and the civilians, doctors, nurses, teachers, attached to each base or barracks.

By the time the Prisoner Guards arrived at most locations it was a question only of rounding up those who had escaped deliberately or had not fallen into the nets of the Spearhead and Support Groups. To the Prisoner Guards also had been given the task of collecting the transport by which to remove the accumulating numbers. The first step, in each case, had been to mobilize the military transport of the barracks or base with the NATO drivers.

175

Into them had been crowded the first prisoners to be rounded up, whether male or female, adult or child, service-man or woman or civilian. Some had managed to grab a top coat to put on over their day clothes if they were still dressed, or even if they were dragged out of bed. Some had had no time even to put on shoes or slippers. The younger children had, in the main, been in bed and asleep, and terrified and distraught parents had tried to wrap them in blankets and to carry them. Some children had lost their parents in the mêlée, and ran screaming in tears, from group to group, until their parents were found or until a Prisoner Guard hit the child into unconsciousness or killed it by the force of the blow. The very old, relatives or friends, were killed outright with any weapon that was at hand, where they stood or sat or slept. The very young, the infants and babies, were picked up by the heels and their heads swung against the walls until they split open like blood oranges, leaving a trail of blood and brains staining the walls and floors, where the bodies had been cast aside.

In almost every barracks and base, there was an initial resistance by the prisoners. Some tried to rush the guards to overpower them, some tried to block the searches by the guards or Spearhead Groups, some tried to smuggle a few of their number through a door or window or into a coal cellar hatch. There were few who escaped.

In some cases, where there was not enough room in a batch of transport to load all the prisoners, the surplus was taken on one side and shot. Where, in canteens, clubs and dining halls, there were any men and women who were incapably drunk or noisy and hilarious with drink, they were shot, the guards losing patience with any one who would cause any problem. Some of the women escaped with their lives — but at the cost of humiliation and degradation.

When the military transport had been loaded to capacity and despatched, the guards searched the nearest streets for German civilian trucks and vans, and ordered the owners and drivers at gun-point to the barracks and living quarters. These men had to watch the scenes of horror while their vehicles were loaded, some unaware up to the moment they saw them that the Pact Forces had arrived.

By midnight, against the westward flow of the vehicles of the

Pact Forces moving on the pre-selected routes, there was an equally large eastward flow of vehicles packed with terrified humans, in each of which the stench of sweat, vomit, urine and excreta become worse and worse as the long drive continued for hour upon hour without stop or rest.

The aim was that by morning most of the man power, as well as the families and civilians connected with the forces, from the twenty-seven NATO divisions, Air Forces and Headquarters should be in transit to East Germany and the prison camps further east.

SUNDAY

2300 Hours Central European Time

Southern Europe

While the Pact Forces in West Germany proceeded virtually unimpeded, movement into north Italy was slowed by the steeper, narrower and more winding roads in Austria. By 2300 hours the leading forces were at a point about 25 kilometres east of Klagenfurt, 60 kilometres from the Italian frontier post at Coccau. Moving through Graz and Wolfsberg, they had covered less than the planned distance but would nevertheless be well into north Italy by daylight. By midnight, or soon afterwards, depending on the conditions of the roads, they would have passed through Villach. By 0200 hours they planned to have reached Udine and to be in the North Italian Plain. By 0400 hours they would reach the outskirts of Venice and turn due west to be beyond Padua, and on the way to Vicenza and Verona, by first light. Meanwhile other forces would go due south to the crossing of the River Po at Ferrara, and through Monselice to Mantua. By early morning on Monday, Pact Forces would have reached positions where they would be in close contact with the Red Brigades in North Italy. They did not expect any opposition at any point on their route. The advance through Austria was delayed only by the roads, which, though good, were winding and, here and there, had steep gradients. In North Italy the Pact Forces expected to meet no opposition until they were well south of the Alps and their foothills as the Red Brigaders were expected to impede the moves of Italian forces.

In North Greece, Pact Forces started to cross the frontier in the Rupel Gap at 1730 hours simultaneously with the attacks in Europe. Within the first hour they were at the crossing of the River Struma on the way to Thessaloniki, 70 kilometres to the south, which they entered at 2300 hours. By then, other forces were through Yefira on the way to Kitros and Katerini in the plain below Mount Olympus, and to Veroia, with the aim of reaching Kozani early the next day. Meanwhile yet other forces had turned east about 40 kilometres south of the frontier, to advance to Alexandronopolis and there north-east up the valley road of the River Evros, to make contact with the Pact Forces at Edirne, in Turkey on the route to Istanbul. The Greek Forces on the frontier, though alert in case of attacks from Jugoslavia and Bulgaria, were no match for the Spearhead Groups and the Pact assault forces which followed close behind. More used to the warmer weather in their homes in the south of the country, some of the Greek troops were overrun in their defence positions as they were sheltering in the warm bunkers, without adequate vigilance.

In Turkey, the leading Pact Forces had, by 2300 hours, met no opposition and expected to be in Istanbul overlooking the Bosphorus by midnight. Other forces would reach Silivri at about the same time, and Tekirdag soon afterwards. Later Pact Forces were to turn south west, at Babaeski, to pass through Hayrabolu and Malkara to Sarköy; and at Havsa to Kavak, and to a point west of Gallipoli, to prevent Turkish attacks across the Dardanelles from the Turkish coast of Asia Minor.

SUNDAY

1700 Hours Eastern Standard Time
2300 Hours Central European Time

The Pentagon, Washington, USA

By 1700 hours it was clear that the 'hot-line' to Moscow and the links to surveillance and communications satellites had been deliberately disrupted. It was impossible to make more than garbled and distorted contact with any military headquarters outside the United States, and the State Department had reported that contact with American Embassies and agencies in Europe was subject to interruptions and interference. Contact with European military headquarters and defence departments had been confused, as the operators could not apparently fully understand what was said, and demands to speak to more senior officers were being met with incomprehensible delays.

The diplomatic and commercial links in America of the European countries had found similar difficulty. On the other hand contact with commercial ships at sea in the Atlantic and with airliners in flight from Europe had been found to be uninterrupted, but some later flights had been cancelled without explanation. The Pentagon communications experts had questioned certain known ham radio operators and had found that they were experiencing no problems and had had exchanges with counterparts in Europe.

Nevertheless it had had to be assumed that so widespread a disruption of key communications could not be explained as accidental, and that therefore the purpose of the dislocation had to be evaluated. The key staff officers servicing the National Security Council had been summoned to the Pentagon main conference room. An Army Brigadier had no doubt of the explanation of the situation.

'This must be connected with Soviet attacks on Western Europe. Can you tell me any other circumstance which could explain what has happened? Can you suggest any other nation that would have been capable of this degree of confusion? My guess is that attacks have started already and that when we get to hear what has happened it will be too late.'

'You can't be sure,' a Navy captain replied. 'There have been no intelligence reports of a Soviet build-up, and certainly there have been no signs of the Soviet fleet moving to war stations.'

'That's right,' an Air Force Colonel added. 'We have no reason to suppose there have been any large-scale attacks without getting some signs of a build-up of their airforces. I've kept the usual check on the satellite intelligence on the location

179

of their Tactical Air Armies. None of them have moved — the disposition to airfields are just as they were a few weeks ago. Maybe the Soviets have something already planned, they may even be carrying out an operation which they don't want to talk about, but that doesn't mean they have attacked Central Europe.'

'I'll tell you,' the Brigadier answered, 'they don't need a navy or air build-up to be able to attack in Europe. With the forces they have, as far west as they are, and in the numbers that are permanently mobilized, they could march into Western Europe at the drop of a hat. And they can march across Western Europe to the Atantic without any build-up. Anyway who's to say that there hasn't been a build-up of ground forces? We wouldn't be able to detect a very careful stepping forward of say fifteen of their divisions, would we? We wouldn't be looking for it at this time of year, would we? They could have moved fifteen divisions closer up to the frontier, dispersing them carefully, hiding the men and vehicles in all kinds of buildings, as part of the preparations for their manoeuvres.'

'But,' interrupted the Colonel, 'you don't mean that they would attack with just fifteen divisions — and no air support — because they can't get more than the minimum support from the airfields way back east in East Germany and Poland.'

'No,' the Brigadier answered, 'I don't mean that they would attack with only fifteen divisions. I mean that maybe fifteen divisions have been moved up close enough to the Iron Curtain for them to have crossed with no warning at all. Then say another fifteen divisions could have been moved up to a line just west of Berlin, and while the first wave of fifteen are moving out of their camouflaged hiding-places, this second wave could be charging down the autobahns and roads to catch up — from 50 kilometres further back. Then behind them — another 50 kilometres further back — straight from their peace-time barracks, another fifteen divisions could have started off.'

'But what about air cover?' the airman asked.

'What about air cover?' was the reply. 'They won't need any air cover tonight. The NATO Tactical Air Forces won't be able to determine in the dark which are the enemy vehicles and which are the friendly. I tell you they don't need any air cover.'

'But what about when it's daylight?' the airman persisted.

'They are not going to be able to hide that number of vehicles by day.'

'No, you may be right — but just suppose they don't even try to hide. This whole thing could be so unconventional that let's imagine that when it gets to be light all they do is to park all their vehicles right in the middle of towns, cities, villages, so that if the NATO Air Forces attack, they have to accept huge civilian casualty rates.'

'Where do you think they might aim to be by then?' asked the captain. 'I mean, at this rate, by the time we know what's happened, it'll be too late to do anything. The US plans to sea and air lift huge forces within fourteen days, but if what you say is right, it'll all be over in fourteen hours.

'I don't say that,' the Brigadier replied. 'I'm just guessing like you, like all of us. But let's see what could have happened. It won't be light till say 0800 hours, that gives them say fifteen hours to travel. Suppose they average 30 miles an hour, that's 450 miles. Hell, that's way over the Rhine — and they'll have overrun all the NATO divisions and most of the headquarters. I tell you Ed, potentially the most peace-destabilizing forces that any side can have are what we all call conventional forces. If the Soviets want to invade, conquer and occupy Western Europe, they have got to have huge conventional forces. Manpower, and lots of it, is what matters, when invasion, conquest and occupation are planned. You can't invade and occupy with huge navies — you can't invade and occupy with air forces. Sure you can threaten, but to capture a territory you have to go in. We saw that in 1945. The Germans were beaten, but we still had to occupy the country. That's why the Soviets have so many motor-rifle divisions. You can't occupy with tanks — you've got to have men out on their feet. That's why the Soviets have built up such huge conventional massed manpower armies — they're not for defence, they could defend with tanks and weapons. No, their massed manpower divisions are for the occupation of Western Europe.'

'So you say,' queried the sailor, 'that all along this talk that conventional armies and weapons are more moral and ethical than nuclear weapons is wrong?'

'Sure it's wrong,' the Brigadier answered. 'It's wrong because if you're dead it doesn't matter if it was a conventional

181

bullet that killed you or a nuclear weapon. Second, it's wrong because it has been a gigantic confidence trick to hide the real motives of the Soviets. It was their campaign, backed by lots of well-meaning, and some not so well-meaning people, to discredit the use of nuclear weapons of any sort, so that they could pretend to some righteousness with huge conventional forces — but really because they had got to have conventional forces to be able to carry out their invasion plans. And, of course, they could adopt a righteous attitude about the neutron bomb, whereas, in fact, their propaganda campaign against it was to ensure that they could still invade and occupy.'

'Well, what's the answer?' the Air Colonel asked. 'Should we have matched the Soviets with conventional weapons? Or what else could we have done?'

'I'm not a politician,' the Brigadier said. 'Come to that, I'm not a statesman either, and maybe I don't see all the angles. But I would say that it's not often in life you can have your cake and eat it. And by that I mean that I don't believe you can have just enough conventional forces and hope for the best. If you have just enough, or probably barely enough, then the politicians and statesmen can say that they will be enough for a successful defence. It's a great word, defence, for a politician, because he hasn't got to do the defending. Anyone who's been really in a war, and seen the death and destruction, doesn't want to defend with just enough, or barely enough forces. He wants to deter the enemy from ever starting a war — doesn't he?'

'I guess we all feel the same,' the airman added. 'I don't think there can be more than a very few thinking service-men who imagine there's any glamour in war now, if there ever was any. I think of it like crime or disease, something which should be prevented and the best way to prevent it is to be really able to deter it. I guess we in the Air Forces and the Navies can still reckon that we can deter an all-out ballistic missile attack on the West. But how in hell could we have deterred this Soviet conventional attack?'

'Well, as I see it,' the Brigadier said thoughtfully. 'I don't believe it was ever sensible to think that any of the NATO countries would ever have had the political will, or even the available economic resources, to raise the full total of conventional mass manpower forces that were really needed. I guess each country would have had to double the conventional forces it had for the Soviet Union to have been deterred by them. Could you see that happening? Why even the United States has announced that only in the event of war would it double its ground forces within a fortnight and treble its air forces within one week. But what's the good of that? The war, if it's already started, which is more than likely, is going to be over before we can even issue the orders to get the troops back from their Christmas leave.'

'So what should have been done? The neutron bomb?'

'Yes, but not just the neutron bomb,' the soldier answered. 'We should have made a much bigger decision a long way back. Just as we had to make the major decision back in the 1930s to convert a basically horse-drawn, horse-carried or foot-marching army into a fully mechanized, armoured, motorized army, so I think the decision should have been made some years ago to convert a conventional mechanized, armoured high-explosive army into a nuclear army with all the changes that that implies. And I don't mean the big tactical nuclear weapons — I mean the really small frontline micronuclear gun shells and mortar shells. That way we could have had the weapon power to deter the Soviet manpower.'

He was interrupted by the airman, who said, 'We are just beginning to get some messages in from Switzerland, which seem to show that the Soviets have moved forces into Southern Austria from across the border with Hungary. Maybe that's why the communications have been cut and disrupted. We'd better go and see if there's more news come in yet. I guess we'll all be busy as hell now. Will the fleet move in the Mediterranean?'

The two men moved out to the Communications Centre, leaving the Brigadier alone with this thoughts. He could imagine what the scenes must be like in the garrisons overwhelmed by attack. But he knew too that his prescription for a viable nuclear deterrent was up against two major hurdles — the first that the politicians would not be prepared to allow the frontline fighting battalions to be given the responsibility for deciding when to use even the frontline micronuclear weapons, and also the statesman's objections to allowing the frontline battalions of other nations to handle such weapons. If the existence of the weapons failed to deter, the use of them might commit the

183

United States to an all out thermonuclear exchange. As against that though, he wondered how many men, women and children were going to lose their lives or their freedom, without being able to offer any resistance.

SUNDAY

2359 Hours Central European Time

West Germany

By the last minutes of Sunday, Pact Forces had reached everywhere beyond the strategic forward and secondary defence lines which NATO had planned to occupy in the event of an attack.

In Denmark they had reached Ringkobing on the west coast of Jutland and, on the east coast, Aarhus, and the crossing to Funen Island and Odense.

In north Germany, they had reached the bridge over the River Ems and the canal at Lingen, Oldenburg, Wilhelmshaven and Bremerhaven.

Further south, they had reached the River Ems and the Dortmund-Ems Canal at Rheine, and had already passed through the NATO garrison towns of Verden, Nienburg, Fallingbostel, Bergen and Soltau.

Just north of the Ruhr, the bridges over the River Lippe and the branch of the Dortmund Ems canal had been gained as had the bridges over the River Möhne, just south and east of the Ruhr. Just west of the Ruhr the Rhine crossing at Neuss had been reached.

A few minutes after midnight Pact Forces had crossed the Rhine at Cologne, Bonn and Koblenz. Ten minutes earlier the Rhine had also been reached at Mainz, the point nearest to the East German frontier, and Pact Forces had moved on southwest past Bad Kreuznach, on their way to Idal Oberstein and Saarbrücken. Some 55 kilometres further south the Rhine crossings at Worms, Ludwigshafen and Mannheim were reached by Pact troops about twenty minutes later.

South of Mannheim, where the Pact Forces had started from frontier crossings much further east on the Czechoslovak

184

border, and where the course of the River Rhine swung to the south-west, they had only been able to attain the strategic crossings over the River Neckar at Neckarelz, Heilbronn, Stuttgart and Nürtingen. Some scout cars had arrived at the Rhine. On the most southern route, south of Ulm on the Danube, the Pact Forces had crossed the River Riss.

In some places the leading armoured cars, scout cars and combat vehicles, travelling independently from a column of vehicles and at their best speeds, had gone faster than had been expected, but would have been without immediate support if they had been attacked by any considerable NATO force. In other places they had been unable to make the same progress, as here and there, they had been impeded by parked German vehicles, or occasionally, by late night revellers returning home, causing short traffic jams. On some of the minor roads, running parallel with the main routes, all of which were being used if only by a few scout vehicles or motor-cyclists, progress had been faster than on the main routes.

The surprise of the advance at that time of year, and the secrecy achieved by the disruption of civilian communications, meant that the West German population in general, and even a large part of the population on or near the main routes, had no idea what was occurring. There were therefore none of the road-clogging streams of refugees which had impeded so many of the major advances of the Second World War. Where the roads might have been blocked by civilian traffic, the motor-cyclists of the Pact reconnaissance units were usually able to divert the civilian cars. Their uniforms were not easy to distinguish, even under the street lamps, so that their waved traffic directions were obeyed without question.

SUNDAY

1830 Hours Eastern Standard Time
0030 Hours Central European Time

The Pentagon, Washington, USA

Three senior officers sat in the Pentagon staff restaurant

185

discussing the military calamity in Western Europe.

'How could we have taken the necessary steps quickly enough to be able to resist a massive Soviet conventional attack?' a Colonel inquired. 'What could we have done, which would have made a Soviet conventional attack impossible, or impossibly expensive?'

'Briefly,' a Brigadier answered, 'NATO should have learnt from Napoleon and Hitler that to try to invade Russia is asking for defeat. They can always use their vast spaces and climate to defeat us. So we should have concentrated entirely on the weapons needed to defend. I know the old saying that attack is the best form of defence, and I believe that attack, and only attack against attacking forces would have been the best form of defence. We should not have planned to invade. So all the forces which exist essentially to defend by invading in retaliation, should have been abandoned.'

'You mean that we should have disbanded the tank forces?' the Colonel asked.

'Yes, I do,' the Brigadier answered briskly. 'We should have abandoned the large tank formations which we planned to use to strike back against an invasion, and if successful, to penetrate deep into the Warsaw Pact defences. But we should have kept the tanks because there would have been occasions when they would have been needed.'

'Do you think that we should have abandoned mobile infantry, artillery and engineer units whose role would be to support a large-scale attack?' a second Colonel asked.

'Yes,' the Brigadier said, 'but I don't recommend a new Maginot or Siegfried Line, or any fixed line. With the introduction of frontline micronuclear weapons, the situation has very radically changed. Where the fixed defence lines relied on steel and concrete to defend, there was no effective means of attacking the attackers. Where the defended areas had more depth to the defences, there was still no adequate weight of bullets and shells to kill the attackers in sufficient numbers. With good planning the attacker was always able to bring such a superiority of numbers against a part of the defences, that the defenders could not, in time, beat the attackers back. Micronuclear weapons have changed all that. The weight of blast and heat and radiation from even one small micronuclear weapon is enough to stop the attack of a whole regiment. Now if the attacker masses his manpower for an attack, he risks having his massed attacking force totally obliterated with absolute certainty. In the past, battles were fought between two opposing lines of forces and each side tried to force a way through the other's line. With micronuclear weapons, war will be dominated by the fact that no longer can the likely success of an attack be estimated by a calculation of casualty rates. There will not be any casualty rates except total obliteration, the only answer to which will be counter-obliteration. So there will be no wars to invade, conquer and occupy, because invasion will have to mean obliteration of the enemy, and there will be no enemy forces to conquer and nothing worthwhile left to occupy. Now we had better get back to the Centre.'

Frontline micronuclear weapon warheads with an energy yield one hundred times less than that of the 20KT weapon used in 1945 on Japan had been developed in the early 1950s. By then the United States had developed a micronuclear warhead with an energy yield of only 0.2 KT of high explosive. Further development had resulted in the production of micronuclear warheads with an energy yield as low as 0.1 KT of high explosive. Even lower yields than that of 0.1 KT had been found to be possible. Calculations showed that moderate or heavy damage to buildings and equipment would be caused by a nuclear weapon with an energy yield of 0.1 KT at 0.34 mile, up to a distance of 598 yards or 546 metres, from ground zero below an airburst. Dug-in defences and equipment would suffer negligible effects at these or greater ranges.

Most battle actions between opposing land forces, whether infantry or armoured, would take place at ranges of 500 metres, the shortest distance except for hand to hand fights, up to ranges of 2,000 to 2,500 metres, beyond which visibility on a battlefield would usually be too poor to ensure accurate shooting. Micronuclear weapons were therefore suitable for use by frontline defending infantry or armoured units. The 'Davy Crockett' micronuclear weapon, with an energy yield of about 0.25 KT, had been fired from a light mortar, manned by three to four men, carried on a jeep and trailer. It had not been issued for general use because of the political implications of even very small nuclear weapons being in the hands of frontline units, and

187

the responsibility for firing them being with relatively junior ranks.

As well as developing nuclear warheads with smaller and smaller energy yields, a selection of weapons, each with a different effect to match a specific military need had also been developed. By adjusting the power of each of the three main properties of a nuclear explosion, those of blast, heat and radiation, the desired effect could be obtained.

One development had been an 'RRR' nuclear weapon — having 'reduced residual radiation', designed to damage by blast and heat with minimum radiation. Its purpose was to achieve maximum effect while ensuring that the target area was safe from radiation, so that it could be occupied by the force which had used the 'RRR' weapon.

Another development had been an 'EH' nuclear weapon — having such 'enhanced heat' that it would be capable of melting, or making partly molten, vital steel components of tanks, as well as killing or seriously wounding the crew inside the armour.

The development which had received the most publicity was the so-called neutron bomb, which was not a bomb but a nuclear warhead for shells or missiles. It was an 'enhanced radiation and reduced blast weapon' known technically as an ERW/RBW. The warhead consisted of a micronuclear device with an energy yield of about 1KT. Detonated at an altitude of 3,000 feet, only a fraction of the blast would reach the ground, but the radiation would penetrate the thickest tank armour, causing radiation sickness to the crews. The radius of effect of the 1 KT warhead was about 300 metres for the blast effect, 400 metres for the intense heat, and 1,400 metres for the radiation effect. Up to a radius of 300 metres, the outer radius of the blast effect, the radiation effect would quickly disable tank crews, who would die within two days, if they had not also been affected by blast and heat. Up to a radius of about 600 metres, about 200 metres beyond the outer radius of the intense heat, the radiation effect would disable tank crews within minutes, and they would die of the radiation effects within 6 days, unless they were within the 400 metre radius of the intense heat effect and had received third-degree burns. Up to the 1,400 metre outer radius of the radiation effect, victims would be disabled by radiation sickness within hours and would die within several weeks.

Because of the reduced blast and heat effects the neutron warhead had the tactical advantage of causing little collateral damage to the surrounding built-up areas, though the intense radiation would seriously affect the ecology of the target area.

The collateral damage of micronuclear devices, with an energy yield below 0.1 KT or less, was equally small, without the hazard, to the side that launched the warhead, of the relatively very wide radius of effect of the enhanced radiation of the 0.1 KT neutron weapon.

SUNDAY

0030 Hours Central European Time

Western Europe

Throughout the evening and early night the Spearhead and Support Groups and the Assault Regiments had been uncannily efficient in picking just the right tactical and technical targets to hit to ensure the maximum dislocation of communications and defence and governmental systems. Telephone switchboards had been sabotaged without trace of the actual damage and in such a way that it had appeared that faults could be blamed, without any suspicion of sabotage. The duty staff in Government Departments had, with only one or two exceptions, been accurately found and killed. Police stations, where reports of untoward incidents might have been received and acted on, had been either eliminated or isolated. In barracks, headquarters and airbases, in the big supply and ammunition dumps, at repair depots, early warning sites and at the offices of security forces and counter-intelligence staff, just enough had been done to ensure that the alarm was not spread early, and that, when it was, action would be difficult to organize.

The fact that it was a Sunday evening and the eve of the Christmas holiday had meant that the key sites were additionally vulnerable. The staff in most places had been reduced to a minimum, was less alert because of the impending holiday and felt more free to find distraction in the special TV programmes. That it was winter and not the accepted traditional invasion time of spring, before the harvests had been gathered, or autumn, when they had been conveniently collected for the invaders' benefit, was an additional reason for some complacency and a lack of the keen edge of alertness which could alone have prevented the widespread success of the sabotage squads. The widespread strikes and go-slows added to the muddle.

Over a period of many years the espionage efforts of the Soviet Union and of the whole Eastern bloc had been ruthlessly and relentlessly probing for NATO's secrets. There had been the notorious early post-war cases of Soviet agents in the United States, Canada and the United Kingdom passing vital information on nuclear weapons. There had been the equally notorious cases in the United Kingdom of Philby, Burgess, Maclean, Blunt and unidentified others, all high-ranking staff of the Foreign Office, who had been Soviet agents since before the Second World War. There had been other cases across Europe of Soviet agents or sympathizers, intent on gaining secrets for the Soviet Union on every aspect of the defence of Western Europe. It had been a determined, detailed, deadly campaign, a secret, stealthy, sinister intelligence-gathering war.

An endless succession of captures of Soviet agents over many years had culminated in the sensational scandal that Günther Guillaume, personal adviser to Herr Willi Brandt, the then West German Chancellor, was an East German agent and had had access to the most secret state papers for years.

Vital West German and NATO military secrets had been passed to East Germany and the Soviet Union. Over one thousand top secret documents had been photocopied in Bonn in West Germany and smuggled to East Berlin. The documents gave the Warsaw Pact High Command detailed information about the plans and equipment of the West German armed forces, and also their knowledge of the Warsaw Pact armed forces.

A significant proportion of the documents dealt with NATO war plans, logistic arrangements and equipment deployment. Among the documents were guidelines for West Germany's defence policy for the coming years; plans for the Bundeswehr; evaluations by the Bundeswehr of its own strength, combat readiness and failings; details of its structure, personnel, equipment and infra-structure; plans for crises, civil emergencies and stand-by situations; arrangements for mobilization and for dealing with movements of refugees; as well as requirements for future weapons.

Later a West German married couple were found to have been spying for Eastern Europe while living under assumed names in Holland, close to the headquarters of Allied Forces Central Europe at Brunssum.

In Paris, Serge Fabiew, the son of a Russian migrant on trial for spying for the Soviet Union for ten years, told how he had been recruited by a Soviet diplomat in Paris. He and accomplices had operated an espionage network that had passed on information about radar, computers and missiles to the Soviet Union.

Almost continuously, there had been a Soviet rescue tug at anchor within 20 miles of the Shetlands. For approximately eight months of each year there had been an Intelligence Collector ship (AGI) off the Clyde Approaches. In addition and sometimes simultaneously, a second AGI spent a total of some three months a year on station off the east coast or, less frequently, the south coast of England.

In Vienna, in the two important United Nations organizations — the International Atomic Energy Agency and the International Development Organization — and in the Soviet Mission, there had been over a hundred Russians, of whom some forty were known members of either the KGB or officials co-opted to help the KGB.

The Federal Bureau of Investigation, in a 'classic spy case', had seized three Russians from the United Nations in New York in the act of collecting secrets concerning the United States Navy submarine warfare projects.

And these were only some of the world-wide activities of the Warsaw Pact nations used to acquire the intelligence information on which to plan their attacks on the West.

MONDAY

Southern England

Major Dickie Dickenson of the Special Air Service Regiment had been on a special assignment, for ten days before the Christmas holiday, with the Italian security police in Turin in North Italy. He had taken with him details of the techniques and equipment which had been so successfully employed against the PLO terrorists at Mogadishu in Somalia. His return which should have been on the Saturday before Christmas had been delayed for more than twenty four hours, because of fog at Turin Airport. Amid the holiday traffic and in view of the shortage of staff at London Airport because of the holiday, he had had further delays getting through customs and security, because of the sensitive nature of his luggage. He was due to go away from the battalion for the Christmas holiday, but could not take with him the top secret documents and equipment, which had to be locked up in the special vaults at the barracks when not in use.

He drove the car into the barrack gates, showing his identity card and special pass to the sentry on duty, and parked his car outside the officers' quarters, where, as a bachelor, he had a bedroom, sitting-room and bathroom. It was not long after midnight, so he felt sure that there would be other officers still up and about, even if it was only the duty officer who would have to be awake and alert. It was the duty officer he wanted to see in any case, to get from him the key to the vaults.

He dumped his cases in his room and went in search of the duty officer and any other who might be awake. After being away for a time he did not know who the duty officer might be or even who the duty stand-by company commander would be. One complete company was always on alert, all the officers, NCOs and men being confined to the barracks for their whole tour of duty.

It was a question of looking quietly into each officer's room. In each he found either that the room was empty or that the

192

occupant was warmly tucked into bed. Unwilling to disturb any of them, and certain that the duty company commander and duty officer must both be in the battalion headquarters building, he made his way there. On the route he passed a half-lit barrack block, the lights at the doors and on the landings still on, for the duty company to be found and alerted quickly in case of emergency. Hoping that he might find someone awake, who could tell him which officers were on duty, he tiptoed his way to each room, to find the occupant in each case sound asleep. It was only after he had nearly completed his tour of the building that he realized that there was a deadly quiet. It came to him that he had not heard deep breathing, nor snores, nor snorts, nor even the noise of a sleeper turning in his bed.

In the next room, he peered more closely at the man in the bed. He bent down and could hear no sound of breathing. He prodded the man and got no reaction. He pulled the bed clothes back and found that the man was fully clothed, but dead. He went quickly back to the other rooms nearby, and found that each man was dead, and convulsed and contorted in death.

'My God,' he said to himself. 'What on earth has happened here?'

His one thought then was to get to the battalion headquarters building, find the duty officer or duty sergeant, and report the tragedy as soon as possible. He pushed his way in through the double doors of the headquarters, where he saw a man standing in the doorway of the clerk's office.

'Do you know what's happened to the duty company?' he asked. 'Has it been reported?'

'Yes,' said the man. 'I do know what's happened — and it's going to happen to you too.'

As he spoke he raised his right arm to point his nerve gas pen at Major Dickenson, who got the full force of the burst of gas at a range of only four feet.

MONDAY

0100 Hours Central European Time

West Germany

Whereas the alert and warning systems against the chance of strategic nuclear ballistic missile attack were sophisticated, as they had to be, expensive, highly tuned and at a constant state of readiness to trigger retaliation, the alert systems and procedures to guard against assassination and sabotage by small terrorist squads and against conventional land attack were in comparison elementary and not highly vigilant. The concept that no warning could be expected of strategic nuclear ballistic missile attack had not been applied to conventional ground forces or the areas behind the front lines. Instead the accepted philosophy had been that, with conventional ground forces on both sides, there would be an adequate period of warning in which to mobilize, reinforce and bring the alert and alarm systems up to a state of vigilance.

So, with just a few insignificant exceptions, the Pact Forces met with no resistance, because there were no units or security forces which were required to be at the level of preparedness which would have at least given a warning. Even that would have been of little value, because the mobilization procedures of the infantry and tank battalions, which would have formed the first line of defence, envisaged that there would be hours available before the enemy could be expected to have penetrated far enough to be able to attack.

Nevertheless there were some setbacks to the Pact's progress. At the Mannheim bridge over the River Rhine, which Pact Forces were crossing at 0100 hours, the driver of a very large and heavy earth-moving vehicle, which the German Police had insisted could only use the main roads after midnight, refused to stop when ordered to do so by the soldier who barred his way. He was an alert Army reservist who quickly recognized the Soviet Army uniform. Keeping his foot hard down on the accelerator pedal, he continued across the main bridge. The huge excavating blade swept three motor-cyclists over the rails into the swirling river below, pushed an armoured car back on

194

top of the following combat vehicle, which itself, slewing side-ways and taking the bridge balustrade with it, fell on to the river bank below, bursting into flames as it hit the rocks. The crew, trying to jump clear, were either killed as they hit the rocks or were burnt alive in the flames. Continuing its progress on the east bank of the river, the machine impacted three personnel-carrying vehicles, one into another, so that all three were wrecked, forming an impenetrable barrier of tangled metal across the road. One of the Russian crew members managing to escape from the wreckage, shot the German tractor driver before he could extricate the blade from the pile of metal. Using the earth-moving machine to clear away the obstacle, the Soviet troops soon had the road clear, but more than thirty minutes' delay had been caused.

In the steeper valleys south of Frankfurt, an armoured personnel vehicle went out of control on a steep hill and ran, at speed, into the vertical stone quarry face at the side of the road. There was a delay in the vehicle column, which was forced to pull to the road side to allow ambulances to drive forward to tend the injured crew.

In Bonn, some members of the GSG9 unit, off duty but alert in case of need, became aware of the increase of traffic during the night, dressed and went out to investigate. With their light weapons they were able to eliminate some half a dozen Soviet motor-cyclists, succeeded in killing the complete crew of two SAM9 carrying vehicles, but were eventually mown down by the machine-gun of a Soviet armoured car.

The major setbacks were caused by the sheer inefficiency of the map reading of many of the Soviet Army junior officers and senior non-commissioned officers. Bewildered by the multitude of major and minor roads, nearly all of a considerably higher standard than those in Eastern Europe, blinded by the excellence and brilliance of the street lighting, to which they were totally unaccustomed, bedazzled by the obvious richness of the villages, towns and cities through which they passed or nearby which they skirted, they frequently lost their way, and only made up the distance lost by travelling during the periods of supposed rest and repair.

By the early hours of Monday morning, the Pact Forces had already achieved a total breakthrough beyond the intended defence lines on the Rivers Leine, Aller and Weser in the north and in the steep valleys of the south, but also, further west, well past the battalions, regiments and divisions, which were to have moved to the defence lines, and even further west to overrun the main headquarters which were to command and control the forward divisions in battle.

SUNDAY

2400 Hours Greenwich Mean Time
0100 Hours Central European Time

United Kingdom

In many households throughout the United Kingdom there were individuals and families still awake and listening to the late radio programmes before going to bed. There were others, working on early shifts, who had been to bed and were rousing themselves to go to work.

Suddenly the blaring pop music faded, the set was silent for a few moments, then the sound came back. A strange news announcer was heard, sounding startled and a little afraid.

'This is the BBC. Here is a newsflash we have just received. There is no confirmation as yet of the details. It appears that armoured forces have been moving across West Germany. They have already reached the Rhine north and south of Bonn. We have been experiencing considerable difficulty in contacting any of our correspondents on the continent. As I said before, there is no . . .' The voice was abruptly cut off and the sound discontinued. Moments later the same announcer was heard saying. 'The following should be noted very carefully by all listeners. A curfew has been declared in all areas of the United Kingdom. No one will go on to the streets. Anyone doing so is liable to be shot. Anyone seen at open doors or open windows is also liable to be shot. There will be a further communiqué later. That is all.'

Bewildered listeners turned to each other, or if alone sat stunned, staring at the silent set.

SUNDAY & MONDAY

2000 Hours Eastern Standard Time
0200 Hours Central European Time

The Pentagon, Washington, USA

During a brief pause from their duties in the Pentagon Communications Centre a group of officers analysed the tragic insufficiency of NATO's response to the Warsaw Pact invasion.

'You said that you thought that the NATO forces could have prepared an impenetrable defence if we had wholeheartedly adopted micronuclear weapons and had equally wholeheartedly adapted our organization and military philosophy. What did you mean?' one Colonel asked.

The Brigadier leant forward onto the table, cupped his hands round a mug of coffee and said, 'Yes, in essence I think that NATO should have built a defended zone, stretching back about 100 kilometres from the frontier with East Germany and Czechoslovakia. Inside this defended zone we should have laid out what I call a 'minefield pattern' of defence — in diagrammatic form looking like a giant cheeseboard. On each black square we should have built a minor bunker to house underground, with underground access tunnels in all directions, and a force of not more than about company strength. We should have learnt the details of the techniques from the North Koreans and the North Vietnamese — you know what I mean?'

The Colonel answered promptly, 'Your parallel with a minefield means that you see the layout as being a deep defended zone, like a minefield, with each bunker being like a mine in a minefield. Presumably round the bunkers there would be real minefields?'

The Brigadier hesitated for a moment and then said, 'Yes, a few perhaps, but the real defence of each bunker would be the micronuclear weapons launched from other bunkers against the attackers. An important point about such a defended zone is that it would be manned not only in a period of emergency, but as normal long-term peace-time dispositions, so there couldn't be many minefields. It must be permanently manned to prevent the possibility of what is happening tonight. Any NATO plan

197

that involves moves, let alone long moves, of fighting units from their peace-time barracks to their battle positions is bound to be running the risk of just such a surprise attack as we are hearing about now. We should have planned on having no warning time. The underground bunkers would not need to be the elaborate concrete fortifications of the Maginot or Siegfried lines, or of the German Atlantic Wall. The bunkers would need to be well hidden. If the job was done properly, using camouflage and deception, such a defended zone of bunkers could be built in such a way that it would be almost impossible to be detected from the air. Look what the North Koreans and the North Vietnamese did. They could do it, so surely NATO could be as efficient.'

A second Colonel broke in to say, 'You are not suggesting that the bunkers should be able to withstand a heavy attack? You visualize the bunkers as being a very extended pattern of watching and listening posts, which defend themselves against minor attacks, but which would be defended against major attacks by the firing of micronuclear weapons from other bunkers nearby. In fact you would see a whole series of observation posts acting also as missile launching sites?'

'Yes, that's right,' the Brigadier said. 'It sounds simple enough, and, at first sight, it might seem to be an over-simplification, but just think how you would plan to attack such a defended zone. First — the NATO forward defence line — except that there would be no line as such in this plan — would be right up to the Iron Curtain. Any move across the border could be detected immediately and obliterated promptly. Second — if a Pact attack was to penetrate a few kilometres — the attack commander would not know what his next objective should be, and if any Pact Forces get obliterated other Pact Forces would not know from where the fire was being directed. Third — the NATO forces would not need to expose themselves at all to any form of attack, and, by varying the position from which our micronuclear weapons were being launched, could make it very difficult to locate the bunkers. And fourth — and I think we must accept that the Warsaw Pact could hardly raise valid objections — we could aim at targets, east of the Iron Curtain, up to the same distance as that to which any Pact Forces had advanced — what I have thought of to myself as

198

being a reciprocal targeting area. And fifth — to elaborate that point further, once NATO adopted micronuclear weapons to arm its frontline troops, it would not need to attack any targets beyond the reciprocal targeting area, and could use the maximum propaganda to stress the fact. If you think about it, the targets deep behind a battle-front have to be attacked when only conventional weapons were in use, because at the frontline the attacking forces cannot be killed quickly enough in sufficient numbers. Against micronuclear weapons — the more forces attacking the more would be killed.'

'How would you expect the Warsaw Pact to have attacked such a defended zone, if NATO had prepared it in time?' the first Colonel asked.

'I don't see how it could be attacked successfully,' the Brigadier replied. 'Surprise would be almost impossible to achieve. A nuclear barrage ahead of the attacking forces would have to cover such a huge area of ground to be sure of hitting the defences, that a thermonuclear intercontinental war would be bound to follow. Besides they would be left with a desert to occupy, and what would be the point of that? And the fall-out which might be carried east might have terrible consequences on the Soviet Union. No — I am sure that once NATO adopted micronuclear weapons and adapted its defence strategy to something like the pattern I suggest, the Soviet and Warsaw Pact conventional forces would be seen to be what they are — a relic of the past, no longer capable of invading, conquering and occupying NATO's territory.'

'I assume the soldiers in each bunker,' the second Colonel said, 'would only do a short tour of duty in such conditions.'

'Exactly,' the Brigadier said. 'The troops for each bunker would serve a duty period in the bunker. They would have barracks and family quarters, but, for a period each year, each unit would be at full alert battle stations in the bunkers of the defended area. When not on a tour of duty in the forward bunkers, they would be in their barracks ready to occupy bunkers further to the rear. Such a defence layout would be difficult, if not impossible, to attack successfully.'

MONDAY

The Kremlin, Moscow, Russia

The President of the Soviet Union had ordered that at 0700 hours Moscow Time, the Defence Council was to be briefed on the progress of the Pact Forces throughout Western Europe. Moscow Time being two hours ahead of Central European Time, it had only been possible to give the position as it was about 2½ hours prior to first light in Western Europe. It would however serve the useful purpose of enabling the Defence Council to decide whether there were any urgent amendments which needed to be made to the original plans.

Standing before a vast wall map, the Chief of Staff first explained that he would deal with the theatres of operations from north to south, taking Norway first. He further explained he would first give the up-to-the-minute position at the time he started to speak, and that, when he had finished with all the theatres, he would go back to give any later information which might have been received in the meantime.

'In the far north,' the General started, 'Kirkenes and the Varanger Halvoya, with the radar and early warning installations are now held by Pact Forces. The North Cape and Lakselv, Hammerfest and Alta have been taken, and so has Tromsö further west.

'In South Norway, Oslo and Bergen have been captured. In Denmark, Pact Forces advancing up the east coast of Jutland reached the Skaw, at the north tip, by 0430 hours this morning. On the west coast of Jutland, Holstebro has been entered. Other Pact Forces on this front are already crossing into Fünen Island.

'In Germany and further west, all objectives have been reached within the last hour and some of them as much as an hour earlier.

'Pact Forces have just entered The Hague in Holland. Rotterdam and Amsterdam were captured one hour earlier. In the south of Holland, Tilburg has been captured. The route has

200

therefore been opened to Walcheren. Turnhout in Belgium has been entered by reconnaissance forces on the way to Antwerp. Brussels has just been taken. The NATO supreme Headquarters at Mons has been captured intact. Pact Forces have already moved south and captured Sedan in France. Luxemburg was taken two hours ago. Longuyon, in France, has been taken within the last few minutes. Metz, Sarreguemines, the French salient west of Karlsruhe, Strasbourg and Mulhouse, all in France, have been entered within the last hour, with no opposition at all.

'The operations in North Italy, North Greece and North Turkey have all gone according to plan.

'All reports are not yet available. But from those we have already received it is clear that all NATO tank battalions have been put out of action. First reports from the Prisoner Guard Organization show that very large numbers of prisoners have already been taken.

'The NATO forward airfields have all been overrun.

'The Soviet Navy in North Norway, and in the Baltic, will be in position by dawn to enter the ports which have already been seized.

'This situation has yet to be confirmed by first light reconnaissance reports. These and other details will be given to the Supreme Council at the meeting, already arranged at midday today.'

The Defence Council dispersed, very satisfied.

MONDAY

0800 Hours Central European Time

Western Europe

As dawn broke over West Germany, the duty aircrew and civilian staff of the NATO air forces, who had not already been taken prisoner by the Soviet Spearhead Groups and Assault Regiments, started to report for duty. At all the Allied air bases, the guards and control tower staff had been killed. Technicians and aircrew, who had reported before first light to

201

prepare the first light sorties, had been killed or captured as they arrived at the airbases. During the night, senior air staff officers had been killed at their duty posts. Others with their families, off duty in family quarters near the bases, had either been killed or been taken prisoner. From air bases, such as that of the British Second Tactical Airforce, at Gütersloh near Bielefeld, the whole military and civil communities had been captured during the night, herded into trucks and buses, and driven to the prison camps. The barracks and houses were empty except for bodies.

Situated at about 200 kilometres from the Iron Curtain NATO airbases such as Gütersloh had been overrun well before midnight. North and south, at about the same distance from the frontier, West German Airforce airbases had met the same end. In Southern Germany the West German and American bases, located far enough east to enable the aircraft to give early support to the ground forces, had also been overrun early in the night.

At all the NATO airfields, the Pact Forces had made no attempt to destroy or sabotage the aircraft. By capturing the main gates, the guard rooms and the control towers, they had achieved their aim of preventing crews and technical ground staff from reaching the parked aircraft in their hardened shelters. By seizing the main ammunition bunkers, they had not only prevented the possibility of any isolated aircraft being armed and made ready for take-off, but had also blocked the chance of an effective counter attack, because none of the allied personnel could obtain ammunition even for their personal weapons, pistols, rifles and machine-guns. The airbase fuel tanks had been special objectives of the Pact Forces which had clear orders to seize all aviation fuel. They had also been given the specific task of ensuring that all runways were free of obstruction, and the landing lights undamaged and ready to be operated.

As the thin winter dawn light spread over the countryside from the east, it revealed nothing that would have immediately indicated that Pact Forces had passed, during the night, across the landscape. Travelling east, along the main routes on which, in the darkness, these forces had made their unhindered progress to the west, were the long lines of NATO military trucks and German civilian transport, carrying the prisoners into East Germany.

Further west, where the Pact Forces had reached their objectives, the signs were few and far between. Wherever possible, to guard against air attack from NATO aircraft flying from bases in the United Kingdom, which might not have been so completely neutralized as those on the continent, Pact combat vehicles had been carefully parked where they could be hidden or close against buildings.

Soon after, Pact combat aircraft came in to land at the NATO airfields close to the Rhine in West Germany and in Belgium and Holland. Uprated MiG 21s, MiG 23s and MiG27s, which had taken off from their airfields in East Germany and Poland, where dawn had been an hour earlier, landed and promptly moved to the positions on the airfields, where refuelling tankers had been drawn up in readiness.

MONDAY

0800 Hours Greenwich Mean Time
0900 Hours Central European Time

United Kingdom

At 0800 hours on the Monday morning, the majority of the population of the United Kingdom were still unaware of the emergency about which only some had heard the bare mention on the radio in the early hours of the morning. Some of the emergency authorities had attempted to take the action laid down for them, but most action was fragmented and useless in the face of the widespread strikes which had immobilized the country.

At the airforce bases which had been hit by Pact spearhead or Support Groups, the vital communications and flight control systems had been put out of action. Where attempts were being made by aircrew and ground staff to get some fighters airborne to discover whether the United Kingdom was threatened, all but a few were cancelled as it was impossible to make contact with the headquarters controlling operations, which had themselves been blacked out.

By midday some small groups of fighters had flown sorties from airfields on the east coast of England, north of the Wash, and from Scotland. These sorties had returned to base when no enemy activity had been sighted.

MONDAY

1000 Hours Central European Time

Mainland Europe

The NATO captives who were among the first to be taken prisoner were packed tightly into all the vehicles that could be commandeered for the task of taking them east.

In all stages of dress and undress, without seats or proper protection from the cold of the winter night and the hardly less cold day, the packed trucks were driven without stops to the nearest railway sidings behind the Iron Curtain. In certain marshalling yards stood long lines of red cattle trucks which had been moved in during the night and early morning to carry the NATO prisoners to new prison camps, specially prepared close to the major cities and strategic areas. The cattle trucks had been assembled straight from carrying earlier loads. They were uncleaned from a mixture of cattle urine and dung, coal, lime or fertilizers. They were not fitted with seats or even benches. They had no means of providing warmth for the passengers. The cracks in the woodwork of the sides and floors did not exclude draughts. The small apertures which allowed some fresh air and light into the interiors were only blocked by metal bars.

The NATO prisoners were brutally herded and harried into the cattle trucks. Children were separated from brothers and sisters, husbands from wives, and wives from screaming, hysterical children, who saw the whole fabric of a happy family life being torn away from them. The urgency of the whole process was two-fold — to load the trucks as quickly as possible and to pack them with as many human bodies as possible. In the crush young children were suffocated, their dead bodies held erect by

204

the pressure of the bodies surrounding them. Women and children had limbs broken by the weight of other bodies pushing them against the flat wooden walls, or, more often, against the interior wooden uprights of the frames of the trucks.

There were no lights in the cattle trucks and the noise made by the ancient wheels, mingled with the clanking of the towing links and hooks, and the metallic clanging of the buffers, as the trucks jerked forward or suddenly stopped, prevented any conversation. There was no food or water to relieve the thirst caused by terror, or the growing gnawing pangs of hunger, particularly of the younger children, who had eaten many hours previously.

Occasionally, through the night, the prisoners were aware that the train was stationary in a siding near a town or village. On one or two occasions, those near the apertures could see the lights of station platforms. In desperation, they had yelled in unison for water and food and to be given the chance to breathe fresh air, but the stop was only temporary and there was no answer to the calls.

By mid morning on Monday the surviving prisoners were in very poor shape. Those who had been captured before midnight had had a truck journey of four or five hours before they had been put on the trains. The journey had been slow and tedious, the age of the rolling stock precluding any speeds above about 50 kilometres per hour. The total journey from the Iron Curtain to the first railyards inside Russia was a distance of about 900 kilometres. It was not to be until about midnight on the Monday that the first train loads would reach Russia.

Throughout Western Europe, Monday was a day of confusion and mounting terror. With the media silent or under the control of Soviet agents, with the heads of state and governments and key officials taken prisoner, with the tight clamp of a total curfew on all the areas occupied by the Warsaw Pact forces or their agents, the populations were dazed with the disaster, unable to make, or even plan, any moves against the enemy.

In the remoter areas of the countryside, away from the key targets, the populations were bewildered, powerless to discover the full extent of what had happened to each of their countries and not daring to travel outside their immediate vicinities to try to find out more details. In some parts of all the countries, there were even small pockets of inhabitants who were still totally unaware that anything untoward had occurred.

MONDAY

1200 Hours Moscow Time
1000 Hours Central European Time

The Kremlin, Moscow, Russia

The President of the Soviet Union took his place at the rostrum to address the Council of Ministers gathered to be informed of the operations against the countries of the North Atlantic Alliance. Adjusting his papers carefully he said, 'Comrades, the Council has been summoned to be given further information about operations against the imperialist powers of the West. Yesterday you were told about certain of the preparations. Today you will be told of the wide-scale success of the Warsaw Pact.

'The success has been due to a number of factors — the scope of the activities to weaken the enemy, the geographical extent of our attacks, the time of year and the time of day for the attacks to start, the scale of the forces deployed, the speed and momentum of the attacks, and finally, but by no means least, the determination of the Warsaw Pact Forces.

'You have already heard of the scale of the efforts of our secret forces to acquire secrets, to subvert or convert individuals, to sabotage plans and installations, to kill or capture key officials and so on. These activities, combined with those of the armed forces have contributed greatly to the success.

'You will be given details of the geographical extent of our attacks — from the North Cape of Norway to the shores of the Black Sea — from the Atlantic islands to the Mediterranean islands.

'We have surprised the enemy by attacking, as we have done before, at this time of year when the Western Imperialists are less alert. And we attacked during the night, which was also a factor in achieving surprise.

'The Chief of Staff will now tell you of the scale of the armed

206

forces deployed and how the speed and momentum of the attacks was achieved.'

The President moved back to his seat, as the Marshal rose, moved to the rostrum, laid his notes out before him and said, 'I will deal with the detailed allocation to the various fronts.

'The Norwegian Front was allotted one airborne division, two motor-rifle divisions, three Naval infantry regiments and all the available ships of the Soviet Northern Fleets and their supporting naval aircraft.

'To the operations into Denmark we allotted one airborne division, three motor-rifle divisions, one tank division, one naval infantry regiment, and all the ships of the Soviet Baltic Fleet and two tactical air armies.

'An amphibious operation against the Danish island of Bornholm will be carried out by Polish forces, separate from the attack on Denmark itself.

'For the operations on the North Central Front in West Germany between Hamburg in the north and Göttingen in the south, we allotted seventeen motor-rifle divisions, eleven being Soviet, three East German and three Polish, and fifteen tank divisions, ten Soviet, one East German and four Polish. East German forces under separate command of the Commander-in-Chief of the East German Army occupied the Western Sectors of Berlin.

'The South Central Front in West Germany, Göttingen in the north to the Austrian border in the south, was allotted twenty-two Soviet motor-rifle divisions and two Czechoslovakian motor-rifle divisions, and twenty Soviet tank divisions and two Czechoslovakian tank divisions. The major concentration of NATO divisions was in this sector, including all the United States divisions. The Central Fronts have been allotted eight Tactical Air Armies.

'The Southern Front, covering North Italy, North Greece and North Turkey, was allotted divisions as follows: to the North Italian front two Soviet and two Hungarian motor-rifle divisions and two Soviet tank divisions; to the North Greek front two Soviet and four Bulgarian motor-rifle divisions and two Soviet and one Bulgarian tank divisions: to the North Turkish front four Soviet and two Rumanian motor-rifle divisions and one Soviet and one Rumanian tank division.

'Six Airborne divisions are allotted to the United Kingdom Front.

'Completing their mobilization now, we have twenty-two divisions in the Leningrad, Baltic, Byelorussian and Kiev Military Districts, six divisions in the Volga and Ural Military Districts and ten divisions in the North Caucasus and Trans-caucasus Military Districts. In all there are therefore thirty-eight Soviet divisions in reserve available to support operations in Europe. We still have five divisions in Afghanistan. There are four Tactical Air Armies in reserve.

'On the Front with China, we have retained the forces there at full strength, that is, forty divisions in the Central Asian, Siberian, Transbaikal and Far East Military Districts, and three divisions in Mongolia. This force is backed by four Tactical Air Armies and nuclear weapons. It is improbable therefore that the Chinese will launch any sort of attack.

'Including eight airborne divisions, four Naval Infantry Regiments and eight assault regiments — a total of about one hundred and twenty-five divisions have or will have attacked the North Atlantic Alliance.

'The helicopters of the Air Transport Force were allotted initially to the Norway, Denmark and Central Fronts. In operations following the first stage, the whole of the Air Transport Force will be allotted to support six airborne divisions to be landed in Britain and two airborne divisions after their first operations in Norway and Denmark to be landed in Eire.

'The operations of the Warsaw Pact Forces, land, sea and air, were combined and closely co-ordinated as you have already been told, with the operations of the International Terrorists, our own deep penetration Spearhead Groups and the Support Groups of urban guerrillas in each of the Western countries.

'There have also been other offensive actions aiding the operations in various ways, sometimes merely by hindering the enemy's operations.

'The Strategic Rocket Force, the Long-Range Air Force and the Air Defence Force, have been allotted tasks to support the mainland and sea operations.

'Now to deal with Northern Europe in more detail. First the Norwegian Front.

'This Front was allotted the Soviet First Airborne Division

to land on Oslo and Bergen, after the Soviet Second Airborne Division had first taken Copenhagen. It was also given first call on the 2,500 Soviet helicopters earmarked for operations in North Europe.

'To ensure early capture of the NATO strategic radar and early warning systems, three Navy Infantry Regiments, carried in helicopters, attacked the Varanger Halvoya Peninsula, the Mageroya Island including the North Cape, and Tromsö including the airfield.

'While these operations took place, a motor-rifle regiment crossed the frontier at three places just north and west of Pechenga to capture Kirkenes, with its airfield.

'The Navy Infantry Regiment on the Varanger Peninsular was replaced by units of the Air Defence Force and Coastal Artillery, backed by KGB border troops and MVD security forces and will take Narvik and Harstad during this afternoon.

'The Navy Infantry Regiment on Mageroya Island is being replaced by a motor-rifle regiment, which by moving well south from Nikel on the Norwegian border, crossed into Finland near Virtaniemi. It skirted the great frozen Inari Lake, crossed into Norway and joined up with the Navy Infantry on Barak and Bukta airfields. From its point of departure at 1730 hours yesterday this motor-rifle regiment had about 300 kilometres to travel. To ensure that the Navy Infantry were replaced on time to enable them to be landed on Bodö this afternoon, a proportion of the infantry of the motor-rifle regiment, normally carried in armoured personnel carriers, was lifted by helicopters ahead of the rest of the regiment.

'Meanwhile another motor-rifle regiment, having crossed into Finland much further south onto the new strategic east—west roads which were completed last summer, has reached Tromsö. Again, as the distances were long and it was essential to replace the Navy Infantry there as soon as possible, a proportion of this motor-rifle regiment was lifted by helicopter. The Navy Infantry Regiment will capture Namsos this afternoon.

'Two motor-rifle regiments moved west from the Leningrad—Murmansk railway, about 200 kilometres south of Murmansk, crossed into Finland onto the main route which the Soviet Union improved for the Finns during these last few summers, to the Gulf of Bothnia, at Kemi, accessible by sea from

South Norway, Denmark and the Baltic.

'By midnight tonight therefore Soviet forces in the North of Norway will have captured all the key installations and ports as far south as Namsos.

'By early this evening ships of the Soviet Navy, with supply and repair ships which have been on exercises in the North Sea, will enter Tromsö and Narvik to replace the Navy Infantry Regiments in both places. Early tomorrow morning these two regiments will take Trondheim, Kristiansund and Alesund.

'That completes the details of the operation from the North, after which we will have occupied all the strategic ports, air-fields and installations as far south as Alesund. Behind our advance round the coast, the Northern Fleet moved out from Murmansk to occupy selected anchorages and bases. With it went the amphibious vessels which will connect the ports and bases, and which will move the supplies to the more isolated, smaller ports needing defence.

'Now for the operations in South Norway. The Soviet Second Airborne Division landed at Copenhagen. A helicopter borne Navy Infantry Regiment landed on North Denmark to secure the sea passage through the Kattegat and the Skagerrak. On the success of these operations against Denmark the First Airborne Division landed at Oslo and Bergen.

'Just before midday when the whole of Denmark had been occupied by the land forces moving north from Germany, the Navy Infantry Regiment in Jutland was flown to occupy Kristiansund and Stavanger in South Norway. As soon as amphibious vessels, which have already sailed from Rügen Island and Stettin, reach North Jutland later this afternoon they will embark one motor-rifle division to be landed at Oslo, to release the First Airborne Division for later operations against Eire. The Second Airborne Division at Copenhagen will also be required for these operations. It has been replaced by a motor-rifle division which advanced north from Schleswig-Holstein.'

The Chief of Staff paused and then commented, 'These operations, and those in Denmark to a lesser extent, are without doubt the most complicated of the whole invasion plan of the Warsaw Pact. The nature of the geography of Norway, the lack of land routes, the extreme shortness of a common frontier, though we have been able to use Finnish territory, all make operations difficult. Of course, the size of the opposition in Norway is not great, and, by achieving surprise, we have been able to forestall the arrival of NATO reinforcements. A very considerable degree of efficiency has been needed to operate at these latitudes in very low temperatures and in semi-darkness for twenty-four hours a day. These operations are vital to the future moves of the Soviet Fleets in the North and in the Baltic. On their successful completion depends the moves of the Soviet Fleets to take Iceland and the Atlantic Islands and so to be able to prevent the arrival of reinforcements from the United States of America.'

After a short break to allow for a change of the wall maps, the Chief of Staff resumed. 'The detailed plans for the operations on the Central Front are contained in the documents which have been circulated to each of you (*see* Appendix A, on page 227).

'You will see that the invading divisions were grouped for command in armies as usual, but that each leading army consisted initially of the motor-rifle divisions advancing on each of the selected routes, with the tank armies following. At later stages of the advance, depending on tactical needs, the divisions were regrouped differently, with the forward divisions, of whichever type, under one army and the divisions further back on the same route under other armies.

'Each army had its own extra troops and units over and above those in the divisions making up the army. Behind the advancing divisions on each route there was therefore a large amount of extra artillery support. Each army commander also had a number of SS-IC 'Scud' nuclear missiles with a range of 295 kilometres. He also had a tank reserve and a large amount of engineer equipment.

'The Front Commander deployed his air armies in advance in co-ordination with the ground forces, to come into action in daylight the following day, if required.

'He had, in addition, longer range nuclear missiles, the Shaddock and Scaleboard, with ranges up to 800 kilometres, as well as, if necessary, a call on the even longer range SS20 multi-warhead missiles sited in the Soviet Union.

'From East Europe into West Germany there were fifteen crossing points in all, including that in the North at Schlutup, where four divisions crossed in their advance to Denmark. The fifteenth crossing point furthest South, the one from Czechoslovakia at Philippsreut, was reserved as an extra route into Italy, on which support and supplies could be moved through Austria to the crossing at Coccau, should the necessity arise.

'You will see from the document you have been given that on the thirteen crossing points between the two I have mentioned, in nearly every case three motor-rifle divisions and three tank divisions advanced.

'From each of the crossing points major traffic routes led north into Denmark, or west through West Germany into Holland, Belgium, Luxemburg and France. The details of the routes are in the document too.

'Each route led to strategic objectives which had to be taken to secure the capture of West Europe. The objectives are also clearly identified in the document as are the deployment areas of the divisions further east on each route.

'You will see that, including the airborne division, there were eight-three divisions involved.'

The Chief of Staff paused briefly to rearrange his papers, and then continued, 'You have already heard how, in the operations in Norway and Denmark, speed was achieved by the use of airborne and helicopter borne forces. The Pact High Command considered very carefully how speed could be achieved in the mainland advance, particularly on the Central Front.

'The Pact High Command took certain calculated steps, all aimed at achieving a conquest of Western Europe with the least possible delay and damage, which might be caused by the need to fight the NATO armed forces.

'The High Command decided on a winter offensive both because it would be more unexpected and because the long hours of darkness would cover the moves of the invasion forces, causing the maximum possible confusion among the NATO allies which would enable the Pact forces to move at their best speed. A winter offensive had the added advantage that the build-up of divisions close to the frontier could be carried out during long hours of darkness, so that by daylight, men and vehicles could be hidden.

'Surprise was achieved by the actions of the Special, Spearhead and Support Groups throughout the NATO countries, and

212

by the very swift advance — averaging 70 kilometres per hour — of the Assault Regiments ahead of the divisions.

'The High Command decided that it would aim to achieve the highest possible speed of advance by the main forces so that by dawn today they would be as far west as possible, astride or beyond the strategic obstacles of the Rhine and the Meuse.

'The High Command therefore decided that, since the heavy tanks were the elements in the land forces which had the slowest speed, these tanks should not lead the advance, but would follow to arrive in time to fight the tank against tank battles, which, if they took place at all, would not occur until after dawn. This decision also had the advantage that, since there was no preliminary movement by any of the tank units, the deception about the intended invasion could be more complete. NATO was likely to assume that without moves by the tank battalions, no invasion was impending.

'The motor-rifle divisions were therefore stepped forward up to the Iron Curtain, without their heavy tank battalions. The speed of advance laid down for the light tanks, the lighter tracked vehicles and the wheeled vehicles, was 50 kilometres an hour, with a gap between vehicles of 40 metres and a rest period of fifteen minutes after every two hours of driving. It therefore took each motor-rifle division almost exactly one hour to pass any given point on the route of advance. Or to put it another way, during the advance, there was one Pact division on about every 50 kilometres on each route.'

'Travelling at an average speed of 30 kilometres an hour, instead of the 50 kilometres an hour of the more lightly equipped units, the tank battalions stationed closest to the Iron Curtain crossed into West Germany between three and four hours after starting.

'For instance, at the Helmstedt crossing, four motor-rifle divisions advanced on the autobahn route, followed by three tank divisions. The last vehicles of the fourth motor-rifle division passed the frontier post at about 2200 hours, four and a half hours after the first vehicle of the first division had started the invasion. Close behind the last vehicles were the leading tanks of the tank battalions of all four motor-rifle divisions. Travelling at the slower speed of 30 kilometres an hour, the thirteen hundred tanks and support vehicles took about four hours to reach the West German frontier post from their barracks in East Germany and Poland. They then took about an hour and forty-five minutes to cross into West Germany, following the motor-rifle divisions ahead of them. Allowing for the rest periods of both the motor-rifle divisions and of their tank battalions behind, four complete motor-rifle divisions moved into West Germany on just this one of the routes available.

'From barracks even further east in East Germany and on the western borders of Poland, other divisions started to move west at 1600 hours as soon as it was dark. With a travelling time, including stops, of about twelve hours, the leading tanks of the tank divisions reached the Iron Curtain at about 0500 hours and were about 50 kilometres inside West Germany by first light at 0730 hours.

'To give you some idea of the speed of the invasion as a whole I will give you, to use as a yardstick, the rate of progress of the leading division on this autobahn. In the first hour from 1730 to 1830 hours it reached the crossing over the Rivers Oker and Fuhse north west of Braunschweig; in the second hour to 1930 hours — the Langenhagen Airport north of Hanover, and the crossing over the River Leine west of Hanover, after a fifteen minute halt, in the third hour from 1945 to 2045 hours — the crossing of the River Weser north of Rinteln; in the fourth hour to 2145 hours, west of Ubbedissen, passing on the way, the next crossing of the River Weser just east of Bad Oeynhausen; after a further fifteen minute halt, in the fifth hour to 2300 hours — a point just north of Beckum; in the sixth hour to 2400 hours — the northern outskirts of the Ruhr, about 2 kilometres south of Lunen; after another fifteen minute halt, in the following hour and thirty minutes to 0145 hours — the crossing of the River Rhine about 10 kilometres east of Duisburg at a point due south of Hamburg; in the eighth hour to 0245 hours — the crossing of the River Meuse north of Venlo. At that point, with the division stretched out astride the vital strategic crossings over the Rhine and Meuse, all the divisions stopped for an hour to rest, carry out repairs and gather themselves for the final stage of the advance.

'The advance started again at 0345 hours and in the next hour reached Eindhoven in Holland; in the hour, till 0545 hours, the complex of roads around Turnhout in Belgium.

214

There, after a further halt of fifteen minutes, this leading division separated, sending one regiment to the Walcheren Peninsula to secure the north bank of the River Scheldt leading to the port of Antwerp and the two other reigments to the port of Antwerp.

'Meanwhile, from their peace-time barracks well to the east in East Germany and on the western border of Poland, the heavy tanks started their long march at 1730 hours yesterday evening. Ahead of the main battle tanks, starting at 1600 hours when darkness had already fallen, the reconnaissance battalions together with the 5-ton cargo vehicles, had already set off. These lighter vehicles moved at the same speed as the motor-rifle divisions ahead of them — 50 kilometres per hour. At predetermined points on the routes forward, the combined reconnaissance and supply columns were joined by extra numbers of 5-ton cargo vehicles carrying fuel. When they reached these supply points the battle tanks were refuelled. One further refuelling halt just east of the Iron Curtain ensured that the tank divisions crossed into West Germany fully refuelled and ready for battle without a further halt. Behind these leading tanks, other tanks were carried forward on tank transporters.

'The halts after every two hours of march were used to replace the drivers of the tanks, as well as to rest the crews and carry out the essential adjustments or repairs. Spare tank drivers had been trained during the previous months so that each tank had a total of three drivers, enabling each to have a rest from driving of four hours between each turn. This ensured that the tanks were driven into West Germany by drivers who had had some rest in the cargo vehicles travelling in each column, instead of in a cramped corner somewhere in the turret, which would otherwise have been the case.

'Food and hot drinks, provided at the roadside at each refuelling stop, also helped to ensure that the tank crews arrived fit for battle.

'The arrival time at the Iron Curtain, at 0500 hours, had been carefully calculated, so that by first light at 0730 hours sufficient tanks had passed the bottle-necks of the gaps through the Iron Curtain minefields to be able to deploy into open battle formation, to protect the moves and deployment of the tanks behind them.

'The High Command knew that most of the NATO battalions positioned near the border were the tank battalions and that, therefore, if they had not been sabotaged or otherwise delayed or put out of action, the main tank-versus-tank battles would occur soon after dawn, in the NATO area closest to the Iron Curtain.

'In the event, except for one or two isolated small incidents, no tank-versus-tank battles have taken place as the NATO tank battalions had been sabotaged and overrun by the assault forces.'

The Marshal paused and then said, 'I will end by summarizing the general position of the Pact Forces on land in Western Europe.

'First, all the motor-rifle divisions have been joined by their tank battalions. The tank divisions have advanced on to NATO territory. There are therefore about 31,300 tanks of all kinds already on their first objectives, with about 1,300,000 men. To this total of men in the divisions should be added the men of the Navy Infantry Regiments and of the airborne divisions. There are, as well, the Army Headquarters which will move well forward with the divisions. Also the KGB and MVD forces, which are taking over the governing authorities in each country. In all there are about 1,500,000 men of the land, sea and air forces on NATO territory, on the objectives given to them.

'All the NATO airfields, civil and military, have been captured. They are now ringed with SAMs of the motor-rifle divisions. Later we will move units of the Air Defence forward to take over these duties.

'Very large numbers of military and civil prisoners are already on their way back to the designated transit cages. From there they will be taken to the prisoner of war camps. When they reached East Germany and Czechoslovakia, these POWs were transferred from vehicles to specially assembled trains. The trains have carried forward ammunition, fuel and other supplies, which will be loaded on to the captured NATO vehicles carrying the prisoners.

'Aircraft of three Tactical Air Armies have been redeployed to NATO airfields and An-22 and IL-76 long-range freighters have taken in the first of the spare crews and technical staff in support.

'As soon as it was clear that NATO air resistance had been eliminated, medium and heavy helicopters of the Air Transport Force ferried forward to the main civil airports of Belgium and Holland one airborne regiment of each of the six airborne divisions to be landed on England.

'The next phase of operations has already started. This is the essential process of liquidating those elements in the captured countries which are known to be hostile. At the same time, in close co-operation with the Pact embassies in every capital city, Liberation Governments, made up of known sympathizers, are being put in power.'

The Marshal folded his papers and resumed his seat. The President moved to the rostrum and surveyed the audience before saying, 'You should be clear about the ultimate aims of these operations.

'The first aim is to take over those NATO states, or parts of states, which are essential to enable us to dominate the continent of Europe. We planned to capture these strategic areas from Iceland in the north to the small part of Turkey which is in Europe, in the south. We have therefore moved against Iceland, Norway, West Germany, Britain, Denmark, Luxemburg, Holland, Belgium, France, Portugal, Italy, Greece and Turkey.

'The second aim is to take over the neutral states of Austria, Spain, Finland, Sweden, Eire and Switzerland, Jugoslavia and Albania together with all the dependencies of the NATO and neutral states such as the Atlantic islands of Madeira, the Azores, the Canary Islands, and the Mediterranean islands such as the Balearics, Corsica, Sardinia and Crete, and the two remaining neutral islands, Malta and Cyprus.

'It was our intention to move with the least possible warning as far and as fast as necessary to dislocate the enemy's defences, to disarm his forces and to take over the power of government as soon as possible.

'We could not achieve the whole of these aims at once. We have therefore first occupied Iceland, Norway, Denmark, West Germany, Belgium, Holland and Luxemburg in the north, and in the south Austria and the northern provinces of Italy, Greece and Turkey.

'Now that these territories have been secured, since their defence forces are no longer capable of resistance and their

217

governments or the district authorities have been removed, we shall occupy France, Britain and Eire in the north, and Portugal, Spain and the southern provinces of Italy and Greece in the south.

'We will then occupy the Azores, Madeira and the Canary Islands followed by the Mediterranean islands.

'Operations against Austria have been incidental to the attack on North Italy. Operations against Finland, Sweden, Switzerland, Jugoslavia and Albania will be ordered when the rest of the continent of Europe has been secured.'

The President, the Defence Council, the Politburo left the hall to prolonged and thunderous applause.

MONDAY

1500 Hours Greenwich Mean Time
1600 Hours Central European Time

South-east England

In the early afternoon MiG fighters of the Soviet Sixteenth Air Army flew in over the coast of East Anglia at low altitude, swooping across the runways of the British and United States airbases. Behind them, hugging the sea and the land contours, came wave after wave of Soviet helicopters, carrying six airborne regiments, one from each of the airborne divisions allotted to the invasion of the United Kingdom. Some of the helicopters flew on to the civil airports at Stansted, Luton and London and to the Royal Air Force Airfield at Northolt in north-west London.

Behind the helicopters, protected by their own screens of MiG fighters, came aircraft of the Soviet Air Transport Force, and medium and long-range airliners of the Soviet Civil Aeroflot fleet, as well as airliners of a number of European airlines which had been commandeered the previous day, carrying the twelve further airborne regiments of the six Airborne Divisions in the invasion.

By 1600 hours Greenwich Mean Time, six complete Soviet Airborne Divisions had been landed at airfields in a broad arc

218

across the north and east of London. MiG fighters of the Air Armies, after completing their escort duties of the unarmed helicopters and airliners, had landed at the airfields closest to the continent, where already transport aircraft had been flown in with technical support crews and ammunition. Fuel supplies everywhere had been captured intact, as had the control towers and emergency generators.

Before dark further reinforcements of KGB and MVD had arrived, to join with the Spearhead and Support Groups which had so successfully secured the key targets. The horrors of terror and cruelty which had subdued each continental country as the tide of invasion had swept over it, now engulfed the United Kingdom as well. Hundreds of thousands of men, women and children who had looked forward with keen anticipation to Christmas were either dead, prisoners or cowering petrified in their homes.

MONDAY

All Day

Western Europe

During Monday, throughout Western Europe, the fifth column of communist sympathizers in each country, aided by the Pact Spearhead and Support Groups, now released from their initial tasks, and instructed by the KGB agents of the Soviet Embassies, embarked on a programme of liquidation and imprisonment of all those who were, or were likely to be, against communism.

The Soviet Embassy in each capital had assumed control of all actions directed against the civil population. The Soviet military units were a law unto themselves in the areas which they occupied. But the KGB agents, with their helpers, had the authority to enter those areas to take the known enemies, the members of the armed forces who were not with their units, the police, the espionage and counter-espionage security men and women, civil servants — all who could have a vested interest or a personal belief which would make them anti-communist. The

219

net was a wide one, and the organization to make it effective had been carefully built up in each Embassy. Special communication links had been established to bypass those of the host country, which, in some cases, had been totally disrupted. Prior provision had been arranged of the transport vehicles needed to pick up those suspected of being capable of and intent on resistance. Each Soviet Embassy, unlike the closed, darkened and deserted buildings around it, became the centre of the only activity permitted under the curfew regulations.

Each Soviet Embassy had also made arrangements for the reception and vetting of those in each country who, as soon as they heard of the invasion or the elimination of the existing authorities, had hurried to offer their aid and assistance.

The known anti-communists were dealt with immediately to ensure that there would be no trouble from them either in the short or long-term. Long deep trenches had been dug in selected, secluded, forested areas. To those the convoys of trucks were driven as soon as darkness fell. At the execution sites, the victims were first made to remove all their valuables and distinguishing documents and to stack them neatly in separate heaps for watches, jewellery, money or papers. Next they were marched in groups of forty or fifty to the edge of the trench where they were made to kneel, facing the dark hole in front of them. Execution was by a bullet from a heavy automatic into the back of the head, which removed the face, making later recognition impossible.

Those for whom immediate execution had not been ordered were taken to the main secure prisons, from which the prison population had been released. Crowded into the cells up to a dozen men, women and teenage children had to share the cramped space on the bunks, tables and chairs, or take their turns on the floor. The first target of the arresting squads, as had been the case in the early days of the revolution in Russia, had been the bourgeoisie and their families — the professional classes, teachers, lecturers, writers, clerics, businessmen, farmers, civil servants and trade union officials. As the numbers of the arrested grew and the prisons became full to overflowing, some were taken out to the forests to be executed, some were moved to deserted military camps and airfields and some were packed into freight trains, trucks, ships and aircraft returning, otherwise empty, to the Soviet Union and its already established slave camps.

Wherever the Warsaw Pact divisions and the Spearhead Groups had taken control, the population, other than those taken as prisoners, slave labour or for execution, learnt the horrors of enemy occupation. Property was looted, belongings destroyed, women raped, and the men who attempted to intervene were either beaten senseless or killed. The Pact Forces lived off the lands they had conquered. What they wanted, they took. Where whole buildings or private houses were wanted, the military forces called in the KGB execution squads, and entire families were removed. By Tuesday the flow of prisoners, those condemned to execution and those being removed to the slave camps, had grown into a human flood of misery.

The long roll call of the dead joined that of the years which had started in 1917, at the birth of the Russian Revolution. The gross total of about 140 million would probably never be accurately verified — too many who might know the truth had disappeared in the tidal waves of extermination which had swept world-wide wherever communism had reached. The cost to mankind had been staggering and was now mounting with every day of occupation in Western Europe.

MONDAY

1700 Hours Central European Time

Eastern Europe And The Soviet Union

At marshalling yards in Eastern Europe the train loads of prisoners were sorted into consignments for each of the big Soviet cities. The dead and dying were taken into the open countryside and theré left for later attention. The still living were at least given food and drink — a hot vegetable and potato gruel dished from huge cauldrons into tin cups and bowls.

Ahead of most of them lay a journey of equal length to the one they had barely survived. But, at intervals, there were prescribed stops for food. At these halts, as far from human habitation as possible, the prisoners were allowed to move not more than 100 metres from the rail track to relieve themselves. Infinitely weary, hungry, dispirited and still, in most cases, suffering from the shock of their appalling fate, there was no risk of any attempts to escape. By chance some families were reunited, others heard that a child, a wife or a husband had been seen in another truck. Some families became aware for the first time of those who had died or had been left dying.

Though in the main the prisoners taken were from the armed forces and their families of the NATO allies, they were by no means limited to those categories. NATO civilians had also been taken, as well as tourists and visitors from other parts of the world. In Norway the Soviet Navy had taken prisoner any Norwegian who had survived the fighting. They were being transported back to the Northern and Baltic bases in transport ships as soon as these were emptied of their loads. In Italy, Greece and Turkey too, prisoners taken by the Soviet divisions were being transferred back to Russia in any available transport, including freight barges which had been moved along the Black Sea coasts in anticipation.

With their own slave labour camps already filled, the Russians planned to hold the prisoners who survived the journey in specially constructed prisoner of war camps.

The heads of state and the high Government officials of Western Europe had fared no better. They had been flown to the main cities of the Soviet Union, and taken to the civil and military prisons at each place. They were given no diplomatic recognition nor special privileges. They were treated individually as criminals, but specially valuable and well protected criminals.

TUESDAY

1200 Hours Central European Time

Western Europe

By the early morning of Tuesday the Soviet Armed Forces were in control of the capitals and central government offices in Norway, Denmark, West Germany, Luxemburg, Austria,

Holland, Belgium and Britain.

During the later morning ships of the Soviet Navy and mercantile marine, carrying sufficient armed forces to overcome any resistance, took control of Iceland, the Azores, Madeira, the Canary Islands, the Balearic Islands, Corsica, Sardinia, Malta and Crete. Two Soviet airborne divisions landed at Dublin, Eire.

At 1200 hours Central European Time, the Soviet Ambassadors to France, Italy, Spain, Portugal and Greece each delivered an ultimatum to the governments to which they were accredited. The ultimatum stated that each country, in the absence of the Heads of State and senior ministers, who had been taken prisoner, had until midnight to appoint an interim government empowered to surrender the armed forces and the state to the High Command of the forces of the Warsaw Pact. In the absence of such a surrender by the appointed time each country was to consider itself at war with the Warsaw Pact and should be prepared to accept the consequences.

At the same time the Soviet Ambassadors in Finland, Sweden, Switzerland, Turkey, Albania, Jugoslavia and Cyprus each delivered a note to the governments of the countries to which they were accredited demanding that by midday Wednesday each government should accept the terms of a close political, military and economic treaty with the governments linked by the Warsaw Pact.

By then the tide of tyranny, which had started as a small ripple in the far north-west corner of Russia in the winter of 1917, would have engulfed the whole of Europe and the islands linked to it.

Late on Tuesday afternoon the United States was able to activate another satellite to restore the 'hot-line' link with Moscow. At the same time they also reactivated command and control satellites by which they could issue instructions to their intercontinental ballistic missile thermonuclear forces.

The President of the United States of America, on a nationwide television hook-up, spoke directly to the peoples of America, and his speech was relayed to the Western Hemisphere, China, Africa, Asia and Australasia. He informed his audience of the magnitude of the disaster which had struck Europe and continued, 'I solemnly declare that the United

States of America and its Allies will not accept the present position as final. I warn the Soviet Union and its Allies that, unless they withdraw their armed and para-military forces from all the territories which they have invaded, within a period of one week from today, the United States will consider itself at war with the Soviet Union and its Allies and will take all the steps necessary, including resort to thermonuclear war, to recover the freedom of the sovereign independent states of Western Europe.'

The ultimatum had little credibility . The threat of thermonuclear attack did not even carry the conviction that there would be mutual assured destruction. The Soviet Union, by the possession of an arsenal of nuclear weapons which more than matched that of the United States, by its air defence preparations, by its development of high energy laser and plasma beams, by its ability to disperse its population in the time available, by the possession of thousands of prisoners and the resources of the continent of Europe, had made itself a far less vulnerable target than the United States.

Two hours later the Defence Council of the Soviet Union issued its reply. 'The Soviet Union, and its allies, exercising their rights under the Charter of the United Nations, have been compelled to enter West Germany, and the nations allied to West Germany, to prevent a resurgence of Nazi power, of which there have been very serious indications in recent days. A friendly act of *détente* made by the Soviet Union and its Allies was rejected out of hand by elements intent on revenge. In Western Europe as a whole, the Soviet Union has had its diplomatic and trade emissaries expelled by Governments clearly infiltrated by Nazi connections. In these circumstances the Soviet Union and its Allies had no alternative but to intervene to save Western Europe from the dreadful fate of being taken over again by the descendants of Hitler's Nazi followers.

'We hold heads of state and government, senior military and civilian officials and many prisoners, men, women and children, of most of the states of Western Europe. We also hold many citizens of the United States of America. These prisoners are held in or near all the major cities and strategic areas of the Union of Soviet Socialist Republics. Any thermonuclear attacks on the territory of the Soviet Union will kill many of these prisoners.

'The Defence Council of the Soviet Union is ready to discuss the terms of a peace treaty with the President of the United States of America, and will immediately return all citizens of the United States of America, now held as prisoners in the Soviet Union, provided that, within three days, a document is received by the President of the Soviet Union, containing a solemn and binding declaration that, in exchange for the return of its citizens, the United States of America will for ever afterwards promise and contract never to engage in hostile activities against the Soviet Union or its Allies.

'Unless such a declaration is received within the time stipulated, the President and Commander-in-Chief of the Soviet Union will order such action as is necessary to secure the safety of the Soviet Union and its Allies.'

TUESDAY

1400 Hours Eastern Standard Time
2000 Hours Central European Time

The Pentagon, Washington, USA

In the Communications Centre of the Pentagon the staff listened to the reply of the Soviet Union. After a silence which lasted some minutes a disconsolate senior officer said to no one in particular, 'It's a monstrous but totally unnecessary tragedy. We should have known that with an enemy as implacably determined on world domination we had no option but to match each and every warlike capability. We had to match subversion with subversion, espionage with espionage, counter-espionage with counter measures of our own, terrorism with extra alertness, propaganda with propaganda, disinformation with disinformation and so on with economic warfare and denial of raw materials and other unfriendly acts.

'On the military side we matched the Soviet intercontinental missiles but not their killer satellites, we matched their theatre missiles but with too few, we matched their battlefield missiles but with aged weapons. Our fundamental mistake, which enabled them to succeed, was that we copied their reliance on conventional weapons, instead of matching that capability with a new concept of defence based on frontline micronuclear weapons. If we had done that this might never have happened.'

TUESDAY

2200 Hours Greenwich Mean Time

London, England

An old man stood looking down into a London street from a darkened window of his home. Below him the street had been filled for some minutes by a long procession of trucks closely escorted by vehicles carrying soldiers of the Soviet airborne divisions which had landed during the afternoon. Each truck had an armed guard sitting next to the driver, but the interiors were in darkness and it was impossible to tell what was being carried.

Talking over his shoulder to his elderly wife in the dimly lit room behind him, he had his own ideas.

'That's twenty-five closely guarded trucks which have just gone past here, all tight shut and without a light to show what they are carrying. It must be a convoy taking the first batches of victims for execution or imprisonment. The pattern is always the same. First the known anti-communists are taken, then those who might be anti-communist and then some of those who had not even thought of being anti-communist, but who are taken as an example to the rest.

'I looked up *The Times* editorial of May Day 1978 which said no communist nation enjoys: freedom of elections; freedom of belief; freedom of religion; freedom of speech; freedom of the press; freedom of assembly; freedom of movement; freedom of property; freedom of employment, freedom to form trade unions; freedom from arbitrary arrest; punishment or impri- sonment, nor does it have representative institutions, impartial laws or independent judges.

'And some say "better red than dead", the old man added gloomily as he drew the curtains carefully and then joined his wife by the fireside.

226

APPENDIX A

Copy Number 99

Main HQ Central Front Forces

Zossen – Wünsdorf

GERMAN DEMOCRATIC REPUBLIC

0900 hours CET 15 Dec 198?

Reference Pact 14

Op Order 6

1. Situation

   a. NATO FORCES – No change from Intelligence Summaries

   b. PACT FORCES

     (1) FIRST SOVIET AIRBORNE DIVISION is to land on OSLO, NORWAY

     (2) SECOND SOVIET AIRBORNE DIVISION is to land on COPENHAGEN

     (3) SOVIET ASSAULT REGIMENTS are to advance on all routes, as ordered, ahead of divisions of Central Front Forces

   c. Later Deployment

     (1) SECOND SOVIET AIRBORNE DIVISION is to revert to command of HQ WARSAW PACT FORCES when relieved of duties in COPENHAGEN

     (2) SOVIET AIRBORNE DIVISIONS are to overfly Central Front Forces for invasion of UNITED KINGDOM and EIRE

     (3) 2 SOVIET NAVY INFANTRY REGIMENT and 62 SOVIET MOTOR-RIFLE DIVISIONS are to come under command NORWAY Front Forces

on transfer to NORWAY

d. <u>Nuclear Weapons</u>

Nuclear Weapons will not be used under any circumstances
without direct authority of Soviet Supreme Command

2. <u>Mission</u>

Central Front Forces to invade, conquer and occupy
WEST GERMANY, DENMARK, HOLLAND, BELGIUM, LUXEMBURG,
and northern and eastern FRANCE up to objectives
previously indicated

3. <u>Execution</u>

a. General Outline - Operation Overlay - Annex B

(1) Phase 1. Capture of all key crossings of Rivers Rhine,
Meuse and their tributaries

(2) Phase 2. Capture of capital cities and main ports
except in FRANCE where separate detailed
orders apply

(3) Phase 3. Elimination of all centres of resistance in
captured territories

b. <u>Invasion Crossing-Points and Forces allotted</u>

(1) SCHLUTUP	- Thirteenth Shock Army	- 3 motor-rifle divisions
		1 tank division
(2) LAUENBURG	- Twentieth Guards Army	- 3 motor-rifle divisions
	Second Guards Tank Army	- 3 tank divisions
(3) HESTEDT	- Eigth Guards Army	- 3 motor-rifle divisions
	First Guards Tank Army	- 3 tank divisions
(4) HELMSTEDT (North)	- Fourth Shock Army	- 4 motor-rifle divisions
	Seventh Tank Army	- 3 tank divisions
(5) HELMSTEDT	- Fifth Guards Army	- 3 motor-rifle divisions

(south)	– Sixth Guards Tank Army	– 3 tank divisions
(6) DUDERSTADT	– Thirtieth Army	– 3 motor-rifle divisions
	Twenty-eighth Tank Army	– 3 tank divisions
(7) HERLESHAUSEN	– Third Shock Army	– 4 motor-rifle divisions
	Eighteenth Tank Army	– 3 tank divisions
(8) HENNEBERG	– Tenth Guards Army	– 3 motor-rifle divisions
	Fifteenth Tank Army	– 3 tank divisions
(9) EISFELD	– Eleventh Army	– 3 motor-rifle divisions
	Seventeenth Tank Army	– 3 tank divisions
(10) HIRSCHBERG	– Twelfth Army	– 3 motor-rifle divisions
	Twenty-fifth Tank Army	– 2 tank divisions
(11) SCHIRNDING	– Fourteenth Army	– 3 motor-rifle divisions
	Ninth Tank Army	– 3 tank divisions
(12) WAIDHAUS	– Sixteenth Army	– 3 motor-rifle divisions
	Twenty-second Tank Army	– 3 tank divisions
(13) FURTH IM WALD	– Nineteenth Army	– 3 motor-rifle divisions
	Twenty-first Tank Army	– 3 tank divisions
(14) BAD EISENSTEIN	– Twenty-fourth Army	– 3 motor-rifle divisions
	Twenty-third Tank Army	– 2 tank divisions

Routes west from invasion crossing-points

(1) SCHLUTUP	– (west route) – NEUMUNSTER – RENDSBURG – HUSUM – TONDER – NORTH JUTLAND
	– (east route) – KIEL – FLENSBURG – AARHUS – RANDERS – FYN ISLAND – ZEALAND – COPENHAGEN

(2) LAUENBURG — south of HAMBURG and BREMEN – NORDHORN –
HENGELO – UTRECHT – AMSTERDAM – THE HAGUE –
ROTTERDAM

(3) HESTEDT — UELZEN – SOLTAU – RETHEM – NEINBURG –
OSNABRUCK – RHEINE and MUNSTER – REES and
WESEL – ARNHEM – NIJMEGEN

(4) HELMSTEDT — BRAUNSCHWEIG – HANNOVER – RINTELN – HERFORD
(NORTH) – and BIELEFELD – BECKUM – HAMM – DUISBURG –
VENLO – EINDHOVEN – TURNHOUT – ANTWERP and
WALCHEREN

(5) HELMSTEDT — south of BRAUNSCHWEIG – HILDESHEIM – HAMELN
(SOUTH) – PADERBORN – DORTMUND – HAGEN – NEUSS –
ROERMOND – BERINGER – MECHELIN – GENT – BRUGES

(6) DUDERSTADT — GOTTINGEN – KASSEL – MESCHEDE – COLOGNE –
GELEEN – HASSELT – BRUSSELS – TOURNAI

(7) HERLESHAUSEN — autobahn E70 – GIESSEN – SIEGBURG – BONN –
AACHEN – LIEGE – NAMUR – MONS

(8) HENNEBERG — BAD NEUSTADT – FULDA and BAD BRUCKENAU –
FRANKFURT – WIESBADEN – KOBLENZ – TRIER –
LUXEMBURG

(9) EISFELD — COBURG – SCHWEINFURT – ASHAFFENBERG – MAINZ
– IDAL OBERSTEIN – SAARLOUIS – METZ

(10) HIRSCHBERG — BAMBERG – WURZBURG – WORMS – KAISERLAUTERN –
SAARBRUCKEN – NANCY

(11) SCHIRNBIND — BAYREUTH – FURTH – ANSBACH – HEILBRON –
HEIDELBERG – PIRMASENS – BITCHE

(12) WAIDHAUS   - NURNBERG - AALEN - STUTTGART - KARLSRUHE
                          - SARREBOURG

(13) FURTH IM WALD - REGENSBURG - INGOLSTADT - ULM - TUBINGEN
                          - STRASBOURG

(14) BAD   - LANSHUT - MUNICH - MEMMINGEN - FREIBURG -
      EISENSTEIN   COLMAR and MULHOUSE and BELFORT

d. Objectives and deployment areas

    (1) Thirteenth Shock Army   - NORTH JUTLAND and COPENHAGEN

                                          Tank division north of HAMBURG

    (2) Twentieth Guards Army   - 1 motor-rifle division at
                                            AMSTERDAM, THE HAGUE and
                                          ROTTERDAM
                                          1 motor-rifle division at
                                          APELBORN, HENGELO and NORDHORN
                                          1 motor-rifle division at
                                          BREMEN, OLDENBURG and
                                          GRONINGEN

        Second Guards Tank Army   - 1 tank division each at HAMBURG
                                            BREMEN and BREMERHAVEN

    (3) Eighth Guards Army   - 1 motor-rifle division at
                                            ARNHEM, NIGMEGEN,
                                          S'HERTOGENBOSCH and TILBURG
                                          - 1 motor-rifle division at REES,
                                          WESEL and west to R. MEUSE
                                          - 1 motor-rifle division at
                                          MUNSTER and RHEINE

First Guards	–	1 tank division each at OSNABRUCK,
Tank Army		NIENBURG, and CELLE
(4) Fourth Shock Army	–	1 motor-rifle division at ANTWERP and
		WALCHEREN
	–	1 motor-rifle division at TURNHOUT and
		EINDHOVEN
	–	1 motor-rifle division at VENLO and
		north of DUISBURG
	–	1 motor-rifle division in area of HAMM
Seventh Tank Army	–	3 tank divisions in area of BIELEFELD,
		HERFORD and HANNOVER
(5) Fifth Guards Army	–	1 motor-rifle division at GHENT and
		MECHELIN
		1 motor-rifle division at MONCHENGLADBACH
		1 motor-rifle division at ESSEN
Sixth Guards Tank	–	1 tank division each at DORTMUND,
Army		PADERBORN and HAMELN
(6) Thirtieth Army	–	1 motor-rifle division at BRUSSELS
		1 motor-rifle division at MAASTRICHT,
		and GELEEN
		1 motor-rifle division at COLOGNE and
		LEVERKUSEN,
Twenty-eighth	–	1 tank division each at LUDENSCHELD,
Tank Army		brilon and KASSEL
(7) Third Shock Army	–	1 motor-rifle division at MONS and
		CHARLEROI

		1 motor-rifle division at NAMUR, LIEGE and AACHEN
		1 motor-rifle division at BONN and SIEGBURG
		1 motor-rifle division at SIEGEN
Eighteenth Tank Army	–	1 tank division each at GIESSEN, MARBURG and BAD HERSFELD
(8) Tenth Guards Army	–	1 motor-rifle division at LUXEMBURG and TRIER
		1 motor-rifle division at KOBLENZ
		1 motor-rifle division at BAD HOMBURG
Fifteenth Tank Army	–	3 tank divisions north east of FRANKFURT
(9) Eleventh Army	–	1 motor-rifle division at METZ
		1 motor-rifle division at DILLINGEN and IDALOBERSTEIN
		1 motor-rifle division at MAINZ
Seventeenth Tank Army	–	1 tank division each at DARMSTADT, ASCHAFFENBURG and SCHWEINFURT
(10) Twelfth Army	–	1 motor-rifle division at NANCY
		1 motor-rifle division at SAARBRUCKEN
		1 motor-rifle division at KAISERSLAUTERN
Twenty-fifth Tank Army	–	1 tank division each at MICHELSTADT, WURZBURG and BAMBERG

(11) Fourteenth Army   -   1 motor-rifle division at BITCHE

1 motor-rifle division at PIRMASENS

1 motor-rifle division at SPEYER

Ninth Tank Army   -   1 tank division each at HEIDELBERG,

HEILBRON and CRAILSHEIM, and FURTH

(12) Sixteenth Army   -   1 motor-rifle division at SARRESBOURG

1 motor-rifle division at KARLSRUHE

1 motor-rifle division at STUTTGART

Twenty-second   -   1 tank division each at AALEN,

Tank Army   DONAUWORTH and NURNBERG

(13) Nineteenth Army   -   1 motor-rifle division at EPINAL

1 motor-rifle division at STRASBOURG

1 motor-rifle division at TUBINGEN

Twenty-first Tank -   1 tank division each at ULM, AUGSBURG

Army   and REGENSBURG

(14) Twenty-fourth   -   1 motor-rifle division at BELFORT

Army   and MULHOUSE

1 motor-rifle division at COLMAR

1 motor-rifle division at FREIBURG

Twenty-third   -   1 tank division each at MEMMINGEN and

Tank Army   MUNICH

e. <u>Advance and Assault forces</u>

   (1)   Spearhead Groups of specialists are to precede armed

         forces on all routes

   (2)   Elements of 7 Assault Regiments are to follow the

         Spearhead Groups on all routes

      (3)   Support Groups of specialists are to aid operations on all routes

f. **Force Reserves**

      (1)   Reserve tank battalions are to move on all routes after tank divisions

      (2)   Reserve motor-rifle battalions are to move with each reserve tank battalion

      (3)   Reserve tank and motor-rifle battalions to be under command leading Army on each route

g. **Artillery**

      (1)   Co-ordination - Reserve Artillery Commander on each route

      (2)   Tactical nuclear weapons are not to move outside the territories of the Warsaw Pact

h. **Engineers**

      (1)   All engineer resources are to be available to be switched as required onto routes where extra effort may be needed

      (2)   Priority of tasks

            (a)   Route clearance and maintenance

            (b)   Minefield clearance

            (c)   Bridge repair

            (d)   Bridge construction

            (e)   Airfield clearance

1. **KGB and MVD**

    (1)   KGB and MVD forces are to move behind reserve units on all routes

    (2)   Priority of tasks

        (a)   Capture and despatch of NATO prisoners

        (b)   Elimination of civil resistance

        (c)   Security of PACT communications

        (d)   Installation of civil authority

Co-ordinating Instructions

    (1)   H hour

        (a)   Phase 1 – 1730 hrs

        (b)   Phase 2 – to be notified

    (2)   Watches to be synchronized on Moscow time

    (3)   Present Starting Points   )

    (4)   Routes to Forming-Up Areas)

)-   At Separate Movement

    (5)   Forming-Up Areas   )

)   Order Number 8

    (6)   Movement to Invasion Points)

4. **Logistics**

    (a)   Separate Administrative Order Number 10 issued

    (b)   Refuelling of all vehicles on NATO territory to be from civilian fuel pumps wherever possible

    (c)   NATO aviation fuel stores to be taken over without damage wherever possible

    (d)   Personnel casualties to be treated at NATO hospitals

    (e)   Traffic control to be augmented by NATO police

5. Command Instructions

   a. Locations

     (1) Main HQ Central Front Forces – Closes present loc:
        and opens in Defence Ministry of Federal German
        Republic, BONN at 1200 hrs D+1

     (2) Rear HQ Central Front Forces – Closes present loc:
        and opens in GIESSEN at 1800 hrs D+1

   b. Electronic Silence

     (1) Silence imposed at 0001 hrs 15 Dec: on all electronic
        equipment except nominated users, RR and air TC
        communications

     (2) Silence broken for all equipments on first contact
        after H hr + 4 hrs or by issue of code word OLYMPICS
        from Force HQ

   c. Code Words

	Code Word	Meaning	Issued By
(1)	OLYMPICS	Break electronic silence	Force HQ
(2)	JUMPER	River Rhine crossed	Army HQs
(3)	SPRINTER	Objectives reached	Army HQs
(4)	RUNNER	Deployment areas occupied	Army HQs

ACKNOWLEDGE

Marshal of the Soviet Union

Commanding Central Front Forces

DISTRIBUTION – Attached

APPENDIX B

WARSAW PACT ARMY DIVISIONS

The types of army units which made up the Warsaw Pact Armies were of four main categories: the frontline troops — the motor-rifle, tank and airborne units; the artillery — gun, mortar, missile and anti-aircraft units; the specialists — engineer, wireless signal, and chemical units; the supporting and supply services — medical units, traffic police, transport units, technical repair units.

A Pact division was the smallest fighting formation which contained elements of all the four categories, and was called a tank division, a motor-rifle division or an airborne division depending on which category of fighting troops was the predominant one in the division. The basic component of the divisions was the regiment, made up of three or four battalions, with certain support elements added. A tank division had a total of 325 tanks, and a motor-rifle division a total of 266 tanks, making it a more powerful balanced division than the tank divisions, which had fewer infantry and artillery support units. The total men in a tank division was 11,000 and in a motor-rifle division 12,700.

Both types of division had a strong battle reconnaissance battalion as well as a considerable amount of gun support over and above the artillery weapons forming part of the regiments in each division. The frontline gun support was provided by two battalions each equipped with 18 122 mm guns and a third battalion equipped with 18 152 mm self-propelled guns. In addition each division had a battalion equipped with 18 BM-21 'Katyusha' 40-round multi-barrelled rocket launchers, capable of firing 720 rockets in 30 seconds, and also capable of firing chemical rockets. Each division also had 4 FROG surface-to-surface free-flight (SSFFR) missile launchers, capable of delivering nuclear weapons.

239

Pact divisions also had immediate field engineer support, with an obstacle-clearing ability, apart from mine-laying, with trench-diggers, bulldozers and explosives.

The specialist units in the divisions provided wireless and radar experts and chemical defence decontamination squads. The supply transport battalion, equipped with 200 5-ton cargo trucks with trailers was responsible for carrying forward to the fighting units their needs of fuel, ammunition and food.

The tank and motor-rifle regiments in the tank or motor-rifle divisions, also had their own regimental support troops. Each type of regiment had a battle reconnaissance company, and anti-aircraft and anti-tank guns and guided weapons.

A tank or motor-rifle battalion, three of which were in a tank or motor-rifle regiment, consisted of three companies, each of three platoons.